THE RAG
PRINCESS

Barbara J. Franzen

iUniverse LLC
Bloomington

THE RAG PRINCESS

iUniverse books may be ordered through booksellers or by contacting:

iUniverse LLC
1663 Liberty Drive
Bloomington, IN 47403
www.iuniverse.com
1-800-Authors (1-800-288-4677)

Because of the dynamic nature of the Internet, any web addresses or links contained in this book may have changed since publication and may no longer be valid. The views expressed in this work are solely those of the author and do not necessarily reflect the views of the publisher, and the publisher hereby disclaims any responsibility for them.

Any people depicted in stock imagery provided by Thinkstock are models, and such images are being used for illustrative purposes only.
Certain stock imagery © Thinkstock.

ISBN: 978-1-4917-2120-9 (sc)
ISBN: 978-1-4917-2121-6 (hc)
ISBN: 978-1-4917-2122-3 (e)

Library of Congress Control Number: 2014901374

Printed in the United States of America.

iUniverse rev. date: 3/26/2014

Dedication

Dedicated to my mother, Dorothy Calling Tetro—my writing inspiration and much more.

Acknowledgments

Husband Milan for his "help, belief, and patience," and to my "most important" sister, Kathleen. I wish to thank Ladette Randolph, Ploughshares, who performed a developmental edit in the early stages and encouraged me to stay with the book. Roger Harris and Dianne Koerner, Indie Author Counsel, I'm grateful. Thanks Glenda Frailin, NWG and Robert, Tozer, the beginning, Donna Dudley and Cathy Simon for help and encouragement. Merrill Crandall, professional therapist and social worker, who talked with me about the predator, thanks. Other thanks go to Tom Hood thanks for looking at the book . Laura Leader, I appreciated your checkups and niece, Kim Greer, your interest. Also, beloved Ruth Wahlgren, now deceased, who helped me with my nemesis, commas, and to the deceased, Jean Clymer, for asking me to write a book and giving me the Union Aid notes. Maxine Fickenscher, always thanks, my church circle-Methodist Gothenburg, son Matt and Lacey and precious Anna and Cora, Molly, my calico, a real trooper, always curled by my side, waiting for this final day when this would be published!—and the Brady people from my home town...

Book One

Secrets

(November 1932, Lincoln County, Nebraska)

Shirley hadn't expected to hear rain pelting the house this morning. Yesterday's forecast had called for a blizzard. Expecting a foot or more of snow, folks had gone about preparing for a big one. Farmers and ranchers had checked on fuel, feed, and other various concerns while the women busied themselves with groceries, canned goods from the cellar, and warm outerwear. Shirley had driven into Brady to go shopping for flour, oatmeal, and other sundry items. She'd stopped in at Edward's Drugstore for a jar of Vanco rub and hand lotion. The vapors would help with four-year-old Howie's croup. Al, her husband, needed the lotion for the cracks in his dry, leathery hands.

This morning, the four- year- old was bright eyed and begging to help get the mail.

Wanting him warm and dry, Shirley lectured Howie as she knelt to button his corduroy coat and buckle his black over shoes. "Howie, do you promise you'll stay out of the water?"

Slipping on Al's everyday coat, Shirley grabbed the umbrella she'd found in a shed out behind the house. Old and scraggly, it was good for keeping Howie dry while she preferred the rain in her face. Walking along, holding the parasol over Howie, it didn't take long for her to become soaked. Meanwhile, mud puddles were sprouting, like magic, all over the driveway, while overhead, huge cottonwoods swayed under the darkened sky.

Fascinated by these mini-lakes, Howie said, "Look," pointing at a puddle. "Mommy, can I go swimming in one of them?"

"Howie, we don't swim in mud puddles. It's too cold. Besides, the lightening is close. Look up ahead." Sitting on a post, alongside a country road, going east and west, the mailbox wasn't far away. Tugging on the boy, while trying to distract him from the mini lakes, they arrived at their destination. Just then, a streak of nearby lightening flashed, startling Shirley, causing her to screech. Alarmed by her reaction, Howie whimpered, "Mommy, you scared me," as tears rolled down his plumpish cheeks.

"We're fine sweetie," Shirley said, wanting to get Howie back inside... Hurrying to open the mailbox, she gasped. — A "violet" envelope jumped out at her— Breathless, she grabbed it, shoving it in one of the coat pockets, and half-way wishing the letter would float away with the rain. Only one person used violet envelopes...Or maybe? Taking a few steps, Shirley stopped, as her fingers reached in her pocket. Pulling the letter out, she dared her eyes to read the name on the return address...Taking a deep breath, she saw that it was Bonnie Jo who'd sent the letter and not the other person. Relieved, she picked Howie up, swinging him back and forth, while the two of them laughed in the pouring rain.

Bonnie, a stunning beauty with wavy black hair, and the oldest of three children, had married this past summer and was living 150 miles east in York, Nebraska. Close to genius, she'd foregone scholarships to two different schools. She'd done this, despite knowing it was an unusual privilege for a girl to attend college. Instead, Bonnie had married Bob Way, her boyfriend, who'd accepted a job at his uncle's neighborhood market in York. Shirley still hadn't gotten over Bonnie's decision. It hurt to think that, instead of building a career, Bonnie was stuck in a mini Airstream trailer. Good heavens! Would there be room to breathe?

Shirley knew it wasn't her business what Bonnie did; nevertheless .... That and the fact that, a week ago, Bonnie had missed Thanksgiving Day. Without her coming home, the holiday had been disillusionment. Bonnie's humor and vitality made even a badly burned turkey taste good. It wasn't that Shirley didn't love all her children equally. Instead, her rapport with this eldest was unusual. An extreme extrovert, Bonnie had a liveliness that touched on Shirley's introversion and reserve.

Al had suggested that Shirley stop living vicariously through this daughter. While Bonnie's marriage diminished this tendency, it remained an issue. However, thanks to Bev Temple, Shirley was finding a life of her own. Bev was the wife of Clark, the landowner for whom Al worked as a hired hand. Not having siblings, the energetic Bev tucked Shirley under her wing, making her a sister. The Dustys and the Temples lived in the same farmyard not five minutes apart, and Bev invited Shirley over each morning; they would sit in the sunroom doing crafts. Bev did enamel paintings called wicker ware. A dab of enamel made vibrant flowers, their favorite decoration. Bev provided the wicker items, such as sandals, little baskets, and purses. Shirley provided the skill and ideas. A far better painter, Shirley could turn out exquisite work in amazing color schemes. Both houses were filled with enamel items. This sort of fun was new for Shirley.

Not long ago, she and Bev had tried millinery. While Shirley looked splendid in any hat she made, Bev wore boxy male-style hats worn way down. Her children teased her, insisting she toss these head coverings away. Shirley silently agreed, thinking they made Bev look like a turtle.

Celeste and Shirley had shared some of their first woman-to-daughter laughs over this "turtle look"—laughs of warmth and intimacy.

Turning to Howie, Shirley asked, "Guess who wrote us? We got a letter from your big sister. We'll read her letter together."

Uninterested, Howie pointed over to the barn where a '25 Ford truck sat parked. "There's Daddy's truck." The truck belonged to Clark; however, Al used it for his work. Throughout the Dustys' married life, Al had worked for as many as three farmers. Shirley, originally a city girl, and Al, a Sandhills boy, had attended the same high school in Lincoln. Ironically, they'd met for the first time two nights before graduation. Until four years ago, they'd lived in the Sandhills.

Hurrying along, Shirley rushed inside the tenant house. One of two homes in the same farmyard, the Dustys' place sat at the west end. The Temples, whose farm was larger than that of average farmers, lived at the east end. Their charming home, a big, three-story with a large front porch, was the nicest place in the neighboring countryside. By comparison, the Dustys lived in a modest, two-story house. A white picket fence with a swinging gate enclosed the yard. Enormous old trees and a large red barn separated the two places. With the farm and ranch set against the south hills, the Dustys had never known such contentment.

Stepping into the kitchen, Shirley laid her wet coat over the back of a chair. Howie, who was in a hurry to go play, dropped his jacket on the floor. A baby at the time of the move, Howie had been a "late" child. Unsure of having another, Shirley had been elated by his arrival. Except for his brown hair, Howie was the image of his father. Only thirty-eight, Shirley longed for another child—a girl or a boy to help with the work.

Picturing herself bathing a baby and rocking and nursing the small infant, Shirley had no choice but to squelch this strong maternal desire. This was partially because of her spells with worry and anxiety. The biggest reason— her thought were interrupted. Remembering Howie, Shirley turned to help him with his muddy overshoes; instead, Howie charged off to the living room, refusing to wait for her help. Pretending she didn't see this, Shirley poured another cup of coffee. Taking a seat at the table, her work-worn fingers tore at the envelope.

Dearest Folks,

I thought I would die Thanksgiving Day. I sat here alone thinking about my mother's mincemeat pie. Bob's uncle made him work until three in the afternoon. He was tired and hungry by the time he came home. Thanks to our economy and this unrelenting Depression, I didn't even have a turkey to fix him. As you can see, I'm in need of cheer. Please, can you come for a visit? Bring yourselves and some of that delicious pie. My homesickness makes me fear losing this baby. With Bob working all the time, this minuscule tin trailer drives me nutty. You have to see it, in order to understand what I am saying.

(Reading ahead, Shirley's fingers began drumming a rhythm on the table.)

My idleness has led to daydreaming. Incredibly, my fantasies have become a reality. They go way back to that day when I was five. Remember us borrowing the neighbor's car, so we could go to Lincoln to visit your sister? When we finally got to A Street, Sylvie was busy, fixing lemonade for her guests. Instead, we visited with Uncle Mack— Mom, I felt so bad for you, but I never told you. Even then, it seemed like our discussing HER was prohibited.

Dad, this part is to you. Even though you won't discuss Sylvie, I'm going to anyway. You know me! I need to express my thoughts; as a married woman it's my right. Instead of going to Sylvie's door with Mom and me, you sat in the car, refusing to budge. Even today, you scowl every time her name comes up. I don't understand the reason for that. You've never met her.

How can you dislike someone you don't know? She's Mother's sister — and in case you forgot, she's your sister-in-law.

Would it help you if you knew how congenial she really was—and is? You won't remember this, but when I forgot my purse and ran back, Sylvie came out and took my picture. She was drenched in 'lavender' and smelled of 'lavender lilac bushes.' She told me that she wanted to drop me in her pocket and keep me forever. That's how my "Sylvie Star" scrapbook began. Every week, I would sneak the newspaper and cut out those society column pictures and articles. It made you so mad, but as I already said, marriage opened up my mouth!

So now to my plan. York is close to Lincoln. Once the baby is born, I'm looking her up. I think she might be interested in having the baby and me in a society page "picture special" with her. We'd call it *Sylvie, Niece and 'Grandbaby*. I remember you saying that Sylvie's only child died. My baby could be a "sort of grandchild" shared by all of you. That way, we'd become a close circle. Mom, it's too bad that you and Sylvie were separated in high school and lost touch. It's time for your reunion and long afternoon talks.

Homesick,

Bonnie

*   *   *

At least our daughter misses us, Shirley thought, setting the emotionally laden (explosive) topic of Sylvie on top of the icebox. It was just that Bonnie Jo had always been so independent. She'd even refused to nurse as a baby. For once, she was in need of her parents. Getting up for more coffee, Shirley speculated on when they would be able to leave. This would be their first visit with Bonnie since her wedding and here she was pregnant. Sitting there, Shirley imagined two things—Bonnie sitting in a college classroom using her brilliant mind and Bonnie, at home with an adorable baby—one that had endless colic, like Celeste when she was a baby.

She was imagining both scenarios when the demons, her secrets, like the flash of lightening, began taunting her. Shirley wished she could put these skeletons in the trash and burn them. Better yet, she wanted to beat them to death. After all, they beat on her day in and day out the way they'd done out at the mailbox.

These "old bones in the closet" were about the unspeakable—about something Shirley *had done* to Sylvie. Bonnie's letter was right. Sylvie and Shirley were totally cut off from each other. The last time they'd spoken was right before high school graduation. Shirley got up, reaching for the envelope and reading the letter a second time. Despite what Bonnie wrote, Shirley knew it wasn't that simple. Al would read the letter and want her to warn Bonnie about Sylvie. Growing anxious, she laid the letter on the table, telling herself this really wasn't a problem—at least nothing she hadn't handled before. As soon as Al read the letter, she would put it away—out of sight, out of mind. With his heavy workload, Al would forget.

Picking up the dishes, Shirley stood at the sink. Busy scrubbing them, she began fretting about something else—the trip. Though she desperately wanted to go to Bonnie's, the issue was affordability. The gas would cost too much. Depression or not, for the Dustys, who lived on a fixed salary, going that far was a problem. With Al's pay, their income left them making the most of every penny. Shirley had her egg and cream money, but that went for necessities. There was never enough left over for fun and frivolities. The exception was their Sunday picnics to the small town parks. With the Depression on, neighborhood gatherings were an added bonus.

Shirley smiled; thinking about how much getting together meant to Celeste, her middle child, who expressed herself in the cutest ways. "I don't see why everyone complains. Rich or poor, we neighbors all get together. For once, people are staying home, and we're all in the same boat."

Celeste, age twelve and naïve, could put almost anyone into fits of laughter. Bonnie, who'd known "all of it" by age eight, told Shirley, "Celeste will get married and have to ask her husband how she got pregnant!"

Moving to the living room and seeing muddy overshoe prints all over the floor, Shirley sighed, bending down to wipe Howie's nose.

"Don't," he said, shaking his head, asking if he could go see his dad, whining when she told him no. Had the day not turned gloomy and anxious, she would have said yes. Darn it, she wanted to go to Bonnie's. How did parents tell a lonely, pregnant daughter they couldn't come? Walking over to the floor lamp, Shirley turned on the light. Taking a seat in the worn out easy chair, she stared absentmindedly at the RCA console. She'd won the console at a carnival drawing up in Broken Bow. The family was thrilled about having a radio. Winter Sundays, after eating Al's chili and playing board games, they listened to radio shows. *Amos 'n' Andy* and *Buck Rogers,* as well as the great dance bands— Duke Ellington and Glen Miller— were among their favorites.

Wishing the music was playing now, she got up and went to the window. Gazing absentmindedly at the nearby hills and cattle, she saw Clark Temple's pickup in the pasture. That was when an idea began to emerge. Yes!

Certain she'd found the solution to the gas problem, Shirley scurried over to Howie. Scooping him up, she kissed him, convinced her answer was just across the way. Incredibly generous people, the Temples didn't owe the Dustys anything extra. Nevertheless, they would insist on their going to Bonnie's. For one thing, Bev adored Bonnie and couldn't stand to see the young wife, her "sparring partner," suffer. Both of them were outspoken and opinionated, arguing over promiscuity (sex), religion, and politics—things they wouldn't have dared discuss in public. In shy Shirley's opinion, these were issues every woman wanted to discuss but put aside as improper fodder for the mind.

Shirley left the room with a lilt in her step and far more vigor than she'd had when she'd entered it. Going to the kitchen, she decided to make an applesauce cake. She and Al would make it up to their landlords. Laughing at herself, for being certain of the Temple's generosity, she danced over to her recipe book on the counter. The potluck at Banner, the country church where they worshiped, was tomorrow. Though still uncertain of herself and bearing the scars of a deficient childhood, the change from the Sandhills, where Al had spent most his life, to here in the Platte Valley, had been a good one. Thanks to Clark and Bev, she was finally overcoming some of her shyness in exchange for friends. The same was true for her daughter Celeste.

Long and gangly, and as thin as a sideways ruler, Celeste was over at the Temples—another overnight. She'd become Ginny Temple's best friend when the family had moved onto the place four years ago. Ginny was also Celeste's first friend. Now eighth-graders, both of them had skipped seventh grade as advised by Miss England, the country school teacher at Union, a mile down the road. Celeste was particularly young, having started school at age four.

Always together, Ginny and Celeste made quite a pair. Ginny, a petite, whirlwind of a girl, with chocolate hair and freckles, owned the stronger, more willful personality. By contrast, Celeste, tall and skinny, with a waif's face, a thick mop of hair, and a layer of baby fat amiably about her face, was the reticent follower. Ginny took it upon herself to lead Celeste around. It seemed Ginny tied an invisible rope to Celeste—the same rope that Bev tied to Shirley. Were folks to say what stood out in Shirley's youngest daughter, they'd mention three things—a slightly jumbled look, her striking auburn hair, and those long, dangly legs. The continuous blushing was almost as noticeable. Ginny, on the other hand, was more of a traditional beauty, without unusual traits.

*   *   *

Celeste pulled her knobby knees up to her chest and smiled across the pile of marbles at her friend. She loved being in Ginny's third-story attic, especially on a wet day like today. The two girls sat playing a game of makeshift marbles and chattering against the sounds of cold rain hitting the roof. Only moments ago, Ginny had talked Mike, her eight-year-old brother, into memorizing a page out of *Tarzan*. That way, she and Celeste could be alone. As usual, *talking* was on their agenda. What they said, no one knew. Just now they were talking about Miss England and how she piled her red hair up on her head and wore beautiful sweaters. Neither admitted to having a crush on her.

Hearing familiar footsteps, the girls looked up and saw none other than Will, Ginny's older brother. A sophomore, Will was a big deal at Brady High School. According to Ginny, if his head swelled any larger, it would explode.

"I'll challenge you girls," Will offered, the same way he told the coaches he'd do anything they wanted.

To Ginny's dismay, this bravado garnered her brother a position as starting quarterback.

Glaring at him, Ginny hissed, "Remove you! Go play with the barn rats." The two siblings shared a competitive barrier between them that maddened their mother.

Grinning, blond-haired Will sat down, cross-legged, displaying the same confident ease that allowed him to throw a straight ball. Ready to win, he took the game into his hands. His first victim was Ginny, who in typical fashion, snarled at him the entire time. "Will," she said, blowing hot air up toward her loose bangs, "leave us alone."

Ignoring her, he pointed at bashful Celeste, who sat next in line.

Knowing the inevitable outcome, Celeste shrugged. *So what if he beats me at marbles?* Accepting the loss, Celeste focused in on his keen ability to concentrate. She lost track of time as she sat studying him while he reviewed the angles and positions of the marbles. Amazed by what her eyes were seeing, she questioned where this boy had been hiding all of her life. His eyes were as blue as heaven and sparkled with humor, while his hands were strong, yet tender. Delightful sensations rippled through her. Unaware of herself, she landed one hand on her dizzy stomach and the other one on a "gone mad," sizzling hot foot. The boy sitting across from her captured her imagination and more. He was dreamy and adorable. She wished he felt the same about her. On the other hand …Did she really wish this? With her shyness, she wouldn't be able to look him in the eye. Besides, he was lost in concentration, not on her, but on the marbles. *Someday I'm going to marry him*, Celeste promised herself.

Briefly, she remembered two summers ago when she and Ginny had played Cinderella. Ginny had worn one of her mother's old gowns, while Celeste had gotten into her mother's pile of rags—torn-up housedresses saved for cleaning. Using her misunderstood creativity, Celeste had made herself a gown by pinning the scraps together.

Celeste was Maid Cinderella, busy assisting Ginny, the Real Cinderella, on her way to the ball. Naturally, who but Will would catch them acting out their skit? Much to Ginny's consternation, he'd mockingly called Ginny an ugly queen, while Celeste was … the rag princess. Ginny had run off to tattle, but Celeste had stayed right where she was. No one had ever called her a princess. Rag or not, she'd been certain that, one day, her prince would await her. Presently, sitting across from Will, she was convinced that he was that prince … who didn't quite know she existed.

When Celeste returned home at noon, she saw Bonnie's letter. Picking it up, she stood at the table reading aloud. "Mom, you're going to Bonnie's, aren't you?" she inquired.

"Celeste, you know we can't. The gas is too much with Christmas coming."

Having said this, Shirley wondered if she had been wrong about Celeste. Maybe she wouldn't retrace her steps over to the Temples to tell about this dilemma.

Celeste, who saw the anxiety on her mom's face, knew exactly what to do. "Mom, I for-got my book at Ginny's house. I'll be right back."

Sometimes it seemed to Celeste as though Mother favored Bonnie. She handled this by saying that she was Dad's girl.

Seeing Celeste leave, Shirley stood crossing her fingers. As she watched her daughter disappear, she thought about the differences between Celeste and Bonnie. Shirley wondered how Celeste felt about her older sister, who favored her dad's coloring and features. Celeste, light in color, favored her. The thing was Bonnie always looked perfect. The family could appear bedraggled but not Bonnie. With a mere half yard of cotton for sewing, she'd turn herself into a fashion model. Her magic was incredible. Celeste even asked, "Mom, is Bonnie adopted? She's not quite like the rest of us."

Shirley had to show Celeste Bonnie's birth certificate for proof; Bonnie was a pure-blooded Dusty. While it was true that Bonnie owned the sparkle, Shirley didn't want this to affect Celeste. She and Sylvie had always shared the same dilemma. Sylvie had possessed the sparkle, using her glamour to hurt and scar Shirley in unthinkable ways.

*   *   *

Around seven that evening, Shirley heard a rapping on the door. Inviting the knockers to come on in, Bev and Clark Temple stepped inside. Bev, the outspoken one, went first. "You're going to visit Bonnie," she said, giving Clark a rib-cracking nudge, the kind that reminded him why they had come over.

A quiet man with a sense of presence, Clark grimaced. Exasperated with Bev's elbowing him, Clark quickly hid his irritation. Switching to a smile, he took command of the situation. "Bev tells me that after Celeste went home, she returned with concerns about you visiting Bonnie. That's not a problem. You'll take gas from the farm tank."

Pretending innocence, Shirley said, "Oh no, you two. Honestly, we couldn't accept help. That's too generous an offer during these times," she added, feeling somewhat guilty while hoping they wouldn't decide she was right.

Wagging her finger Bev, a plucky one, said, "You will go!"

Al, still wearing his socks and work clothes, walked into the kitchen. "The least we can do is to offer you coffee and blueberry crisp. We're going to repay you. Give me some extra chores," he said, motioning the couple over to the kitchen table.

Clark chuckled. "You're already working overtime. You and I both know that. Just go and have fun."

Celeste, who was in the other room, celebrating the outcome, began cheering when she saw the faces of friends, Ginny and Mike. Even though it was Saturday evening, with church in the morning, the Temples would be there until midnight talking, playing cards, and having a snack, along with Mother's dessert. She and Ginny were getting two nights, in a row, to discuss themselves. Mike could read or to do a puzzle.

* * *

With all in order for the trip to York, things changed the night before. Around 3:00 a.m., Celeste's screams awakened the Dusty household. Going straight to Celeste, Shirley found her sitting upright— her eyes— two pools of terror. Crying out, she said, "You can't go to York. You died in a storm. I saw the accident happen!" Clinging to her mother, Celeste was adamant that her parents stay home. Shirley held her close, reassuring Celeste.

"We'll be fine," honey.

"No, it was too real," she sobbed.

Feeling inadequate, Shirley embraced Celeste, holding her tightly. "Go back to sleep. It was just a dream," she said, giving her back extra pats.

On returning to bed, chill like sensations rippled through Shirley… Cuddled close against Al, she wondered…Could Celeste be right?

The next morning, Celeste's feelings hadn't changed. Tears flew as she ran out the door to the car. A Nash automobile sat waiting to take her to school. Shouting a final time, Celeste's words boomeranged through the screen door, "If you don't care what happens, I don't either. I can be a happy orphan."

Shirley, who was worried about Celeste, sought comfort in Al's reassurance. "Shirley, Celeste is overly sensitive. She's a worrywart and a lot like you. She'll be fine."

Shirley felt better but refused to leave without setting the book *Heidi* on the table. She'd bought it for a Christmas gift. Taking a pen, she left a note inside. "See you tonight, sweet child. Love, Mom and Dad."

Taking extra care with her appearance; Shirley wore her best emerald dress and a matching coat and hat. She'd sewn her dress on her aged Singer. Her chestnut hair, worn in swirls that fell to her shoulders, glistened softly in the morning sunlight. Getting in the car, she scooted over close to Al. Thoughtful and handsome, with coal black hair and olive skin, Al possessed a unique combination of intelligence, tenderness, and good common sense. Only minutes before, he'd set the mincemeat pie, along with Bev's gift, a basket filled with meat, in the trunk of their 1925 Pontiac. The car, a source of pride, was from an old man who'd wanted to repay the Dustys for their kindnesses.

The couple took delight in getting away from the farm, thankful for such a lovely morning for traveling. With the country's economic situation, the Dustys only made it as far as Brady, nine miles north, once a week. Today's longer journey allowed for time together, accompanied by laughter and gaiety. The trees, thick with frost, turned the world to white, appearing like sparkling diamonds, dripping from the limbs, as they drove from one small town to another, following the Platte for a ways.

They were just past Kearney when Al brought the dreaded subject out of hiding.

"Shirley," he said, "Bonnie's letter mentioned her desire to look up Sylvie. This worries me; you know I'm right. She hurt you. And another thing. Both of us witnessed what she did to Ida Lord, the old woman she lived with. Do you remember Ida's thin, onion-like skin? Her arms had those bruises and rips, and her money had all but disappeared. If Bonnie befriends Sylvie, she could hurt both her and the baby. Tell our daughter the truth about her. Sylvie might appear on the society pages, but don't fool yourself. She's still the same Sylvie. You've got to tell her today."

Unprepared with excuses for why she couldn't tell Bonnie, Shirley's chest felt as though her secrets were about to jump out of her body, exposing themselves. With a rehearsed smile and a parched tongue, she managed, "Al, not today. We came to have a good time. Why upset Bonnie? We seldom see her."

"How could you upset her? She met Sylvie once. Good heavens, dear!"

Shirley ran her sandpaper tongue along her upper lip, trying to come up with a logical excuse for not telling Bonnie the truth. How could she tell Bonnie about her sister after what she'd done to Sylvie? On the other hand, what if Al was right? If he was, Bonnie should maintain a safe distance from Sylvie.

Those things she'd never told Al –misdeeds that involved both Al and Sylvie—caused Shirley an extreme amount of distress. Al would never forgive her for what she'd done. Instead, he'd walk out on her. Too afraid, she'd never confided in anyone. The only person who knew anything was Bev Temple. Bev knew a small amount — only what Shirley had chosen to tell her. As a result, she'd spent endless years suffering. Now, riding along beside Al, a startling thought came to her. What if she risked confessing everything? …It would be like taking years of unceasing weight off her back. Such an idea caused her to wonder if she was going mad. Petrified by this impulse, she was speechless.

She sat, absentmindedly, playing with her pearl hatpin. Using it as a needle, she poked it endlessly in and out of her coat. Despairing, she toyed with telling him the truth. If only she could tell him what she'd done- explain things- and he would go on loving her. Al and the kids were the biggest part of her "insignificant" life. Why he loved her was still a mystery, even after all these years. He'd been popular, talented, and the grandson of wealth. Never mind that his grandfather had spurned him in the end. Al's share of the vast sums went elsewhere. By comparison, Shirley had lived in a shed turned shack as a girl.

"Al, please, we can talk about Sylvie another time. This is the only outing we've taken in ages. Don't ruin this trip. I'm sorry, but I refuse to discuss Sylvie today," she said, jamming the hatpin back into her hat.

Determined, Al put his foot down, refusing to accept this. "Shirley, you do this every time. We don't get anywhere. I'm not going to drop it. I made my decision before we ever started out. We'll skip going to Bonnie's if you insist on not telling her about Shirley. I'm concerned that Sylvie will get ahold of the baby when it's born. If we get to York, and you haven't agreed to tell her, home is the other way. That's how worried I am."

While Al drove on in silence, Shirley continued to play with her hatpin, as if obsessed with the task. A Godly woman, Shirley questioned what right she had to discuss her sister's anger. After all, she'd caused Sylvie's fury, long ago, during their final weeks of high school. That was when Shirley had repaid Sylvie for a lifetime of cruelty and rejection; her sister had physically hurt her and shamed her over and over. Ultimately, Sylvie had stolen Shirley's youth.

However, what about today–years later? Sylvie, who had become a well-known socialite, would never hurt Bonnie. Just look at her; Sylvie headed charities for goodness sake! It was Bonnie's right to meet her aunt. The two would likely become friends … And yet…what if Sylvie was still mean? In high school, she'd hidden her deadly streak under a charming façade.

Shirley's mind began racing, this way and that, back and forth–spinning out of control. Finally, within ten miles of York, cautious and uncertain–trapped, but imagining life out of the cage, she began talking—slow and tentative at first. "Al, I'm going to sound a little looney. Even I can't make sense of what I feel or think. Though I'm careful to praise Sylvie, I…I suppose I have undeserved anger towards her. She didn't like me as far back as age five. In her eyes, I was Celeste—skinny and pale, a shy girl on the sidelines. I was a ragamuffin. Bonnie was beautiful. I was bashful like Celeste. Sylvie ordered me to stay away from her. I was Shirley White, a piece of trash. If the kids at school found out that I was her sister, she'd become trash."

"Ha! I'd gladly drop her in the trash," Al scoffed.

"Seriously, do you know how she became Sylvie Lord, Ida's granddaughter? Al, we seem to have danced around this part of the story."

"We've avoided talking about that part because of the awkward way, in which, we met. It's easier to stay clear of certain areas that involve Sylvie. I was amazed when you finally opened up and talked about her hurting and taunting you when you were little. Go ahead and tell about how she came to live with Ida."

"Sylvie and I were fourteen the year we moved to Lincoln. Mom was severely alcoholic, and we were all but destitute. Grandma brought Mom and us two girls from California by train. It took Grandma's last pennies, along with some church help, to buy our tickets back. Sylvie, who was always interested in money, had built this delusion. She thought we were traveling to Nebraska to meet a grandmother who was wealthy. Was she ever surprised?

"I'll never forget Sylvie's eyes when she saw our new home. Grandma lived in a shed—worse than the nearby shacks. Sylvie saw the "shack" and flew apart. Chickens were all over the place … The next day; Sylvie refused to say where she was going. That afternoon, she found Ida Lord. A rich recluse, Ida was out picking weeds. Sylvie got down and finished for her. Can you imagine her helping anyone? She convinced Ida to let her move in and assist her. Sylvie told the poor woman she'd work as a maid of all things. She came home just long enough to pack. Even then, Sylvie wanted nothing to do with me. To her, I was poor Shirley White."

"Not at all surprising!" Al sneered. "It was disgusting the way Grandfather adored her. She always took that path from Ida's that led over to his house. I wanted nothing to do with her, but the old cuss shoved her in my face."

Seeing Shirley's clamped jaw, Al asked, "What is it? What's wrong?"

"Sylvie came to me two weeks before graduation. She talked on and on about the two of you, saying how you sat on Ida's porch every night. She said how wealthy you were and how rich she would be as your wife. She spoke endlessly of everything you had planned for her—parties, clothes, jewelry, cars. I reached my limit. I'm docile, but as you know, I have a breaking point. "

Exasperated, Al pounded the steering wheel, shaking his head.

Taking a breath, Shirley gripped her shoulders, hugging herself. "You're going to leave me when I tell you what I did."

"Me leave you? Are you joking?"

Not hearing him, Shirley rushed her words. "I stayed in the distance, making sure Mom and Grandma were kept away from her. The whole thing was senseless. She never saw them anyway. She said that you'd walk out on her if you learned she was a White,

Wanting to buy time for talking, Al turned into a lane that led to a farmer's field. Finding a spot near some trees, he parked the car. Opening the door, Shirley gulped in the fresh air before continuing. "After I learned about the accident, I asked the policemen to drive me to Ida's. I…I had no reason to tell Sylvie about Mom and Grandmother. Sylvie didn't care about them. My only reason for going over there was so you would hear her real name. I told the policemen who she was on the drive over. I was certain that the police would question her identity. I wanted you to leave her as soon as you heard her say that she was a White. I assure you, I didn't do this with thoughts of us falling in love. I did it to hurt her. I felt it would serve her right. I didn't even know you, Al. We had one class together, but you never saw me." Shuddering, Shirley stepped out on the hardened stubble lined fields, walking a ways, before turning to look at Al.

"Wait up," he said. "We need to talk." Following along to where she stood, he said, "I can still see that old woman shuffling out to the porch, telling the policemen about Sylvie's crimes against her. As for your sister's name, that wasn't a problem. You were a White, and I married you. I never loved Sylvie. I didn't even like her. Her lying and abusing Ida– those things were more than I could handle."

Shirley, whose hands were clasped tight, appeared to be somewhere else.

"What," Al asked, puzzled over Shirley continuing distress? "What did you do that was wrong?"

Sinking to the ground, Shirley covered her face with her hands. Al knelt beside her. Gently, he removed her fingers, holding them in his, despite her tears.

"There's more. My sister said she was pregnant with your baby and how you didn't know. She was saving this news as a surprise graduation gift to you. The baby was Donnie; the one who died in that fall. You never would have left, knowing she was pregnant with your child. I knew this, and married you without telling you. I'm a monster," she sobbed.

Al put his arms about her, pulling her close against him, while wiping her eyes. "Shirley, you're mistaken about everything. First off, she told me she was pregnant right away."

"You knew?" she asked, looking at him questioningly.

"The baby wasn't mine."

"But Sylvie said it was. I'd never seen her so thrilled about anything."

"My crazy grandpa refused to accept that I wasn't the father. He and Sylvie came up with ludicrous stories about how I got her pregnant. The rich old coot…Ha! How he could have thought that basketball players made politicians? — I finally agreed. I felt confusion over abandoning a child about to be born. It bothered me. Maybe it was fickle and wrong of me, but between Ida's bruises and seeing you, I told her to find the real father." Tempted to tell Shirley the name of the father, Al decided against it. "In the end, things worked out for the best. Sylvie did herself well in picking Mack. Not a bad catch," he said.

Unremitting, Shirley continued with another confession. "Even with what you've said, I took a child's life. If you'd married her, Donnie wouldn't have been around those stairs that were being worked on because …"

"That's nonsense Shirley, and you know it. Why do you persecute yourself?"

Neither spoke as the morning went silent, then, hesitantly, Al disclosed a suspicion he'd never shared. "Shirley, I'm not at all sure that Donnie fell."

"Al, she would never do that," Shirley said her nervous laughter, trickling off with the morning breeze.

Rising, Al reached down; taking his wife's hands, he helped her up, thinking Shirley even more beautiful in the clear morning air. Though her cheeks were blotched and her eyes swollen, neither lessened her beauty. Wondering if he should have said that, he added, "But that boy's death is in no way your fault." As was his nature, Al wanted to reassure her. "Say Shirley, seeing as how this has been intense, we'll wait a couple of weeks to tell Bonnie? It's imperative to write the truth." Smiling at her, Al motioned his head towards the Pontiac, his way of saying they were done with the issue for now. "Let's enjoy ourselves. We have a great day ahead of us."

In the car again, Shirley shifted in her seat, facing Al. "Why didn't I bring this up sooner? I really thought that, if I told you these things, you would leave me. The tragedy lies in my not sharing these happenings sooner."

Dear Shirley, "Rejoice. I have no misgivings. Stop creating tragedies."

Shirley was rummaging in her purse, looking for her comb, when Al said, "I forgot one thing. You talked about being like Celeste. That bothers me. What did you mean by that?"

Shirley began combing her hair. "Bonnie is the pretty one. Celeste has the beautiful hair, but so much of her is me."

"Shirley, Celeste is adorable. Someday soon, she'll be the beauty that you are now. Your sister was jealous. Though you're twins, you look nothing alike. Believe me, you're by far the loveliest. But really, it doesn't matter who's prettier. You were both children, deserving of love and warmth. Our daughters deserve the same unconditional love? Tell me why it was that neither your mother nor grandmother stepped in? You were just a young girl when Sylvie began tormenting you."

Shirley gazed out the window. Saying what she felt was difficult. Discussing her feelings about Sylvie was nearly impossible.

Looking straight ahead, Al answered for her. "Shirley, your mother and Grandma Bristol let Sylvie beat on you. I think they did it so that you'd stay and care for them the way you did. Sylvie knew that. I worry about our dear Celeste. I hope she's able to see herself realistically. Your eyes need to smile when you look at her. Speaking of looking, my eyes tell me how gorgeous you are in that green. You wore a ravishing rose to the courthouse, in Broken Bow, that day. When I asked you what you wanted for a wedding present, you said a cherry tree, garden seeds, and a garden. When you asked me, I said that I wanted you. As I remember it, we both got what we wanted. Next summer, let's return there for a day. We can pick cherries and well…" Al raised his eyebrows playfully. "I think you know the rest.

"I would have married Sylvie and been miserable. It was when I saw you in the moonlight at Ida's, that I for sure changed my mind. You were wearing that soft cotton dress and those *Cinderella* type shoes. Your hair was back on one side, and the moonlight enhanced your features. You looked at me for the briefest moment and stole my heart. You were tall and slender, with that full mouth and those shy but inquisitive eyes. Something gave when our eyes met. It might have been that sweet, humble way of yours. I thought I would die if I didn't get the chance to touch you. And then there you were at the dance the next night. Even then, before I'd taken you into my arms, I knew I'd found my life mate. I have no regrets. Sylvie got my inheritance and Ida's house and a world of greed and emptiness. I got you."

Shirley recalled the dance and how she'd obsessed about going. She'd been in grief with the tragedy happening the night before. The only reason she went was in hopes of seeing that boy from the night before. She'd wondered if she only imagined he liked her and felt that she might never see him again … unless she went to the dance.

*   *   *

Bonnie flew out the door to greet her parents when they drove up. News, laughter, and surprises filled up the morning at Bonnie's. Al and Shirley stood back, wanting a careful view of Bonnie's protrusion. Amazed that, at seven months, she'd only gained fifty-five pounds, Al voiced his concern, saying the baby might be malnourished. Shirley suggested the possibility of the baby being born too small. In a wink, all three were doubled over laughing. Fifty-five pounds was nothing over which to sneeze. Bonnie would need to diet!

Next thing on the agenda, Shirley wanted a closer look at the small trailer with its aluminum siding. Finding herself unprepared for anything so small, she asked, "Bonnie won't you be a bit crowded once this child comes?"

Bonnie moaned. "I wish Bob wasn't working for that tightwad uncle of his. I don't know what he was thinking when he bought this tin can trailer."

Al, normally one for jesting, glanced sharply at Shirley. "True, but remember, Bob's doing his utmost to get you by in this depression. People are out there starving, Bonnie. I'm lucky to work for Clark Temple. He furnished the gas from the farm tank to get here. Be grateful that Bob is diligent and loyal. If not, you'd be without this home."

"I know, but I find my days boring. I should have gone to school. Being stuck in this tiny trailer is awful."

"Bonnie, you chose this life. Make the most of it," Al lectured in fatherly fashion.

Shirley winced. Why couldn't Al understand Bonnie's aspirations? Disturbed, she rose, disappearing into the miniature bathroom. Downhearted, she sat and cried. Bonnie should have followed through with her education. This was no place for her to be living. Taking her hankie, she blew her nose. Even now, Shirley dreaded ruining the fairy tales Bonnie had built, around Sylvie. What if Bonnie didn't believe Shirley when she warned her about Sylvie? Jumbled, Shirley was once again uncertain about Sylvie. Although Al had just convinced her of the dangers surrounding Sylvie, maybe Al was too judgmental– or maybe even jealous?

Fleetingly, Shirley thought about the enjoyment she got from Bonnie's scrapbook. Though they'd avoided discussions whenever Al was around, she and Bonnie had managed to bring Sylvie up from time to time…No one knew this, but during the school year, while Bonne was at school, the scrapbook had become Shirley's favorite pastime. Reading about Sylvie was like reading a fairytale, especially when it was a twin sister, and your own life was ordinary by comparison…Shirley frowned. Totally extinguishing Sylvie would…

Struck by what felt like a zap of lightning, Shirley had the answer. *Sylvie!* She knew who it was that would help Bonnie with the cost of going to college. Sylvie continued to adore the girl she'd once met. Over the years, she'd sent Bonnie four cards. As soon as Sylvie saw Bonnie again, she'd fall in love with the beautiful young wife and mother. Shirley would bet money on her sister saying yes to helping with her education. Sylvie's husband, Mack, with his three drugstores, was the reason for Sylvie's elaborate lifestyle. Later that day Shirley would share her solution with Bonnie. Other than turning to Sylvie for assistance, Bonnie was without means for escaping this dull life of hers? Assertive and bright, her daughter could handle Sylvie should she became manipulative.

Following lunch, Shirley and Al, with Bonnie as their guide, took a brief auto tour of York—brief because of the scarcity of fuel and money. Returning home, Bonnie and her mother looked at Bonnie's small collection of baby blankets. They were lying folded in a nip and tuck cupboard. That's when Shirley gave her a handmade, yellow baby quilt. Each block was a small fan design. These she'd made using leftover scraps of this and that. It was Bev who taught Shirley how to quilt. Shirley's ability to work a needle so skillfully baffled Bev. It took mere hours to teach Shirley how to weave the thread in and out of the fabric.

Around three thirty, following coffee, Al up and went downtown. He wanted to stop in at the market to see Bob and his workplace.

Still enjoying coffee, Shirley's finger began tapping on the small table. "Bonnie, have you possibly considered financial aid for school?"

"Mother, are you nuts? Who has any money?"

"Well …" Shirley's fingers began tapping faster and harder. Attempts at initiating ideas made her nervous. "Bonnie, there is someone who still has money."

It was the way her mother said *someone*, emphasizing it, that told Bonnie who Mom had in mind. Bonnie's eyes filled with life as she listened to her mother. When Shirley was done explaining, Bonnie smiled. "You're the genius, Mother. Not a bad idea. When the baby is a few months old, I'll call Sylvie. I'm excited; I'll get to reunite with my idol."

*   *   *

With daylight passing into darkness too quickly, the three of them shared a supper of fried cornmeal mush and baked apples. They were about finished when sleet began pinging on the side of the steel colored trailer. Within moments, the sleet turned to sheets of ice. Shirley would gladly have taken a blanket and bedded down for the night, but Al insisted— He and Shirley needed to head for home. "I have work to do, and Celeste is anxious to see us. She needs to know we're back and safe."

Still, Bonnie begged them to stay put. "We can call the Temples so that Celeste knows you are here. With that ice, the roads are dangerous."

Even Bob, down ringing out customers at his uncle's neighborhood market, called, saying the radio reported statewide ice storms.

Nevertheless, Al vetoed any mother and daughter objections by saying that farmers always went home and that one day away was enough. He knew how to drive in this stuff. He'd driven in far worse. No problem.

After several kisses and hugs and a host of good-byes, they were off for home.

Both Al and Shirley compared the day to a purple pansy bouquet, the kind that was their favorite. Coming as no surprise, the roads were treacherous. Al swerved more than once on the invisible black ice. Several cars were in the ditch. Temperatures were dropping. Overconfident in his driving, Al reached over to pat Shirley. "We'll be home in no time," he said.

Nervous over the roads, Shirley used talking as a means of distraction. "That baby is going to look just like our Bonnie. I think she's happy but homesick. I would love her back home for a month or maybe forever." Bouncing her fingers on her knees, Shirley asked, "Where are we? I'm worried about Celeste."

"We're just east of Aurora," Al answered, concentrating on driving.

It was then that Shirley froze, sensing they were about to die. Panicked, she turned toward Al to tell him, but it passed. It was just one of those silly moments, she told herself. They weren't dying after all. Or were they? The premonition returned. She needed to tell Al one other thing. Time was running out They couldn't die without her confessing everything to her soul mate. This last sin was a problem—one that caused her to dread death.

As she watched the faces of Celeste and Howie float before her eyes, Shirley wanted to be there for them, but knew she couldn't. Unsuspectingly, overcome with calmness, Shirley began. "Al, please listen. You need to know one other thing," she said. "Back when Celeste was a newborn, I had no one there besides seven-year-old Bonnie and my colicky baby. The land was dry and dusty, and you were working long hours. The loneliness was unbearable. I tried to think of someone who could visit with me, but there was no one. As hopeless as I felt, Sylvie came to mind. I even thought of going to her home for a break, as if she would have had me."

"As if I would let you go, darling."

"One of the Sunday papers had an article about Sylvie. It said that Sylvie wasn't able to have more children. I felt horrible for what I had done. I thought that, if she'd married you …"

Al chuckled. "There you go again. You thought I wouldn't have been fixing any stairs and Donnie would still be living. It's hard for me to imagine a man like Mack, who's busy with three drugstores, remodeling those steps. I would think him too harried with other responsibilities."

"Let me finish. I wanted Sylvie for a sister. I was that frantic. My longings portrayed her as being a good friend. In desperation, I wrote a letter, the kind that most sisters could send in good faith. I can remember the words like it was yesterday." Shirley crossed her hands as if praying. Then exhaling, she quoted the letter. "Dear Sylvie, I miss you and am profoundly sorry. Please forgive me. I want to strengthen our relationship. In a demonstration of my love for you, I am going to give you my most precious gift, Celeste, my sweet newborn and Bonnie, the child you met, and any more that I'm blessed to have. I want them to go to you should anything happen to Al and me. Your sister, my love, Shirley."

Shirley, who could still feel the imminence of death around the corner, said, "It's over with us, isn't it, Al? Even if Donnie wasn't yours, I did the unpardonable."

"My precious darling, I married you for better or worse. It would take more than what you did to make me leave. We all do those irrational things. Besides, I know how much you love the children. It's just that you're too impulsive. As far as that goes, it doesn't hold any weight. Your letter wasn't legal or signed by witnesses. All these worries of yours are unnecessary? Did the clever wizard write back?"

Shirley clutched. "I wrote her four times trying to reverse what I'd said. Eventually, a terrifying letter came back from her. It read, 'Shirley, I'll be here waiting. Your gift was surely generous. Sylvie."

Turning to catch Al's silhouette, Shirley heard the tires screech and Al's shouting, "Hang on!" A farm truck appeared, veering over to the wrong side of the road and crushing Al and Shirley's car.

The couple, who had met each other on Ida's porch the night of her mother's car wreck, died instantly. The other driver, a farmer, also died.

For Al and Shirley, love had been tender from the start. The night after first seeing her, Shirley stood in the gymnasium at the May Dance, wearing her rose satin gown, with graduation just a day away. Al's hands were shaking when he went to ask her for a dance. Hearing her say yes, he reached out for her waist. With his arms about her, they danced under a crepe-paper sky with a glitter moon and stars for lights.

Amid the spell of romantic jazz and lavender scent, he spoke to her. "I'm not Howard Anderson. I'm Al Dusty from Arnold and the Sandhills. My mother's name was Lizzie Anderson. She died when I was born. I might as well tell you that my parents married shotgun style. Grandpa Anderson said for me to use my middle name, Howard, the name my mother had picked out for me. An annulment was in the making between mother and father. I came here after Dad drowned on a cattle drive. I'm returning home to the Sandhills. I don't know what you would think of those barren hills. By the way, you can be the first to call me Al, if you'd like."

Blushing lightly, she replied, "I'd like that, Al. The hills sound nicer than waitressing. As for me, I never met my father. In my case, there was no marriage. I'm Shirley White."

Taking a big chance on the integrity of their hearts, they drove to the hills of sand and grass and cattle. By the next afternoon, they were man and wife.

The first summer was an experiment in kissing. They discovered a hundred different ways. He liked the open French; she preferred his nibbling on her upper lip Al and Shirley's relationship was an once-in-a-lifetime love. They were soul mates until the end. One of the saddest things for Al had been that Shirley's Grandmother had known about Sylvie's crimes against Shirley. Instead of doing something, she'd made Shirley forgive. She had used Bible verses in order to frighten Shirley into submitting. Hell was the price for fighting back.

*   *   *

Al knew that marrying Shirley, a woman made fragile from the difficulties she'd faced growing up, didn't mean a life free of problems. She had her issues. Though she'd gotten better, Shirley had times of anxiety. While emotionally trying for him too, he knew of no other woman he wanted. The good times were worth the difficult moments, and even though Shirley was a bit of a lost soul, Al never lost patience with her. His tenderness grew from the sight of her scars—scars he'd never forget.

> The funeral for Al and Shirley Dusty
> will be held at Banner Church, Tuesday
> morning at 11:00. Pastor Broadwater will
> give the eulogy and conduct the service.

Following the funeral, interment was at the nearby country cemetery. Bob and Bonnie served as the strength for Celeste who was crying so hard she could barely stand up. Howie was asking for Mommy and Daddy. The temperature was below zero.

Later on, folks said it was all they could do to keep from crying at the sight of Celeste's coat, the sleeves too short, the buckles of her black rubber overshoes broken and hanging to the side. "But then that's what this Great Depression does," folks said to each other.

During the funeral service, something murky was happening elsewhere. No one knew of the letter, except for a woman named Elvira and one other, the recipient of the letter, Sylvie. Bev Temple knew only what Shirley had chosen to share. The recipient was on her way to see a judge, good for favors, and his helper, Elvira.

While the four years on the Temple ranch had been near idyllic for a family of individuals who reached out and enjoyed their roles in the rural community, including and especially Shirley and Celeste, an unraveling was about to begin for one of them. As time passed, the letter would affect the lives of every remaining Dusty.

*   *   *

Celeste found *Heidi*_after school that day. Despite Mother's note, Celeste blamed herself, thinking her harsh words and anger had caused God to take her parents from her as punishment. Bonnie stayed an extra week to work with Celeste's traumatized spirit. Meanwhile, Bonnie was fighting her own bout of self-condemnation for having written and demanded her parents visit. In her mind, she had taken Howie and Celeste's parents away from them.

As soon as the Temples learned of the accident, they made their home open to Celeste and Howie. Who could do a better job of loving and raising the orphans? Celeste and Howie were like their own children. An unusual friendship had struck up between the two families, considering the economic differences between them. Bev and Clark were very attentive in seeing to the needs of Celeste and Howie. Bev's open arms held the kids, fresh sheets awaited them, she fixed warm nurturing meals, and Celeste could sit in the tin tub as long as she wanted—sometimes crying her tears into the warm water. Ginny was there beside her mother, offering to play games, tell stories, romp in the attic.

In time, Celeste joined her but not at first. Life was too hopeless for play. She still held on to the belief that she had affected Dad's driving. Yet, gradually, her days improved, and she was able to distance herself from the dream and the wreck. Finally, in the third month following the accident, she began to show gradual improvement.

*   *   *

Bev heard the screams and came running to Celeste's side. "What is it? What is it?" Bev asked. Wearing her oversized robe, she patted

Celeste repeatedly while Celeste's terrorized eyes looked into Bev's eyes. Bev wondered, when, if ever, this would end. "

Celeste cried out in small hiccup-like sobs, "The "orphan women! Who's taking Howie and me? We have no home! Are we going to the orphan women?"

Celeste, Bev squeezed the girl. "No, baby, you and Howie are here to stay with us. This is your home."

"Two orphan ladies came to get Howie and me," Celeste cried while Bev rocked her back and forth and assured her of a home, saying they would celebrate over Swiss steak.

The unofficial birthday celebration would be extra special; Bev got a rose for each of the children, including her own, since they would be like siblings. She slipped hearts in with the roses, bought red vases for each of them, and along with raspberry rhubarb pie, she made chocolate truffles. She couldn't resist cuddly bears. In time, she and Clark would do an official adoption. Because of the economy, Bev and Clark dipped into their extras' fund without hesitation.

Ginny slaved over a poem. That night she recited the words she'd written.

> "Welcome
>
> Like the sunflower's smile
> And waters clear and blue
> Like grasses growing green
> We love and welcome you.
> Trust me when I say,
> You have become part of us
> A family that will never let you down
> Or lead you astray.
> From this moment on-
> You are here to stay.
> Welcome to Temple family."

After a big teary applause, Bev and Clark welcomed the children into their home, a permanent part of the family. Clark gave Howie a miniature picture Bible and Celeste a girl's Bible with a golden cross on the zipper. She had one just like it. The cross on this Bible was bigger than on the

Bible he'd already handed out to the Sunday school class. Apparently, he'd forgotten. Ginny, who got the giggles, pretended it was about something at school that day. Passing her laughter over to Celeste, she caught then, but in her cautious, light voice thanked this kind man who was to be her new father. Next, Will, not expected to take part, surprised everyone. After grabbing and popping a balloon, he turned to Howie with a little car. "Pal," he said, "welcome, little brother."

Celeste, who saw another gift, crossed her fingers so tightly, under the table, she might have broken them. Would Will offer something to a screwball like her?

"Celeste, this one is for you." Will handed her a box with three lace hankies, all different colors, from Edward's Drugstore in Brady. Looking down, she tried to hide the tears. There wasn't a chance of her eyes meeting his.

She hadn't looked at him since the day she'd declared herself in love. Will, confident as ever, eyed her. In his mind, she was dissatisfied with the hankies. He reached over for the box. Quick as lightning, Celeste jerked it away from him. "I…I love them," she murmured choking and sniffing. Thank you." Later that night, she laid the white one, aside in a powder jar, for when they married.

Ginny glared darts through Will. She wasn't one bit happy over her brother's show of generosity—a display she felt was more to impress their folks than welcome either Celeste or Howie. Celeste, with her sensitivity, felt these looks of Ginny's as keenly as if a porcupine had struck; this was the reason she'd never told Ginny about liking Will. He had been their enemy ever since the Dustys moved onto the place.

The school's Valentine's Day was tomorrow, and only Bev dared make the cookies, for the country school party, a project she had taken on back when Will was in the first grade. Goodness, next year the girls would go to town school. Just twelve-years-old, Celeste, who was already young for her grade, would definitely be the youngest. This concerned Bev, who thought Celeste too young. A vulnerable child…What about boys!

The recipe for the prized cookies came from her mother, who got it from her mother, Bev's grandmother, who, as far as Bev was concerned, possessed a great deal more common sense than her daughter did. The daughter was, of course, Bev's mother. Bev was not afraid to tell this to anyone who displayed the slightest interest in the two women. Since didn't happen, Bev never got to share this, or the fact that she, not her mother, used the recipe.

Howie sat nearby on the floor with a set of wooden blocks. Bev was surprised at how much she enjoyed the little guy. Before long, he'd take his afternoon nap. Though scolded herself— she should look forward to her time alone—impossible.

Busy at work, Bev stood at the counter doing out dough hearts and singing to Howie. The boy's spirits were back close to normal. With Al and Shirley passing that November, Christmas had been unbearably sad. No, things were brighter, like frosting before the final glitter. This holiday would be fun. Like herself, Celeste seemed better. Bev didn't know which thing had made her happiest-had it been that the Temples were giving her a permanent home or those lacey from Will? Were they really worthy of the girl's tears? Then again, Will had been a stinker to Ginny and Celeste. To have a teaser and pest do something nice…well, it got to everyone. She was glad to see his emergence as a thoughtful son and citizen. As much fun as he could be, she'd had her doubts about how he'd turn out. He'd gone from a cocoon on a tree, to a butterfly.

One of the reasons for Celeste's strides forward was Elle Pederson, a woman in Union Aid. Elle had overheard Bev discussing Celeste's guilt with Jenny Anderson, in at the grocery store. Rolling her cart over, she joined them. Incredibly, the same thing happened to her, as a child, just before her Mom and the baby had been killed in a tornado. Elle, a young girl, of nine, at the time of the incident, had been told by Mother to apologize to her brother for a nasty remark. It concerned an arm he'd lost in a farm accident. Sick of all the care and attention going to the younger brother, she'd refused; instead, she'd accused Mon of being "the cruelest person on earth."

Ellie's mother had told Ellie that she wasn't acting like herself and to say she was sorry and that she loved her brother. Instead, Ellie had run to the barn right after she'd stuck out her tongue. Distraught, she'd fallen asleep; a storm roaring past had awakened her. Later, she'd found her mother and brother, lifeless under some trees.

Ellie had come to share this with Celeste. She was planning to have her over to her magnificent home, in Peckham Township, a short ways south of Brady… Bev was certain that Ellie would cure Celeste's guilt.

Bev was on her twentieth heart shaped sugar cookie when a couple of doors slammed shut. Who would that be? She slid the dough onto the cookie sheet. "Howie, I'll be right back," she assured the boy. Walking along to the foyer, Bev's doughy hands took ahold of the glass doorknob, opening the heavy Oak door a crack. What was this?

A frosty puff appeared, then disappeared, each time one of the women took a breath. Upon seeing Bev, they curved their frozen lips, making a smile. Neither woman even faintly resembled the other one. My goodness. Who could it be? It surely wasn't one of those peddlers who sold vacuums or encyclopedias or cleaning supplies or Bible conversion stuff. It wasn't gypsies. You wouldn't drive a car like that and need to sell those things, but just in case, she was prepared to say, "Go away! No thank you. I have my own things and need none of yours. I have my stores, my church, and my catalogues. Peddlers not needed."

However, one of the women, the flashy one, was no ordinary person. She looked like one of those fancy ladies from the city. Who was that drab thing with her? Bev questioned them, but what about herself, a stocky woman dressed in her blue plaid housedress and torn white apron? She hadn't put on makeup and didn't intend to. Clark wasn't as interested in her lips or hips as he was in his crops and livestock. That was just fine with Bev.

Although she didn't exactly like the looks of these women, she had to admit to a certain amount of intrigue. The fancy one had quite the garb— a green and black wool dress that came as an ensemble. She wore a matching suede skin coat and a big green hat with mink trim and lime and black flowers. My stars! Bev thought. What sort of milliner had done that one up? As though that were not enough, she had stacked black suede high heels. Might as well put a magpie in the flowers to finish her off. The other one, dowdy and ordinary, had an older brief case about to burst, a wool scarf, and an old plaid coat. Her eyes appeared to rest on the lenses of thick magnifiers. Interestingly, the exquisite one had taken what Bev figured would amount to three tubes of lipstick and worked them onto thin lips. Bev thought that Fancy Lady might as well bite the stuff off. Another thing, Fancy Lady had those bulging kind of eyes. She'd be a perfect understudy for Bette Davis, whose eyes had a bit of convexity. Was that the word for curve? "And you are?" she asked none too friendly. A woman should always know her company before buttering up.

Fancy lady took the lead with a smile so wide Bev thought it would crack her cheeks. "I'm Sylvie Sobori and this is Elvira, a helper, who rode along with me from Lincoln. "Don't let that over-stuffed satchel of Elvira's scare you. She's not selling anything. Tisk, tisk," she chortled.

Paying no heed to this, Bev squinted, her hand placed on her forehead, trying to recollect who the stylish woman was. "You are…ah. I remember now. You were in the obituary and would be the sister of Shirley. You were the one who wasn't at the funeral. Bonnie looked forward to your being there… Step inside where it's warm. And what is it you want?"

"It smells blissful in here," Sylvie said, pretending like she didn't hear the question. "That smell is ecstasy. What is that?"

Bev appreciated her baking and nothing delighted her like people eating her creations. Sometimes, when folks passed by, they stopped, just to see what she had on hand. Always welcome, they stayed for a couple of hours. Bev got carried away with entertaining, which meant that snacking led to talking. Nothing like sharing a little gossip over rolls.

Preparing for these unexpected guests, she said, "Let me take that coat. Then we'll talk about my dough out there in the kitchen." Bev had taken notice of the Packard parked by the gate. That told her that Sylvie wouldn't steal anything or cause big problems. Besides, bad people never came to the country anyway. One didn't hear of a farm family being robbed or murdered. It might just be fun to find out about this fancy woman while she baked and they tried her cookies.

Elvira, the one with the satchel, spoke out. "Mrs. Bev, you have egg dripping from your apron. I just thought you'd want to know."

"Yes. I know that." Bev chuckled, wiping the egg up with an old, torn hankie and then picking at the flour crusted to the bottom of her apron. "Like I tell Clark, my husband, I purposefully wear my ingredients about the house. That way, I can offer a cookie whenever someone comes to the door."

The eccentric woman chortled at Bev's corny joke while Sylvie stood there, eyeing Bev's huge collection of United States plates and souvenir spoons. Bev, who took this as her being awed, jumped in. "Would you like the stories on those? My neighbors bring them from everywhere."

Sylvie chortled. "And you just wish they would stop this sort of thing? You do, don't you? By the way, there's a picture of you over here by the plates. Is that your husband or son?"

The young man was Clark, her husband, who was older than Bev was. "That's my husband, Clark. It's last year's church picture, and yes, people do tell us that *we* look extraordinarily young." Feeling clever, Bev said, "Let's have a cookie. Sylvie, what brings you here? I assume you have questions about Shirley, who was my best friend and the most wonderful woman I've known."

"Uh-huh. It's good to see where my sister lived. She liked a plain life. The farm would have been perfect." Before Bev could comment on the fallacy of calling farm life plain, ordinary, or boring, Sylvie had a request. "I see that you have coffee over there. I really don't drink coffee, but I would put you up to fixing a cup of hot tea. All I need is some hot water, a tea bag, sugar, cream, a tea hook, and two napkins. I forgot. Give me a spoon. Tea is much easier to fix than coffee."

This wasn't exactly what Bev wanted to do in the middle of baking cookies. While she made the tea, Sylvie went to remove her hat, returning with a headful of curled black waves. Bev wished she was as slender and pretty. Instead, she was stocky, with rosy cheeks that matched her strawberry blond hair.

Sylvie bit out a small bite, leaving the bulk of the cookie. Good society women followed this rule. Sylvie claimed to buy her own brand of cookie, a pecan thing, which she purchased from a market in Lincoln. "I choose not to spend the day overheating my kitchen when I can trot down the street for cookies and lose calories while I go."

Bev, still heating the water didn't hear this offensive remark; instead she Sylvie began scrutinizing her kitchen. Noting this, Bev asked Sylvie what she thought of her rooster collection, the one that lined the counter and a long shelf…twenty roosters, salt and pepper sets, and an extra rooster container for cookies.

"I think a Puss and Boots cookie jar would be nicer. If roosters are what you want, there are plenty outside. One of them was on my car when I came. He flew up to get warm and scratched the paint."

Bev secretly wanted to laugh at the arrogant woman. "You mean to tell me that the paint isn't any better than that? Why do they make such cheap stuff?" *I put you in your place*, she thought, feeling better and saving a rise in blood pressure.

In some ways, Sylvie was the equivalent of Bev. One was rural and the other citified, meaning they thought differently. One was friendly but cautious, the other, rude, a component as inherent in her as flour is to bread. At present, Sylvie was saying that city women had no time to spare, which could only mean that countrywomen owned slack hands. Bev was preparing her attack when Howie came walking in from the front room.

"Howie!" Sylvie bellowed, flinging her arms wide open. Horrified, Bev watched, wondering if Fancy Woman was a member of the hawk family, those preying birds that flew about grabbing up food. Now, Sylvie's fingers were patting his cheeks while Howie batted her hand away.

"Don't," he ordered. When that didn't work, he started crying.

Oblivious to Howie's discomfort, Sylvie ignored the cries of a child she didn't know.

It dawned on Bev that, during the entire time Shirley and Al had lived here, Sylvie had never visited. She found herself with a growing distaste for Sylvie and, likewise, for Elvira. Swooping down, Bev took Howie's hand so they could go upstairs for his nap. As she was leaving the room, she heard Sylvie saying, "Howie! Oh, you are a cute one. I love you already," she cooed. "You don't look a bit like Shirley, do you? I have always wanted a boy. Wait till I get these hands on you, you little doll."

With each step she took upward toward the second floor, Bev's alarm, which had just gone off down below, grew louder. Something felt ominous, like dark clouds that smelled of danger.

"I'll be right back," she yelled over her shoulder as she and the little boy went upstairs, where she covered him with a blanket, telling him to rest for a while. "If you take a nice nap, you can go out to feed the pigs when Will comes home."

Bev bent over, kissing his forehead. He was such an easy one, a lot like Mike. Will had been quite a different story—bullheaded and willful.

As Bev headed back downstairs, those feelings, dark and threatening, returned. Were these women withholding something? Were they the orphan women in Celeste's dream? What about the creepy, leather satchel that the magnifiers woman was carrying? Did she have hiding inside of it? Bev smelled evil around her. It was as strong as a skunk's spray.

The word, *steal,* jumped out at Bev was … What were these women stealing? Suddenly, she knew the answer. These women were here to take Howie and Celeste. Pinpricks vibrated up and down her spine. Hurry! Hurry! Celeste's dream frightened her. That briefcase that hung on the arm of "musty lady", probably held papers. Her breath grew shallow.

Entering the kitchen, Bev boomed, "It's time you tell me why you're here! We've been beating around the bush long enough. I hope it's good. Frankly, I have my doubts."

Sylvie rose. "Did Shirley tell you about me? On the other hand, maybe Bonnie did. I spoke to her after the funeral. She met me one time when she was five. Did she mention my phone call by any chance?"

Bev could feel the thumping of her heart. She remembered Bonnie's call to her some days ago. "Bev" Bonnie had said, "My Aunt Sylvie, Mom's sister, called. Sylvie asked me how Celeste and Howie were doing."

Clenching her fist, Bev knew what she should have done. Why hadn't she called Lexington or North Platte—county seats? She should have reported having the children the next day. Furthermore, she could have laid claim to these dear, innocent kids. Bonnie had said that this Sylvie had borne a baby who had died. Sylvie had even asked Bonnie about the Howie and Celeste's where-a-bouts. Bonnie had told her about the children being happy at the Temples—the perfect home and that no one knew their needs like Bev and Clark.

Now remembering back, Bev realized there might be an obstacle. Some time ago, Shirley had confided in Bev. The two had been painting the Dusty's picket fence when, out of nowhere, Shirley had confessed, "I'm going to tell you something, but you have to promise to keep this to yourself. If this got back to Al …Well, he's funny when it comes to my sister." Shirley had gone on to say that she'd been depressed and written Sylvie. "I offered my children should anything happen. I wanted to do right by her. She's my infertile twin. She had one son who died. He fell down some steps. I'm talking about her three year old. The boy's name was Donnie." Bev had attempted to get more detail, but Shirley had closed up the way she was prone to do with "touchy subjects." Bev had gotten a bad taste in her mouth, wondering if Shirley was hiding a problem. Until now, she'd forgotten the incident.

As it was, right this minute, the kids were nobody's, no one's property. Without the legal form, they were nameless. What would Shirley want for the children if she was watching? Bev thought a heart attack would strike her. She'd promised Celeste a home here. Why hadn't she gone and finalized the adoption or done something to make having the kids more than some done deal in her own mind? Her mind was not the same as a signed, legal paper.

Bev looked from Sylvie to Elvira. Elvira had removed papers from her "stuffed" satchel—smelly and cracked. "What are those papers?" she asked. Her heartbeat had gone to her throat, and her tongue was stuck to the roof of her mouth. Before Elvira could answer, Bev accused, "You had them assigned to you!" Bev knew that Sylvie was capable of doing that. She was wealthy and knew the right people. Shirley hadn't said anything bad about Sylvie, but her own instincts told Bev not to trust this woman. "I think I should call the police."

Elvira, the placement worker, remaining unfazed, said, "The problem is that these kids were left her at your home without someone like me to do the work. Had you or Bonnie reported where they were living and done the legalities, fine. However, you failed to do so. Those youngsters could have died and who would have known? I won't slap your hands unless you put up a fight. The kids will have an excellent home with their closest relative, the mother's sibling. Bonnie can't do it. Her home is unfit for her own baby. Those bitty trailers, no bigger than a bathroom, are an awful shame. However, don't worry," Elvira said. "Sylvie will be paying her a nice sum for as long as the kids live in Sylvie's home."

"No!" Bev wheezed. Bonnie would never do that. "I'm calling her right now, and we'll settle this. Besides, why does Bonnie need money if they are legally yours anyway?"

Sylvie stepped in. "This is legal. Elvira said it all wrong. I feel that if I am giving the kids a home, Bonnie should also have something. Times are tough. Go ahead. Call her then. Ask her," Sylvie said. "She knows I'm a good person."

"Wait just a minute," Bev said. "She would have told me that the kids were going. She explained about telling you that they have a good home here." Fearing that they were right, Bev dialed 0 despite her doubts and had the operator call York.

"Bonnie," Bev asked. "Did you sell your brother and sister?"

"Is Sylvie there already? Bev, I was going to call and tell you that Mom left a letter telling her she could have us should anything happen. Sylvie showed me the letter." Bonnie's voice was shaky, like a leaf hanging loosely on a tree in the autumn breeze. "That's something that Celeste doesn't need to know. It might bother her. Anyway, Mom spoke well of Sylvie," she said breathlessly.

"Your mom told me about that letter. I knew her well. She didn't mean to write it. She wasn't feeling well at the time."...Though Shirley hadn't exactly said that, Bev needed to say something to change Bonnie's mind ... "Bonnie, did you accept payment in exchange for Howie and Celeste?"

Gaining confidence and slightly belligerent, Bonnie expressed her viewpoint. "Bev, Mom liked her. The only reason they grew apart was that

Sylvie lived elsewhere. Mom went to Lincoln to visit her, but, unfortunately, she had company that day. I know because I was along. Mom liked the Sylvie scrapbook I made," Bonnie said, eliminating certain essential facts; for example, she *didn't* tell Bev that, while Dad wouldn't discuss Sylvie at all, mother seldom discussed her sister.

"Another thing, Bev," she added, "Mom wanted me to borrow money from Sylvie for school. I can pursue a career and give my kids a good life. Meanwhile, Howie and Celeste will be able to have everything they need. I mean, why break your pocketbook when Sylvie will take them on trips around the world? Ginny can come visit—"

"Bonnie Jo Dusty, this isn't about money! You know that. This is about love and familiarity and safety," Bev said, choking on tears.

"Bev, I didn't mean anything by that. It's just that this would make Mother so happy. We've never known Sylvie."

"Bonnie, please refuse her money. You don't know if this is legal. You don't even know Sylvie. I don't like what I see. The worst is my promising your sister, Celeste, that this would be her home. That's what you told me. The kids love it here. Please."

"I did, but Bev, think about it. She's an important socialite. Sylvie wouldn't lie. You should see all the charities she's headed and everywhere she's been. I truly meant to get you called, but Carson was sick. I've been feeling so guilty about the car wreck. I insisted that Mom and Dad visit. I took Howie and Celeste's parents from them. Now, by giving them to the closest thing to Mom—her twin, I'm giving them a present. Don't push me, please. I'm sorry, but I'm not changing my mind. You know how badly Mom wanted me to continue with school."

"If you needed money for your education, you should have come to Clark and me. We would still be willing to help."

"Bev, Carson's awake, and he's still half-sick. I have to go. Good-bye."

Consumed with anguish and disgust—furious was more like it—Bev hung up the phone. Things smelled of dishonesty. She felt like she was in a dimly lit courtroom, where men struck deals. Desperate, she cried out, "Please. Please! I will go insane if you women take the kids. Come look." Bev scurried over to the flowers and vases from her party. "See … the paper hearts." Racing her stout, overheated body to Celeste's room, she brought down the teddy bear and Ginny's poem and two new outfits she had sewn.

The women gave her sad looks, maintaining that taking the children with them couldn't be prevented.

Elvira kept shuffling the typed and signed papers she'd taken out of the satchel.

Why, oh why, didn't Bev know where Clark was?

Close to hysterical, Bev shouted, "Sylvie, you should be ashamed of yourself. You never came to visit her or to do a thing for her kids. Now you want them for life. You know nothing about these kids—not what they eat, how they love, what they love, what they need, what stage they're at in their grieving, what they laugh over, nothing. And yet you're willing to take them. Why? This is going to kill those kids."

Ignoring Bev, Elvira asked, "Bev, can you tell Sylvie a little about Celeste?"

Bev was still thinking about what to say regarding Celeste when Ginny and Celeste came in out of the cold. At a glance, both girls knew Bev had been crying.

Puffing with self-importance, Elvira stepped forward. Without further ado she said, "This is Sylvie, Shirley's sister, and she's come to take Celeste and Howie home to Lincoln. You need to go pack. We only have twenty minutes before we leave."

Ginny, cried out, "No! You can't. I don't believe you. Mom?"

"I'm sorry," Bev said. "I did everything I could."

Hearing this, both girls began to wail. "Please," Celeste sobbed. "I don't want to go. I live here. You promised! These are the orphan women. Please, Bev. Don't make me go. This is my home. It's Howie's home."

"Mom, she's my sister," Ginny cut in. "You said so. This is cruel. You can't do this to us."

The cries, pleading, and accusations continued for a good while. As the girls argued, the two women sighed and grunted and made unkindly comments.

Finally, Bev, who was covered by a rash and frantically itching, convinced the girls to go pack Celeste's things. Bev was fearful of Elvira; she believed the woman could take her own children.

The girls packed Celeste's knapsack—a 4-H project Celeste had made using her mother's worn-out nightgown. The size of the knapsack had shocked everyone! She had more than doubled the dimensions, wanting as much of her mother's worn flannel gown as possible. The adult leaders had been touched to tears.

Still not back downstairs after ten minutes, Elvira barged up the stairs with Bev following. Before Bev could stop Elvira, the social worker was scolding Celeste and saying she would regret it if she didn't come. "You've had plenty of time," she said.

Coming back downstairs, Ginny cried, "Don't let them take Celeste and Howie."

"Please listen to me," Bev said her face a mask of desperation. "Sylvie will be a better mom than I can be. She's related to you, Celeste." Bev knew she wouldn't be better but was at a loss for words.

"Mom didn't have a sister," Celeste lied. "She never mentioned a sister."

"She's more than a sister," Elvira said. "She's your mother's twin, and you're Sylvie's niece."

Fibbing, she said, *"Sylvie has even done the adoption work for you and Howie."*

Adoption? The room went stone silent but only for the duration of a heartbeat.

"Please," Celeste sobbed, looking at Bev. "Don't you want us kids? We've lived here for the past four years. Dad worked for Clark. Mom loved you," she wailed.

Bev, whose pain was colossal, mouthed, "I love you," just as the social worker grabbed Celeste's arm, tugging on her.

"She's got her own kids," Elvira said, yanking her from Ginny. "Say good-bye. We've a long drive ahead of us. Celeste, you have a beautiful home awaiting you in Lincoln. Most kids in your shoes would be tickled."

Desperate, but frightened for her children, Bev turned away, weeping.

Book Two

Trials of a Rag Princess

(1933--37, Lincoln, Nebraska)

Sylvie, who was running over with complaints about the snow, headed across country driving towards Gothenburg. Howie sat up front between the two women. Celeste sat alone in the back. In need of a Kleenex, she grabbed the yellow hankie, the one from Will. Certain she'd forgotten the other handkerchiefs in the rumble, her tears made it hard to see the hills to the right or Banner Church to the left. Before she knew it, the Packard was crossing the Platte River into Gothenburg.

The car was heading toward the edge of Gothenburg when Elvira twisted around, facing Celeste. "Aren't you an eighth-grader? And doesn't that make you too old for that crying behavior?"

Elvira turned to Sylvie. "Isn't she too old?" she asked.

"Elvira, what do you mean?" Sylvie questioned. "That girl lost both of her parents, and now she's leaving everything she knows. When did you ever do anything so brave?"

Pressing her lips together, Elvira could have been mistaken for a wooden stick.

Likewise, Celeste was surprised. She hadn't expected such a supportive answer from Sylvie. Back while they were driving the country roads, Sylvie had said that people had to be crazy heathens to choose a life that included dirt and gravel. She said that, in the city, trolleys, along with paved and cobblestone streets, were the only way to live. She voiced distaste over Shirley's gardening and having raised chickens, saying, "Such a mess." Celeste had wanted to tell her that Dad had taken over the butchering because killing the birds had bothered mother.

Mother had fears about dying; Dad had said this started with Celeste's birth. Hearing Mother voice her worries had bothered Celeste terribly, even causing nightmares.

As it was, Bev had tried convincing Mother that she was fine. In her innocence, Celeste prepared to tell Sylvie a story about this. Instead, Sylvie was asking her a question.

"I'm betting you'd like to return to the Temples' home, even if it amounts to leaving Howie with me?"

Quickly wiping her face on her coat sleeve, Celeste asked, "Do you mean it? Wouldn't it hurt your feelings if I went back?"

"Celeste, you're only twelve years old. I imagine that, right now, you can see Bev finishing up with those cookies. Also you and Ginny would be doing those sweet little valentines to your friends."

Celeste was amazed. Could Sylvie read her thoughts? These same ideas had run through Celeste's mind. "How did you know what I felt? Would you really take me back?" she asked, wondering if Sylvie might get mad if she knew how badly she wanted to return.

Quickly Sylvie slowed the car and turned off on the last street in Gothenburg, digging through her purse.

"What are you looking for?" Elvira asked. "The cigarettes are in the trunk."

"Found what I wanted," Sylvie cackled, fingering a package of gum and then passing the package around.

Celeste, who was anxious to start back to the Temples, gave Sylvie an extra big smile. She knew about Mother and Sylvie not talking to each other but also knew that Mom had said it was because they lived apart from one another in high school. It was Dad, who'd never met Sylvie that confused Celeste. She'd known better than to ask him why. One time, out in the barn, she'd seen his rat poisoning on a special feature about Sylvie. Bonnie had thrown a real temper tantrum.

Celeste rejoiced over the fact that Sylvie had turned around and was heading for the Temples. Coming to the highway, Celeste stiffened when Sylvie turned left. Celeste didn't understand. The other way, a right turn, led back to the Temples.

"Sylvie, we're going the wrong way. The Temples are a right turn." Could Sylvie have been joking with her?

"Celeste, you took me serious? I was kidding. I thought you knew. Why did you ask me in the first place? I didn't drive all this way just to go back. Why would I return you? You're my child now."

Celeste plummeted downward, wanting to put her hands in her face and scream. Howie, on the other hand, was having a fine time up front. The women were smiling at him and he had some small cars to play with. Almost dusk, it felt even darker and colder than it already was. The day had just turned three shades gloomier. Unsure of what was happening; she saw the sale barn, a sight that caused her to remember the pigs! She'd forgotten to tell Bennie or the others good-bye. Clark had presented her with Bennie, a runt, late that summer. He'd been no bigger than her hand. She'd bottle-fed him until he could survive with the others. Grief cut through her. Bennie would cry when she wasn't there to greet him. The thought was more than she could stand. Of all the miracles and magic on the farm, pigs were her favorite. She never tired of their fuzzy pink snouts or how her favorite pigs had litter after litter of minute runts.

Celeste gasped when she remembered the next thing—a precious, sparkling, event, something so unbearable, she'd put it out of her mind and at a distance. She couldn't mention the play or the dress or she would never stop crying. It'd been dreamlike. Miss England, her teacher, had made her, Celeste Dusty, the Valentine Queen for tomorrow's play that the twenty-six children were putting on for their parents. Celeste supposed it was because of her parents' death. Even so, it didn't matter. Ginny always had the leads, and this time the star was to be Celeste. Ginny was playing the king. At least they'd laughed, because Ginny was almost a head shorter, and the man was always taller. Thinking of the dress broke her heart. Miss England had made the gown, keeping the design a secret. The costume was sure to be exquisite. Celeste would never have another chance to be a queen.

Briefly, she forgot herself, remembering today's play practice when Miss England had yelled, "Ginny and Celeste! Stop throwing the glitter at each other. It's to sprinkle on the parents tomorrow. We'll run out, and a few lucky parents won't get doused with love." The red glitter was the love. At the end of the play, *Kingdom Searches for Love*, the two girls and Jack, the only boy in their class, would do the honors.

"Sylvie," Celeste said, returning to the present. "The school play is tomorrow, and I have the lead. I'm the Valentine Queen. We've practiced for a month. Could we possibly go?"

"Well now," Sylvie said, tossing her words back to Celeste, "so you're an actress? I was Cleopatra, the Egyptian Queen, in our school play. You should have seen me up on the stage in my gorgeous outfits. I was dating the love of my life. He thought that I was fantastic, but then someone stole …"

Gripping the steering wheel, the veins on Sylvie's wrists popped out, and for a moment the car veered to the side of the road, bouncing back on, petrifying everyone half to death. No one said a word, but Elvira put her scarf on, tying and retying it three times, before taking it off to clean her classes—using it.

Continuing with her blabber—"I wore a wig. I'll tell you some of my lines…."

Fifteen minutes later, Sylvie was still talking about Cleopatra. Finally during a break for a breath, Celeste edged her way into the conversation.

"Sylvie, excuse me, but I wonder, is it possible for us to discuss going to my play?"

"Elvira, I'd say the leading lady wasn't really so interested in my starring role."

"But I was. It's just that I'm the queen. I have the most important part. I don't think they can have the play without me. Everyone is so excited to do it. Please!"

"Well," Sylvie said, nodding her head, "I know of one thing that would get us to your play for certain."

Celeste leaned forward; wanting Sylvie to hurry and say what it was that would get her to the play.

"Do you have the gas money?" Sylvie asked with a wry smile.

"No," Celeste said, blinking hard.

"Too bad about that." Sylvie looked sideways at Elvira. Then taking the subject on a 180-degree turn, she rambled on. "Did you know that when I was eighteen, I had a baby? When he was three, he fell down the stairs. He died. Nothing in the world compares to what I lost. People can say they're grieving hurts, but let me tell you, nothing hurts like losing a child. You need to face your loss. Leave the grieving to those of us who will never stop hurting. It was so unfair to me. I can still remember his funeral. There were about five hundred folks there. Isn't that right, Elvira?"

Sylvie had caught Elvira off guard. Only a handful of people had been at the closed casket funeral. Sylvie had been imperative about saying who could attend. She'd wanted to continue hiding Donnie from the public.

"Yes, that's right," Elvira, conceded. "It was a sad, sad situation, Sylvie."

"About that play tomorrow, I allowed that we could go if … if you have the gas money. Do you have the money?"

Celeste wrapped her nose in the collar of her coat and covered her eyes with her hat. There was only one thing she could do. She wept, biting her bottom lip, causing blood to trickle down her chin.

Knowing she had to think of something else, Celeste's thoughts went to Miss England. Did Miss England hurt the way she did? After all, the teacher's fiancé, Frank, wouldn't marry her as long as there was no money and making a living was nearly impossible. Frank had come to the school door to talk to her the day the banks had locked their doors. Celeste had overheard him. "It doesn't look good," he'd said, to Miss England, his voice hard and crackled. "I could lose the farm. We'll have to wait to marry. The banks shut their doors." Fortunately, the two lovers were still together. Frank came each morning to get the coal from the little coal house. After that, he carried in water for the day.

Celeste switched her mind to a good memory—the Harvest Festival in Gothenburg, which lasted three days. The citizens and organizations saw to a carnival, displays, and food booths, with their delectable smells, for the duration. The event began with a long parade of various floats and bands, including the fire truck, tractors, horses, Pony Express riders, kids, organizations, and even dogs and cats. People decorated the stores with collections, quilts, china paintings, and other interesting things. Corn shocks lined the streets and highways. Bands from area schools marched along playing their songs and what have you followed, with busy fingers gathering up penny candy thrown from floats.

There were little horses to ride and a rodeo. Guys spent too much trying to win a prize for their sweethearts. They tossed darts, whizzing them at balloons, and swung the "eerie diggers" in hopes of bronze horses. The women were lucky if they could land a dime in a bowl. Of course, they had watermelon-eating contests and pie-throwing events and the brave singers up above on elevated planks. Although everyone was suffering through the country's depression, people still consumed the fun at the carnival. One lady had gone with a dime to split between her five children. At the end of the day, they chose to spend the coin on a merry-go-round ride for the youngest, deriving pleasure while watching the toddler laugh.

Celebrations like this allowed folks to have fun close to home, with all the families—rich and poor alike—in the same boat. Down at the school, families met on Sundays to play games, eat homemade ice cream, or have a good old-fashioned cakewalk. Baseball was popular, either at the church or down at the school. Girls fixed box lunches, and the Brady men met to play donkey softball. Mother had joined Union Aid at Bev's encouragement and loved the women. They catered to the Nebraska Children's Home by sending food on a milk train and assisted with all kinds of aid such as polio drives and natural disasters. They put on a yearly ice cream social and craft bazaar. Each summer the families met for a pot luck picnic. Wedding showers were held for the daughters and sons of the members. That was Mom's first and only club, and seeing her mom with good friends had made Celeste happy.

Celeste sighed. There were so many things that she would never forget. She hoped she'd be going home in two or three weeks. Will was already on her mind. She supposed she didn't dare ask Sylvie how long this stay was going to be. Shivers ran through her when she thought of what the answer might be.

*   *   *

Elvira turned to the backseat, trying to remember where she'd put her briefcase. Seeing Celeste, she knew as sure as they'd forecast snow that Celeste was the wrong kid for Sylvie. The gangly urchin, no fatter than a sideways leaf, was surprisingly cute. Elvira had heard about Shirley's deficiencies for several years now. For sure, this girl wasn't what she'd expected. However, Elvira supposed there was no way that Shirley could be that bad either. If she was, Sylvie wouldn't have needed to put her down all the time. Elvira was constantly amazed at Sylvie's imaginary powers. If she wanted something to be a certain way, it became as she wished. Sylvie had turned Celeste into Cinderella, the maid, the one who existed before the prince came. That was where she'd keep her for as long as she could.

It was obvious that, when Sylvie had taken her first look at the auburn-haired girl, she'd repainted her face to that of an Ugly Duckling. Anytime Sylvie called someone a tomato, potato, carrot, or cucumber, it was because she was jealous. How many times had she said that Shirley was nothing but a dry, white onion, a smelly one? Another woman had become a pickle. Howie would have it good, but Celeste was in for a prison of hell already. The problem was that Celeste looked like the woman who'd become Cinderella and stolen the handsome prince. Shirley had indeed taken the only man that Sylvie had ever loved, Al Dusty, alias Howard Anderson.

Elvira rented an apartment above Mack's drugstore, where the women first met the summer after Sylvie's high school graduation. Sylvie rented the apartment next to Elvira's. At the time, Elvira worked with a children's society. Eventually they fired Elvira for accepting a bribe. Presently, she worked down near the capital, as an assistant for a washed-up old lawyer.

Other than Sylvie, for whom Elvira did favors, like those today, she had no friends. Elvira fed off Sylvie. In return, Sylvie kept Elvira unknown from her highly prestigious world. Elvira, who knew this and more, didn't let that part bother her.

Because no one read Sylvie the way Elvira did, Elvira helped Sylvie get a clearer perspective on herself. As dignified as Sylvie appeared, she oftentimes felt like a version of paints mixed together. No one but Elvira would have guessed this. And no one but Elvira could say what color Sylvie was on any given day.

*   *   *

"We'll be in Kearney soon," Sylvie said. "Do you have a place you like to eat, Celeste? Girl, do I need to repeat my words? I bet slipping off is one of the symptoms of losing your parents. Am I right, sweetie?"

Celeste relaxed. She liked the name sweetie. It told her that Sylvie honestly liked her. "I haven't been this far from home. This is my first time in Kearney. We never ate out when we went places. We took our food along. Any café will be fine."

"Goodness, I didn't know there was anyone who hadn't eaten out. Wouldn't Howard take you?"

Confused, Celeste said, "I don't know Howard."

"I meant to say Al," Sylvie said. "I knew a Howard Allen."

Celeste laughed. "Dad was Allen Howard. I wonder if they knew each other." It was just a feeling, but something clicked in Celeste's mind. She hadn't the foggiest notion what it was.

The group of four was about to get out of the car to go inside for their evening meal when Celeste remembered Sylvie's question. "Mom and Dad ate out on their anniversaries. Once, we ate in Gothenburg at the café and in North Platte at the Tomahawk, just over the bridge, leading into the town. It was exciting, but we didn't eat out that much."

Elvira and Sylvie glanced at each other, smirking and rolling their eyes.

"With Mom and Dad, it had to be really special. We did eat out for Bonnie's marriage. I suppose you might not call it true eating out, but Mom and Bev fixed sandwiches and chips for the guests. They also baked a bunch of cakes."

"Celeste! I asked a simple yes and no question. Try answering in seven words or less. It's a good social rule for children. Actually it's a game."

"That sounds like fun. I hope I can remember."

"Are we hungry?" Sylvie wanted to know as they scooted into a booth at a pleasant family-style café.

Celeste feared making the wrong choices. Though starving, she didn't say anything about her growling stomach. She'd missed her usual after-school snack—grahams with milk and sugar that she and Ginny enjoyed first thing home. Putting the thought aside, she worried about how much her meal should cost. Waiting for Sylvie to give an amount, Celeste almost asked just as the waitress came. The girl was wearing yellow earrings and a black mesh hairnet. "What you people ordering?" she said, chewing her gum.

Annoyed by Celeste's interruption, Sylvie put her finger to her lips. "Hush," she glared, while the waitress popped her bubble gum, waiting for Sylvie to decide. Sylvie's long red fingernail went from one menu item to the next as she picked, chose, changed, and then repeated this pattern, finally saying, "I'll have the catfish. No, wait! Give me the chicken platter, but substitute the fries with an unsalted, unbuttered, catsup-loaded baked potato. And, uh ... exchange the cottage cheese, for ... hum. Do you have pineapple or ... Wait a minute. I know what I want. I want the coleslaw without sugar in it, just the vinegar and mayo dressing. Now let me think ...what do I want for bread? I believe I'll take the wheat. No ... make that a no salt, no butter, Parker House roll with jelly. Or would I rather have toast? Make that plain white bread toasted. Strawberry jelly."

The waitress, looking vastly confused, had a big twist of disgust about her mouth. Screwing her face into a frown, she blew out air. Then chewing her wad again, the waitress repeated, "That's a baked potato, cottage cheese, wheat roll, and is that all?" With that said, she popped a bubble that almost broke in Sylvie's face, making her just nervous enough that she didn't dare ask the waitress to repeat her order. Meanwhile, a music box began playing something by a singer with a Rudy Valentino voice.

Though starving, Celeste sat straight as a board, not looking at the menu. She didn't want to make the wrong choice and risk upsetting Sylvie.

The waitress walked over by Celeste.

"How much ..." Celeste started to ask.

Sylvie put up her finger. "Hush, child."

The waitress stood there with her pen and paper, still chewing her gum. This time, she blew a bubble that covered her nose, popping it back into her mouth.

Celeste wasn't surprised when Elvira duplicated Sylvie's order down to the two pats of butter less butter and the same jelly. By now, Celeste couldn't resist the chicken. It even came with a scoop of chocolate pudding pie, a dish Celeste loved.

"I'll have the chicken but without any substitutes," Celeste told the waitress with pride. Until now, she'd always had to consult with adults who said, "It costs a bit too much. Get the malt or the grilled cheese. Better yet—get water and a grilled cheese. You can have Kool-Aid when we get home."

"What about drinks?" the gum popper asked.

It was coffee for the women and milk for Howie.

"I'll have a grape pop," Celeste said, hoping she'd done the right thing. Faking a brave grin, she glanced at Sylvie.

Sylvie's big lips were partway open. Her bulging eyes stared at Celeste, who looked away and back. Stammering, Celeste said, "I … I don't have to … to get that. I'll run and tell the waitress."

"Goodness, Celeste! Don't embarrass me. Sit and be quiet. You don't need to be stuttering."

"I…I don't need chicken," Celeste continued to stutter. "I t…thought since the two of you ordered it, I'd do the same. Please let me change my order."

Sylvie, who had just drained her glass of water, began bathing Howie, using bountiful amounts of spit. "Howie boy, you're so dirty. My goodness, let's rub a dub behind those ears and get those fingers. Sweet, sweet child, didn't they bathe you? I should say not. Either that or maybe they dipped you in the tank."

Sickened by Sylvie's spit all over Howie, Celeste needed to laugh for fear of coming undone. Sylvie dabbed her saliva all around his mouth.

Horrified, Celeste giggled. "Sylvie, you look like the Temples' barn cat, Stripes, when she bathes her kittens. She sticks her tongue out at least two inches and wipes it all over each kitten like this." Celeste imitated Stripes. "Sylvie, you'd make a great mouse cat for the Temples."

Elvira had to bite her tongue to keep from giggling. Sylvie a farm mouse cat? Holy smokes!

Scorching, Sylvie's eyes could have drilled holes through Celeste, who had no idea what she'd done.

Howie asked, "Sylvie, are you Stripes, the rat cat?"

Fortunately, the waitress brought Howie's meal out early. Setting Howie's food down, Sylvie asked Elvira to feed him. She was unexpectedly in a bad mood. Memories were swamping her. Looking at Celeste brought those memories back. The girl was the image of her mother.

Though she'd never admit it, she knew that Shirley had had the potential to be stunning. This and the fact that Shirley had walked off with her fiancé—had downright stolen him, was something she would neither forget nor forgive.

While Sylvie sat sulking, Celeste had her eye on the waitress. As far as she knew, Dad had met her mother waitressing. Celeste was thinking about her mother. Mom would have been far superior to the woman with the yellow earrings and hairnet. Dad would never have fallen for that Miss Bubblegum. No way! He was against gum and popping those bubbles. Some girl had left her gum in his hair during a dance. His dad had tried cutting it out and had left a hole in his head. Celeste broke out smiling at the memory.

* * *

Sylvie was back on the road and just west of Aurora when she broke the silence; Elvira had just checked the back seat. "Elvira, you sure they're asleep?" Sylvie asked.

"I'm sure. Can't you hear that stuffy breathing sound kids make?" Elvira tucked her smelly feet up under herself. Preparing for the car ride, Elvira rested them on the plush velvet. Seeing this, Sylvie swallowed hard.

"Elvira, I saw you fishing for a smoke in that ashtray right outside the restaurant door. You dropped it when you saw me looking. Embarrassed you huh?"

Mortified, Elvira said, "You're wrong. I was reaching for a dime."

"You expect me to believe that, old girl? Ha!"

As they rode toward Lincoln, Sylvie said, "I didn't know that my Howard came from those silly Sandhills. Lizzie, the one who died giving birth to Al, had a one-night stand after she saw Al's dad riding the broncos. She got turned on watching his arm flail around in the air. I guess we all have our different things, right, Elvira. What's yours?"

"Sylvie! That's enough," Elvira wheezed, turning ashen.

"Calm down, Elvira! My Howard took Shirley home to the Sandhills. Later they moved over to where the land turns to clay there in the Platte Valley. Shirley led her life on that forsaken land with nothing but cows."

"I liked what I saw today—nice and open, horses, the Platte River, and the tractors. Why, I saw a John Deere, and a…"

"Since when have horses and tractors been your thing, Elvira?"

"I used to ride …"

"Comments, unwelcome. William Anderson was crazy. That rich old man wanted Howard to run for president. He chose me to escort Howard to Washington. Can you imagine? Instead, Howard had a sour attitude. 'No,' he said. 'I want to go home.' I told Howard, 'You will become a name in Washington.' By then, the old man had Washington embedded in me. I wanted Howard, the money, and the position, but I ran out of time. There was only one way to rope the boy I loved and the life I wanted."

"For sure, for sure," Elvira said, untying her soiled wool scarf.

Sylvie, who saw this, wanted to brush off the car seat. Back at Bev's, Elvira must have eaten six of those sugar cookies. Sylvie had just happened to glance at Elvira's remaining bite. It looked foreign, as if covered with coconut. Curious, she'd watched as Elvira raised it to her mouth. That's when Sylvie knew. The coconut was dandruff. Sylvie's stomach quivered. "Elvira, please get those legs shaved and take care of that dandruff. The stuff is raining out of your hair."

Just then, Celeste coughed. Hearing her, the women panicked. Elvira was on her knees, with her head hanging over the backseat, faster than she'd ever done anything. Seconds ticked by before she said, "She's sleeping."

Sylvie wiped her sweat-ridden forehead. "Let me continue; stop interrupting me. Howard and I were on the porch, with me pregnant, planning our nuptial when my *sister* came strolling up between two policemen. I was about to wet my pants. Her role was to make sure that no one gave my identity away and—"

Celeste coughed again, shifting sides.

Elvira followed the same routine. "She's asleep."

"Keep her quiet. I'll have a heart attack … Now then, Grandpa was a large man who chewed cigars, played cards, and bossed folks around. When he got excited, his bushy white eyebrows rode up and down like those bucking broncos. I never knew if I liked the looks of those eyebrows. They gave him a lot of power."

"Sylvie, let's get through this story."

"There I was, eighteen and stylish, with the world in my pocket. Somehow, Shirley forgot to stay her distance."

This time Elvira coughed. "I must be catching what the girl has."

"Just be quiet. I'll never forget how mad I was when one of the policemen turned to me. 'Miss Sylvie White?'" he asked.

"I denied it of course. I wasn't going to let them know. 'My name is Sylvie Lord,' I said."

"I have to have a smoke," Elvira interrupted. "Please, Sylvie. Let's smoke. I'm hyperventilating. I might as well put my breath to use."

Sylvie ignored her. "Ida Lord appeared just then. Usually, by evening, she was foggy. That night was different. She said, 'Sylvie, you tell the truth. You know who you are. You're a White.' Next thing I know, the police are checking her for bruises. Howard's right there and furious. He called me a calculated liar. There on the porch, with the world watching us, he said the baby wasn't his. 'Find the real father,' he said."

"Dear, dear," Elvira wiggled. "You must have been getting a sore throat." Elvira felt her own throat to see if she was the one getting a bad throat. Nerves did that to Elvira.

"Two weeks prior, Howard and I had taken the Fuller to a country pond. I had suggested we go for a *dip*. Well, Elvira, put you in my bare feet and bare body. I dipped for an hour while he read Defoe by candlelight. Grandpa had told Howard that, by gosh, the baby was his, and it was time he became a father. Grandpa had also told him that kissing could cause my condition. Pooh! That's what the girls at school thought back then and some still do. Howard bought it. How dumb was he? Never mind. I loved him and always did."

Elvira couldn't help herself. "Sylvie, how many times have I told you? I get the squiggles when you tell this stuff. Keep it to yourself. My interests don't include a naked Howard."

Feeling defeated, Elvira was unsure. Was she or wasn't she interested? There were those dreams. *Let it go*, she thought, knowing she would take her doubts to the grave. In the dark, a tear rolled down her cheek. What would it have been like with a different mother and father? Happier, she was sure. At least men wouldn't have frightened her, and she wouldn't have those empty hours of longing for the phone to ring.

Sylvie continued with her chatter. "Like I said, Howard called me a liar. Later that night, he walked out. I came close to doing Shirley in after the police left. I hunted her down and squeezed her throat, but someone heard and came toward us. I ran before they got there. A week later, I learned that Howard was Al Dusty and married to Shirley! They were hiding out in those Sandhills. I was livid. At least I got his inheritance."

Elvira wanted more. "Oh, do keep on. What a delicious story!"

"Delicious? I never recovered. Furthermore, in all that time, Howard never touched me that way."

"You don't mean that!" she gasped. "I know everything about you! Or do I?" Elvira was mortified that she might not know EVERYTHING."

"It was Howard's grandfather." Sylvie muttered—without so much as a wince. "I needed money, and I thought that if the baby was his; the kid would look like Howard." Sylvie waited, expecting an immediate response. None came.

Finally, in the stone silence of a winter night with only the hum of the Packard's engine, Sylvie Sobori did the hardest thing she had ever done. She reached over and shook Elvira's hunched shoulder. "It's okay, old girl. You know more than anyone else about me, and that's more than even I know about me."

Peering through her bifocals, Elvira smoothed her blouse. Gazing ahead, she fought off a smile.

Sylvie continued. "I was pregnant without a boyfriend. I applied for a job at the drugstore and got hired. Mack a big gentle St. Bernard came with it, feeding me green slips of paper. I suppose, I'm luckier than most, but sometimes I think I should have picked an assertive one, a border collie, with some zipper zapper in him."

"No," Elvira said, sounding annoyed. "I don't think so. You had your baby with which to contend. Remember, I was your midwife. Donnie was born up there at my place. Besides, Mack gives you the world."

"Yes …Yes, I had my baby boy. Poor little fellow. Three short years and he died! I don't believe I have mentioned this, but he never looked like Howard. Of course, it wasn't that I wanted Donnie to resemble him. I just thought…" Changing directions, Sylvie said, "As for the fall down those basement stairs, I can still hear Donnie's head cracking."

Looking over in the dark, Elvira watched Sylvie hand. It appeared to be strangling the steering wheel.

"All he did was fall down those basement stairs. I will never understand Mack. He forgot to block off those stairs he was rebuilding. Never mind. I have a new son back in the backseat. As of now, his name is *Howard."*

"Of course. Of course. Sylvie what do you say we get those cigarettes you had me buy?"

Sylvie pulled over while Elvira raced back, taking the carton out of the trunk.

Lighting a Marlboro, Sylvie said, "The problem with Celeste, asleep back there, is that I want a debutante. I'm unsure about her cutting the mustard." Softening, Sylvie reached up, patting her hair. "Ginny would have, but unless something big happens, I'm stuck with that bumpy carrot back there. She's like her mother. Onion would be a better word. They give off a smell," she cackled.

*   *   *

They rode in silence enjoying their smoke rings and the circles of swirling they made, contenting themselves for several miles. When they reached the outskirts of Lincoln, Elvira said, "Remember that day when I brought the papers from my meeting? They were about folks with no conscience? To us women, this was a spooky new discovery," Inhaling, she glowed over talking about something as immense as psychiatric knowledge. "Do you suppose that's what we are? We seem charming, intelligent, and without care. We might steal, we might lie, and we might ..." Elvira giggled. "I clearly recall Donnie's accident. Of course, the pay I got from you and Mack didn't hurt."

Elvira sat remembering that day Donnie's had died. It had been on Sylvie's birthday. Elvira, who'd been the supervisor of the child society at the time, had called around noon, saying she would run a present over at 2:00p.m.. By the time she'd arrived, Donnie had fallen down the stairs. Sylvie, who was wailing when Elvira a got there, nevertheless finagled Elvira, into doing and saying certain things. She'd gotten Elvira to ride along to the hospital. Furthermore, she'd talked Elvira into saying she'd been there and seen the fall.

The thing that still puzzled Elvira was how Mack hadn't been anywhere in sight. A pile of clothes had been sitting beside the stairs— nothing else...No hammers or nails, no carpenter. Elvira hadn't returned to the house for a year. By then, the stairs were all new. How then, had Mack's remodeling thee stairs killed the child?

"Elvira!" Sylvie snapped, jolting Elvira back. "I wrote the check. Never, ever mention the money again. I loved my Donnie to pieces, and every time you bring him up, you break my heart." Sylvie tapped the steering wheel. "You know what, Elvira? Shirley was afraid of me, and you'll be more than afraid. You'll regret what I'll do to you."

"Oh," Elvira said, shivering in her coat. She was happy they were back in Lincoln and parking in front of her upstairs apartment. "I'll just get what you owe me and be going." Elvira didn't want to stick around. She knew Sylvia's pattern of speech. Tonight her friend was on the crazy side. What Elvira wanted to know, more than anything, was if Sylvie would ever confess. She would bet her life that Sylvie had pushed the young squirt.

What struck Elvira was how composed Sylvie could be in public? She never erred or made a slip. No one out in the world would guess her truest motives or that she had rages, or paid people to do her dirty work. There weren't even a handful of folks who knew Sylvie intimately.

Sylvie rummaged in her purse drawing out an envelope. "Elvira, take this. Here is cash for you and that lawyer you work for. You certainly made those papers look official. You learned a lot from having been the head supervisor for that child society. The money will come in nice for you. See you later."

*   *   *

Sylvie's mansion, once Ida's home, impressed Celeste on one level and made her lonely on another. Ginny's house no longer reached the clouds. This one did. In fact, it went clear up to heaven! Downstairs, Celeste found room after room with dark wood, wallpaper, and mirrors. Wall decorations were in perfect balance, and an open staircase wound up to some mysterious place. She would have liked to wander about counting fireplaces while visiting statues. Instead, Sylvie introduced Celeste to Uncle Mack, a strapping man with a stout belly, dark hair, and a lazy smile–somewhat older looking.

Getting out from his chair, Mack stood up for the greeting. "Celeste, how was the trip here?"

"It was kind of fun. I—"

Sylvie upended Celeste, grabbing the flannel knapsack out of her hand. Earlier that day, while packing the knapsack, Ginny had said that she was adding a valentine for Celeste. Now, hours later, Sylvie sighed. "Mack will take this awkward bag up to the second floor. There is a small cubbyhole in the ceiling where he will put it until tomorrow."

Celeste didn't like that Sylvie called her treasured bag *awkward* and would have explained, but Sylvie grabbed her arm. "Come," she said, sounding impatient and heading Celeste up the open staircase and down a long hall. "Wait till you see your room. I've redone the colors and purchased a bedroom set," Sylvie said animated and inspired.

"Pink?" Celeste asked. "I've always wanted pink."

"Look," Sylvie said, excitedly opening the door. "See your surprise!"

Celeste expected a doll collection. She could hardly wait. Opening her closed eyes, she almost grew dizzy. Lavender was everywhere. There were lavender triangles; lavender flowers; circles, squares, and more triangles—all lavender. Everything was lavender with bits of green mixed in, along with white stripes. Celeste blinked, rubbing her eyes, desperate to keep from toppling over. Fatigue, anxiety, and this crazy zoo of lavender shapes crowded in, making her stomach whirl and churn.

"And …?" Sylvie asked, waiting for her approval

Still whirling, Celeste managed, "Bonnie would love this. Lavender is her favorite col—"

Just then, something warm splashed on Sylvie's suede shoes. Glancing down, she saw what had been Celeste's chicken supper on her heels. Celeste had just thrown up all over her new shoes.

"Lord, child!" Sylvie exclaimed, kicking them off her feet. "Pew! Didn't your mother teach you to use the toilet? It is right through that door," she snapped. Leaving Celeste standing there in shame, Sylvie raced downstairs to get Mack to clean up the mess.

Meanwhile, her embarrassment was so great, she wished she could die, Celeste snuck into her bedroom. From there, she heard Mack and Sylvie in muffled sounds. "It's a mess. Childish! She ruined this new carpet."

Waiting until Mack and Sylvie had gone back downstairs, Celeste found her nightgown. She put it on and crawled in under the sheets, where she lay on the most comfortable bed she'd ever felt. At least one thing was right. Still, she was horribly humiliated. To have thrown up on Sylvie was murderously embarrassing.

Celeste was growing blurry and fading away when Sylvie showed up. She laughed and bounded down on the mattress as though nothing had happened. Taking a seat in the midnight dark, Celeste felt Sylvie's smeared, red lips pecking against her cheek. "Child, a strange house must feel a little spooky," she said, giving Celeste minor chills.

Still, Celeste was amazed. How could Sylvie stand to kiss her after what had happened in the hall?

Sylvie wasn't done. She was saying more than merely good night. "This house must feel funny to you after those few square feet you lived in. I saw that little place where you lived. You were a bunch of squished ants. You were, weren't you?" She followed this with a witchy cackle.

Feeling defensive against Sylvie's insults, Celeste said, "We did fine in that house. My mom, Bonnie, all of us liked it. We were happy. Mom liked farm life, the fields, the gravel roads, and she really loved Dad." There! She'd said what she needed to say.

The room was silent for a bit, before Sylvie said the strangest thing. "So why can't I love Mack even though he gives me everything?"

Proud for inclusion in this enormous revelation, Celeste sat straight up, ready for a long mother-to-daughter talk. However, she was too late; Sylvie was already clicking down the hall.

Sylvie was wearing her huge, flowery lounger and sipping coffee when Celeste appeared, following a restless night. The little girl rose early and chose her valentine outfit—a red skirt with a frilly, white blouse, clothes that bolstered her spirits. She'd bathed and washed her hair with the Soft Glow shampoo sitting in a wire basket. There was no lock on the bathroom door, so she'd pushed a chair against the door, praying that no one entered. Celeste figured she'd pass out and drown if either Sylvie or Mack saw her unclothed. The perfect bath was Bev's big tub, sitting behind long curtains in the kitchen.

She would certainly impress her new acquaintances at school. As Sylvie's niece, others would crowd about wanting her to be their friend. No one needed to know what Sylvie was like. Anyway, this situation would get better. Today she'd be attending a school about five times the size of Union—a hundred kids she supposed, instead of the twenty-six she saw every day at country school.

She'd awakened at three that morning and cried her heart out. Missing the play had come as a huge blow. Unable to find comfort in any form, crying had become her only solace.

"Good morning, Sylvie. I chose this to wear to the Valentine's Day party at school. Bev got it for me. She got it in a different color for Ginny. Her blouse is red with a white skirt. I like mine best. Bev bought this whole thing and my shoes and Ginny's clothes for nine dollars. She ordered them from Montgomery Wards."

"Celeste, say it in six words or less. You could have said it all in twenty seconds. About the outfit, did she buy it last year?"

"No. She didn't shop for me until Christmastime. My things were getting too small by then."

"That skirt is too short. I think you've outgrown it. Wear it today. Tomorrow we must do something with you. We'll give it to mission works."

Celeste was crestfallen. "This is too short? It's my favorite one."

"You need some new outfits."

"I get some new outfits? That's going to be fun!"

"Celeste, grateful, is a better word. Clothes cost money, and money is scarce now. With the rate at which you grow, this is going to be a poorhouse. Now get your cereal. You can reach better than me with those long fingers."

Just as Celeste finished filling her bowl, a smell hit her in the face. It made her stomach whirl. She was terrified she'd get sick again.

"Something wrong?" Sylvie sniggered.

Celeste pointed at her nose, trying to stay pleasant, believing that if she wrinkled her nose, Sylvie would call her persnickety. The next thing she saw was Sylvie's long, red nail pointing at the wastebasket. There sat the shoes! They were the shoes she'd lost her chicken meal on. Celeste had never felt such enormous embarrassment. Her eyes were brimful with tears, and her cheeks burned. Last night—hadn't that been enough?

"Finish eating." Sylvie said. "There will be no snacks. No snacks, no accidents, no fat girl, and no getting sick. Before you leave this morning, come and fetch me. I have a map for you to follow to school. Mack drew it."

The radio had the wind-chill at ten below. Celeste hadn't brought the right clothes. Walking alone was something a kid never did the first day at a new school, no matter who you were. "Thanks for the map, but please go with me," Celeste begged, desperate.

Sylvie's headshake told Celeste her answer. She reminded Celeste to go to the office first thing. She was walking down the front steps, leaving, when Sylvie stuck her head outside, yelling, "When you get to your classroom, look for Alice and Serena, two girls who are daughters of two of my bridge friends."

Terrified Celeste's exposed fingers and legs were red in some spots and frozen white in others. When she finally saw the school, the kids were running inside. What did that mean? Entering the building, she saw a door across the way and a sign that said "Office." Crossing the hall, she knocked.

"Come in!" a woman shouted. "The door's supposed to be open!"

In a moment, Celeste was staring into the face of an obese secretary. "Are you supposed to be in class?"

"I … I'm new," she stuttered. "M … My aunt is Sylvie S … S …" She couldn't remember Sylvie's last name and panicked.

"Where are your gloves? Your fingers look like frostbitten popsicles. You forget to wear them?"

"I don't have any," Celeste said, wiping a tear that was falling from her left eye. She was using the hankie from the box Will had given her.

"I don't think I've seen you. You're new?"

"I'm from Temples' farm. I am living with my Aunt Sylvie S … Sylvie, who got me yesterday."

"I wouldn't remember her name, either, if I'd come alone. Can you tell me something about her? If you can, I'll let you warm your fingers."

"I think my Aunt Sylvie's last name might be Society. She's a friend of a lady with a lot of leg hair who works with kids who are getting adopted."

"Her? That would be Elvira. She worked with kids until … Yes, that's Elvira. That name rings a loud bell. Your aunt's last name is Sobori."

*   *   *

Returning from the school's office, Sylvie lit up for a smoke; Bonnie was next on her agenda. Puffing, she dialed.

"I'm so glad you called," Bonnie exclaimed, tossing her hair back. "Carson just went down for his nap. Do you have the kids?"

"Uh-huh. That Howard is so cute."

"You mean Howie."

"No. I mean Howard. It's more professional sounding."

"Maybe, but he knows Howie. That's what the folks wanted for him."

"Providing I am to keep Howie, his name will be Howard."

"I … I certainly hope you're keeping him," Bonnie said, confused about what she really wanted for the children. Who could have been better than Clark and Bev? Money, like Sylvie's money, didn't buy happiness, did it? Bev had told her it didn't. Bev had also accused her, in a roundabout manner of selling her brother and sister for money.

Bonnie supposed Howie wouldn't care what his name became. He was still quite young, but she thought this name changing strange. Howie was malleable. He'd do all right. She supposed that now would be a good time to bring up Celeste's guilt.

"Celeste had a nightmare," Bonnie said, filling Sylvie in and ending with, "She's not to be blaming herself. I let her know she wasn't the cause of anything. Mom was concerned about her when she and Dad drove off that day. Mom and Celeste were a lot alike. They even looked alike."

"Celeste needs to deal with the dream. Harder things have happened. I didn't have it easy, and neither did your mother. We survived."

Sylvie's words were like hard rocks landing on Bonnie's heart. Sylvie's reply reminded her of Bob. He claimed that Al and Shirley were overly nurturing, too much so. He'd been raised by his grandmother because of a sick father and a mother who'd run off and married another man. Nothing had come easy for him.

"I'm just an overprotective older sister," Bonnie said, not meaning it. She wanted to tell Sylvie that what she said was the final word.

"I was surprised at what she had in that knapsack. It was old candlesticks and some …"

"Sylvie, the candlesticks were a gift to Mom from a lady in her Union Aid club. They are old but precious. They have a story. They came over from Sweden with a woman named Nellie Sandstrom. Let Celeste have them for now. They'll be comforting to her."

"Well, I suppose she can have them a short time. They look like junk to me. Now for the childish stuff, it goes to the attic. She needs to be maturing and toughen up a bit. I know what life can deal out. Your mother wasn't the one who left home. I did."

"Mom had a hard life. She cared for her mother, cleaned her messes, and didn't always have food. Mom didn't have it easy." This topic was one that agitated Bonnie. Also, why did Celeste need to grow up so fast? "Could Celeste have the things in her big flannel bag, that knapsack, for a bit, until she gets used to your place? Twelve isn't that old, especially considering the loss."

"You're saying I can't raise a child who's lost her parents?"

"No. Please! I'm glad she's there."

"Good. I think I'm superior to those foster homes. I didn't do too badly raising myself. By the way, I have a close acquaintance at the head of placements, should your children ever be in need of foster care. All I have to do is say the word and…"

A sudden attack of panic snuck up on Bonnie. "Goodness, you did an excellent job of raising yourself. I'd hate to compare my successes to yours. Celeste would fall apart in one of those foster homes. We're so fortunate to have you, Sylvie."

"I'll do my best by her, dear."

"I'll come see the two kids on Sunday. Bob's driving into Lincoln."

"Bonnie, I would have thought Bev told you. I want her to get used to this home. Seeing you would interfere with her adjustment. Hold off a little while, maybe a year. Then we'll see."

"A year is too long, Sylvie. It would kill all of us. The folks just died."

She waited for an answer but got none; Sylvie began discussing Howard. Bonnie didn't think she'd ever met anyone who could out manipulate her like this. Oh Lord, what had she done?

"Bonnie, would you like to raise the kids, or would it be better to keep getting that forty dollars each month for as long as the children are in this home?" Sylvie asked brusquely.

Bonnie sputtered, "You're sending that every month?"

"That's my plan, but it means you stay clear of my decisions and stay away. You can write letters, but I need to get these children acclimated to my parenting style."

Times were barren and she and Bob were barely surviving. Sylvie was a successful woman, who, after all, wouldn't fail the children. They would carry her name. "I understand," Bonnie said. "You're right. You do need your space for mothering them."

"That Howard is adorable. He'll be easy to bring up ..."

"So will Celeste."

*　　*　　*

Sylvie was having her noon soup while talking to Natasha, cook and housekeeper. "Natasha, I adore Howard. That boy will start school next year. Celeste is the child who annoys me. She got me called in to talk to the secretary who called saying, 'Mrs. Sobori, we hate to bother you, but we need you to come register this frightened girl. She says she's living with the Society family, and we think she means you.'"

Curious, Natasha raised her eyebrows.

"I went to the office, where I was greeted by this secretary."

"How'd they figure out who Mrs. Society was?"

"Celeste said I was the woman whose best friend was Elvira, the child worker with a lot of leg hair. That's how! I told the school secretary that Elvira is not my best friend. Can you imagine? Why would the school think I would know her?"

"Everyone knows that you know her. It's a small town," Natasha said, smiling at her boss. It tickled Natasha to see Sylvie humiliated for once. While honored to work for Sylvie, she found Mrs. Sobori overly haughty and gossipy.

"Natasha, I said, 'Celeste, no wonder your hands are freezing. I have gloves and more gloves all over the house, begging to be worn.' In response, Celeste looked at me. 'I didn't hear them begging,' she said. Natasha, the vibes are not good."

"You take care of you, Sylvie. You've had pneumonia twice," Natasha said, realizing the rewards that accompanied coddling Sylvie.

*   *   *

Sylvie sat in her easy chair up in her bed, making a list of expectations for Celeste. Each day, she took a few minutes to enjoy the logs as they crackled in the fireplace. Snow was falling outside. The girl's carrot face was just like Shirley's. She hoped Al and Shirley were watching from wherever they were—maybe hell. She certainly hoped so. "Ha!" She chortled.

There would be no Bonnie and family at Christmas. That would be breaking her rules. It would be best to say the children weren't home when their families and friends called. After all, they must become acclimated without confusion. She would groom Howard for politics and Ce-leste could be the debutante.

Walking over to the window, she glanced downward, past the cold ground. Speaking aloud, she said, "Hi down there. You two don't need any fireplace where you are. Ha! Did you watch your girl walking to school this morning? It was a cold morning. Oh, you two have a nice evening now. Be sure to make frequent visits. I'll put on some nice shows for you. You can ex-peat to see Celeste, my costar." She laughed. Being dramatic was certainly fun. It'd been a long time since she'd done any acting.

*   *   *

Celeste was almost as frozen as she'd been this morning. The sidewalks were icy, and she was trying to guess at the streets. When she knew she'd taken the right route, she sighed with relief, letting herself review the day that had just past. By now, Celeste knew who the girls Sylvie had instructed her to find were—Serena and Alice. She would sooner poison herself with arsenic than approach them. They were gorgeous and perfectly dressed—two tiny movie stars. That's how the day had seemed—impossible and hopeless.

What would Sylvie think if she saw her standing alone at recess? Sylvie wasn't a bad person, just a rich lady who was hard to please.

It seemed that she'd spent her day watching hundreds of kids running up and down the halls like armies of ants, she a stranger among them. No one said hello, which left her stranded and wondering what to do with her hands. She'd hung them at her sides, held them behind her back, used them to pull on her dress, ran them though her hair, yet still she'd been unable to get them to feel at home or comfortable. Out of options, she'd scratched herself on her fingers and then pulled on her nails, also biting them. The feet were good for drawing designs in the snow.

When the lunch hour came, Celeste took her tray, wondering where she should sit. She'd felt self-conscious and alone in the big cafeteria. At Union, she would have been sitting with Ginny and the other girls, each trying to get Miss England's attention, asking her if she wanted something from their lunch pail. All Miss England ate was an apple and some cheese.

A boy flew by, bumping Celeste hard and splashing soup onto her fingers. It burned, forcing her to set her tray down beside a group of four girls. Smiling, she'd inhaled, trying to quell the pain. "I burned my finger." She chuckled. At least it was something to say. Good, she'd said her first words to kids her age. It was a start for someone as shy as she was.

The heavyset one had smiled back, such a relief. Did she have a new friend?

Now the fat one was asking, "What did you expect, standing where we walk? No one's supposed to be there. Was he supposed to walk through you as if you were a ghost?" Her smile had changed to a scowl while the others laughed.

"I didn't know. I'm new."

"Where are you from? I suppose it's some hick little town?" The same girl laughed at her.

"I'm from the country. Brady is the closest town. Gothenburg isn't far away. It's big."

"She went to a country school," the cutest one said. "So, where's your lunch pail?"

"I don't have it. I wish I did though. We ate with our teacher and she didn't eat much, so we tried to give her our food."

"That sounds entertaining. What's that cute outfit you're wearing? I suppose it's also country school?" a girl with a ponytail wanted to know.

"I was supposed to be in a play this afternoon. I'm Queen Love and had the lead. My parents died, and I've been living with my best friend, Ginny Temple. She was to be King Love." If nothing else, Celeste could tell this group about this play. Taking a seat at an empty spot, she said, "My teacher was making my dress. It was to be a gown with glitter hearts."

"Your teacher sewed all your clothes?" a girl asked, wrinkling her nose.

A boy down a few chairs yelled, "Do the cows get to come to school, too?"

Laughter rang throughout the cafeteria.

A third girl who'd been gawking at Celeste said, "There's a table over there for kids from weird places. Go sit with them. See, over there." The girl pointed at a table full of children with physical issues. One slept while another kept saying something that Celeste couldn't understand. A cross-looking teacher, appearing bored, sat with them. Celeste's head began to swim.

Embarrassed and feeling that she might cry Celeste had moved to a spot where she could eat all by herself.

Glancing at the map, certain she was almost home, Celeste wondered about the school party and how the play went. Momentary memories of her and Ginny and good times swam through her mind. Even the good was painful. Among her comforting memories was that of moving from the Sandhills to the Temples' farm. She'd only been eight years old, and to this day, memories of moving brought warmth.

1928 The family left Arnold that morning, with Mom promising everyone a treat with her egg money on reaching Brady, not far from their new home. Arriving there, around 11:00, in two vehicles, with Dad and Celeste riding in the truck, the family stopped at the filling station for sodas. Taking their drinks out to the sidewalk, Celeste and her mom watched as the young attendant eyed Bonnie, and they listened to Dad, who was busy telling a station worker about the 25 Pontiac. Even now, Celeste could hear her father talking—"It came from a man named Ambrose. He was the father of my latest boss, a Jerry someone." Not a man to give out names, Dad continued, "Ambrose went up there to finish his days peaceably. Ha! It didn't work. Jerry was a mean one. I took over pulling the old man out of the mud. That way, he could drive to town. Wife Shirley here, she was the one he loved like a daughter. She had him over each morning for chatter and breakfast. We didn't expect anything. A good man does that for his neighbor. We said we didn't want a thing. Heck, even though we told him that, he didn't listen. He left us this car, a beautiful blessing. He was a real good fellow. You don't meet many like that."

The gas station restroom was a special treat for them. Celeste was tired of those smelly outdoor privies. After Celeste, it was Howie's turn. Spit up dribbled down his front, earning him a sink bath. Leaving the station, headed south, they crossed the Platte River. Two old men were fishing on a bank and a group of boys were wading, trying to grab minnows. Meanwhile, cottonwoods, vinery, and wild roses grew randomly along the riversides. The water, a good source for irrigation for the farmlands, was flowing full and fast that morning, thanks to spring rains and heavy snowfall up in the mountains the past winter. Running hither and thither, the water wound around sandbars, heading east.

The cornfields, laying another mile south, had tractors—the Farmalls, John Deere's, Allis-Chalmers, Massey-Harris's, and Oliver's—rattling row to row. Meanwhile, Celeste wondered if the family looked a little strange. Dad had converted the ancient Model A into a contraption that resembled a truck. This bizarre-looking vehicle was overflowing with the Dustys' possessions. The couch sat tied up on the roof, with the "born again" wagon following behind. Bonnie found this in a ditch of water when she was out looking for lost cows. The chickens were caged in the back with Dad hoping that the wind wouldn't scalp their feathers. Mom was planning to make new pillows. In his opinion, she needed to double the feathers.

It wasn't long before they saw tall hills, full of cattle. Some were standing up on cliffs along the sky. Their calves stood beside them. Down below, fields curved smoothly around the hills. "I've never seen anything like this," Celeste said. "Something's about to spring forth like flowers popping up through the dirt."

Dad laughed; his daughter's joy pleased him.

"Look!" Celeste pointed. "Over there—it's a schoolhouse with nice swings. I don't like school, but I have a feeling that I'm going to like this one. There's a miniature house with a cute roof. It's for the coal." The school was freshly painted with a pump for our water. A red-headed woman was going inside. "She might be my new teacher next fall," Celeste said, "Oh, no! She's looking my way. I'm ducking down."

"You're missing the Oregon Trail marker out front," Dad said. "It was the first cross-country trail and went for two thousand miles. Before that, people went by water. Fur trappers made the trail. Later, the emigrants took it to Oregon. They brought along livestock. At night, the circle of wagons served as a fence or corral to keep the animals together. You're lucky to have that bronzed piece out in front of your school. They built the trail before 1850. It isn't quite a hundred years ago. Say, we only have a mile left to go before we're home."

There it sat, just inside the drive—their new home. As soon as Dad stopped, Celeste was off to explore the farmhouse. Her dream had been to live in a two-story house like this one. Inside, Celeste discovered a kitchen and a washroom for separating the milk and cream. Mother liked her cream money for extras. The first floor had a living room with a bay window. Celeste could use that for her stage. Upstairs, Celeste found three bedrooms, one of them for her and Bonnie. The thought of sleeping upstairs, eye level with the treetops, thrilled her. A big branch stuck out just beyond the window. Wouldn't Mother be thrilled when Celeste flew past the living room? Celeste would be mother's little fairy. "How awfully wonderful," Celeste said aloud.

Back outside again, Dad and Bonnie were taking the haphazardly packed boxes inside. They'd barely begun when a blue-eyed, blond-haired boy, muscles flexed, walked up to Al. A younger girl tagged a ways behind. "Sir," he said, "name's Will Temple, Clark's son. Be glad to lend you a hand with the boxes."

Dad grinned. "I'm not used to having a boy your age wanting to do a man's work."

"I'm not a boy. I'm ten years old." Will was obviously insulted.

"Quite right about that," Al agreed. "You have some good muscles there. Start with any box you want to carry."

Anxious to show off, Will hoisted one box on top of another, blinding his sight of anything in front of him. He'd taken two steps when he tripped. The top box went flying. Fortunately, Al caught it. Laughing, he said, "Lucky thing I was here."

Will, too embarrassed to look at Al, charged on down the sidewalk, depositing his only box inside the tenant house

*   *   *

A petite girl, with dark braids walked up to her. "I'm Ginny Temple," she said. "Who are you?"

"Celeste. Celeste Dusty," a shy voice answered.

"How old are you?" Ginny asked. Her long, ribbon-tied braids dangled to the tops of her shoulders.

"I'm eight. I'll be a third-grader."

"Me too. We'll be in the same class together. There will be five of us, counting you. Four girls and one boy. I don't like him though. He picks his nose. Mostly, I don't like boys no matter who they are."

"I don't like them either." Celeste hadn't given them thought either way. *In her opinion, girls caused the problems.*

"The school's down the road a mile. We'll walk together every morning."

"We will? I mean, we will." No one had walked with her at her old school. *Celeste was always the invisible one—except when her clothes got too patchy. Then the kids teased her.*

"I came over to see if you could play. Like dolls?"

"Mine's packed in a box. I'll never find her today." Celeste's eyes flickered *as she'd looked away. As soon as Ginny learned about her dirty doll, the friendship would end. Oh, well. They weren't friends yet anyway. Celeste had never had a close friend. "I'll have to ask Mom if I can play."* Celeste paused. *She might as well tell Ginny and get it over with. "My doll isn't pretty. She has bad hair, an eye is missing, and one leg is gone. A dog attacked her."*

"Ouch!" Ginny exclaimed. *"We can have a hospital. We'll play Civil War nurses. I'd love to be Clara Barton. We did her in school. I was Clara, and several of the boys were injured soldiers. Will, my crazy brother, the one helping your father, was a doctor. Some of the girls were nurses, and some were wives. We cut up old sheets for bandages, using water from the classroom pump to wash the catsup off the patients. We also fed them soup."*

"Why the catsup?"

"Blood. We used chocolate cookies for dirtying the soldiers."

"You really do things pretty real. Were you scared they'd die?" Celeste *smiled, knowing better.*

"No," Ginny laughed. *"The stage was our hospital. We heated the bandages over near the stove. When it was all over, the parents had a potluck. I wore a Red Cross outfit that Mom made. I should show it to you sometime. We can both be Clara, and the baby pigs can be our patients. Or we could use dolls. Let's ask if you can play."*

Yes, Celeste could play as long as it was all right with Ginny's mother. Ginny assured her that her mother would be relieved.

"Let's skip," Ginny sang out. *"Wait. I have a question. What color is your hair? It's the same as your mom's. She's pretty."*

"It's auburn and snarled. Auburn is brownish red."

Ginny reached and patted it gently. "Let's skip."

The two were off, Ginny reaching for Celeste's hand, whose heart began singing. Could this be her first friend?

As they passed a small grove that sat between the two houses, a huge, three-story farmhouse came into view. "It's a farm palace," Celeste said, awed. "Your roof goes clear up to the sky. We could walk off it and go running in the clouds. Maybe we'd meet an angel."

They came to the large porch. "Come in. Mom's baking cookies. Let's get one and go back outside after we get my dolls. Smell the cookies?"

"Yummy," Celeste said, following Ginny through an oak-trimmed house with a foyer, an open staircase, a fireplace, and charming built-in bookcases. Wilted iris and mail were on the table, and clothes lay heaped on the couch. A breeze was coming in the window. It looked a little like home. Celeste was thinking how this was the finest house she had ever seen when she saw a large derriere sticking out from the oven. Celeste could see two large, rippling legs and a girdle. How embarrassing! Celeste was afraid she would start giggling from nervousness. It was like when the pastor's mother had fallen on ice and her dress had come up over her silk boxers. The pastor had set her upright, his own mother.

The woman took the sheet of cookies out of the oven, stopping to push the damp strawberry blond bangs off her forehead. Then, without an introduction, she said, "Well, I see that Ginny's friend is finally here. You're Celeste, aren't you? Ginny has been bugging me every day with, 'When are they coming?' By the way, I'm Bev, this kid's mother."

"Mom, you don't have to tell everyone everything I say," Ginny scolded, half laughing, half pouting while Celeste took the cookie Bev handed her.

After the girls had finished their cookies, Ginny led the way to the attic playhouse to get a few dolls. They were planning to take them to the haymow. However, Celeste had never seen anything like the attic and wanted to stay and play. There were hundreds of books, including Robert Louis Stevenson's poetry, The Tale of Peter Rabbit, Raggedy Ann and Andy stories, and more. She had a paper circus set, a Lionel train, doll buggies, wooden dollhouses, the Effanbee dolls, and raised patterned porcelain china dishes. Ginny had to drag her back downstairs, promising they would come back soon.

Bev, who was still working in the kitchen, had a message. "I'm making these cookies and a casserole for Celeste's family. I plan to do lemon bars if I can work it in. Time is running short, but I figure Shirley is going to find it impossible to move in and cook the evening meal, all on the same day. It gets too confusing and hectic. She'll be lucky if she can find anything to eat amid the clutter and unpacked boxes. Everything scatters out here and there. Ginny, as to your asking about another cookie, you girls can each have one more cookie, but only one. I want to save plenty for snacking."

While she spoke, Celeste took in the details of Bev's kitchen. Done all in white with yellow accents, its charm came by way of crocks, roosters, a wooden *pie cupboard, wooden cabinets, a Monarch stove, and beautifully patterned linoleum. Her goods were stored in the pantry and a chunk of ice from the ice house was laying on the counter ready for the icebox…*

Celeste worried about Bev seeing her mother's mess. Packing, no matter how many times Mom did it, never got easier for her. There weren't enough boxes, and as Dad put it, Mom waited until the last minute and then found herself short of the time needed to sort the things she packed. The cereal was apt to be in with the pajamas. This morning, they'd found the biscuits under the brassieres. "Finders keepers, losers weepers," Bonnie had teased. Celeste had figured that, when it came time to fix supper, the pots and pans would be scattered here and there, making it nearly impossible for Mom to cook or Bev to get in the house. While some folks ate in restaurants, Celeste had no expectations of eating out. The Dustys couldn't afford such luxuries?

Somehow, the thought of Bev getting mad at her or anyone had scared her. Celeste had been nice enough but not exactly sweet. Shy didn't describe Ginny's mom, to her chagrin. This woman seemed sort of like a charging bull. No, that was wrong … Determined was a better word, Celeste decided, afraid Mom would shrink in Bev's presence. Still, it was nice of Bev to make things easier for her. Wanting Bev to understand what moving was like, Celeste said, "Mom isn't the best mover, so you might find a mess. Otherwise, she's wonderful."

"Oh, now." Bev's eyes shone. "So you think you have to protect your mother by preparing me? Your mother and I are going to do just fine. I've met you, and that tells me she's special."

Celeste blushed, beaming with pride.

True to her word, Bev delivered the casserole and bars, plus the cookies, around 5:30. Celeste, who had come home by then, knew that the supper would spell the end of her new friendship. While Bonnie was popular and everyone liked Dad, Celeste had always felt that people treated the family as transients. No one had ever asked the Dustys to their home. At church, they sat in a pew by themselves. Celeste knew they didn't make a lot but wondered why that mattered. People were to love their neighbor as themselves, and the Dustys were good people. Dad or Mother would do anything for others. Mom even fed the hobos who were out of food.

By the time Bev left the house, everyone was more than ready to sit around the table to rest and eat. Mother had managed to put several items in the enamel cupboards, including plates. Taking their places, Al said grace. "Thank you, Lord."

When they said, amen, all but Howie joined

In the silence, only a country breeze blew the curtains about, Dad took the plates and filled them with Bev's goodly sized chicken noodle casserole with mashed potatoes. Other sounds were Howie banging his fork on the high chair, silverware on graniteware plates, chewing, and requests for more. Occasionally, Celeste had gotten up so she could stare out the window at the greening valley and canyons to the south.

Suddenly, Mom, normally quiet, piped up enthusiastically. "Bev Temple invited me over to her place. I'm going to have coffee with her tomorrow. She's making cinnamon rolls and will tell me about their Union Aid Society. Can you believe that?"

*   *   *

Memories! Finding it hard not to cry, Celeste used her coat sleeves as tissues. Sylvie's house was just coming into view, and Celeste feared that Sylvie would say something if she saw her bawling. Opening the door, she thought of her brother and his warm snugly ways.

There, not six feet away, sitting at a little table, Howie twisted around, putting his arms out. "Celeste's home."

On hearing his greeting, music to her ears, Celeste ran towards him. "Howie, I'm so glad to see you, little buddy." Grabbing him, she hugged Howie tightly.

They were still embracing when Sylvie walked into the room. Looking pristine, she was holding a plate of sliced apples, vegetables, and crackers, smeared with peanut butter. Some had cheese slices and bits of meat. Starved, Celeste had forgotten the snack rule. A little something to fill the hunger and things would be all right. Everyone needed time to adjust. A few crackers would work a miracle. She took three crackers, each overflowing with peanut butter and an apple slice. "Thank you," she murmured, swallowing a bit too much.

Sylvie, who saw the peanut butter smeared on Celeste's skinny, dry hands, gritted her teeth. Everything was wrong with the girl. That silly skirt was even more ridiculous than it had appeared this morning. Moreover, by now, the blouse looked like a wrinkled square dance outfit.

Celeste grinned at Sylvie, about to thank her again. Instead, two cold eyes pierced through her like the sharpened points of darts. For a split second, she recalled those eyes somewhere in the past. She would have captured and kept that thought if not for Sylvie's fingernail waving in her face.

"Celeste Dusty! What are you doing? That food is your brother's and mine. Unlike you, we haven't had any lunch. We were downtown shopping for clothes for Howard."

"I-I thought these were snacks. W-we always had something to eat at Bev's." Tears spilled over.

"I have order and rules in this house, Celeste." The sight of Celeste's face was an immense repulsion. She wanted to hit the girl. If only Celeste could exude confidence like that found in daughters of friends over at the club. What was she going to do about her fancy friends meeting this strange niece? Celeste was gangly and awkward. Her tangled hair was her only asset. Looking more closely at the hair, she noticed something sticking to the strands—something white. "What did you get in your hair?" Sylvie snapped.

"We were making hearts for our mothers, and I know you're not my mother, and mine didn't turn out so good… It's that my head itched, and I went to scratch it and got plaster in it. I'm sorry. At Union, we would have laughed. W-we even had a paste fight. One day, when Mrs. England had all this flour and water left over, we went outside and got …" Celeste giggled. Then, without warning, her eyes grew moist. She remembered her friends and the tractors humming in the distance and, most painfully, today and the play. Her young mind wandered. "I wonder who played me. Ginny and I were to sprinkle love glitter over all over the parents."

Sylvie jumped in. "We were talking about my meal and Howard's meal. Now you've gone from food to paste and love by way of glitter. I don't care about your play, paste, Mrs. England, Bev, or glitter. I want you to go upstairs and wash your hair. And when you are done, clean your room."

"I did clean it," Celeste said, swallowing and remembering how much Mother liked her cleaning, even when she couldn't do some things well.

"You need to get a hold of yourself. I might as well be honest. I have problems with you."

Celeste dried the tears as they escaped from her eyes. How was she going to be perfect? She'd come close before the accident. Now it was impossible. Things weren't working the same. She wished she was a car. If she was, some mechanic could do an overhaul and fix her, including her broken heart. Just then she realized what Sylvie had said. She'd called Howie, Howard.

"You called Howie *Howard*. Why?"

"It's more professional. Someday, he's going to go to Washington to be a politician, a senator at first."

In a split second, Celeste lost herself. She stood there in a frenzy of anger. "You don't know him. How can you say he'll be a senator? You met him just yesterday. He's only four years old. Don't try to change us. We don't belong to you."

Turning, she ran up the stairs, where she fell into a deep sleep, sobbing her way to a coma-like state. In less than twenty-four hours, her world had turned around.

*   *   *

She was still sleeping when Sylvie brought a plate of steaming food up. It was stroganoff, which was new to Celeste's taste buds and delicious. Sylvie explained more kindly why snacking was not done in this house. "Girls are expected to be thin if they're to have a debutante party. Popular girls are thin, beautiful girls are thin, and debutantes are popular and beautiful and thin."

Celeste started to ask what *debutante* meant.

Instead, Sylvie began expounding on how the "in-group" always dressed well. She also announced that she'd found some clothes for Celeste. Getting up, she returned with four puffy bundles of cellophane, each tied with a skinny ribbon. "I kept busy all day on you, as well as your brother. You didn't give me a chance to tell you that. Each package has an entire outfit of parts that match. One is a jumper and top with matching socks. The next is a red and blue frock with a matching hair bow. After that, we have a blue plaid skirt with a blue vest and with shoes that match. Now, on closer look, I can see those will be too small for you. Lastly, you have another jumper with matching bells. That one is for the coming Christmas."

Celeste said she hoped she didn't grow too tall for the holiday outfit. "Christmas is almost a year away. Could I wear it now?" she asked, wondering why the clothes had those packages. Then she saw a tag, Henrietta's Attic Specials. Prudence Henrietta was one of the girls she was to have met today. "Are those clothes from Prudence's house?" She almost laughed. To her, it sounded so absurd—*new clothes from Prudence's attic.*

"Sylvie, Prudence is one of the cutest girls in the room but not very nice. She passed a note that made a weird girl cry."

Sylvie waved her hand. "Pooh! Celeste, these clothes belong to Prudence's older sister Lynne. There are eight girls in the family. Their mother, a friend of mine and a lovely woman, decided to sell these so that the more *unfortunate* could have clothes."

"Am I one of those?"

Sylvie stopped talking just long enough to give it some thought. "Ask me in a month. I'm inclined to say you are. I explained your growth as being like that of a snake, thin but long and still growing—in the rapid stage. She thought we could go up above to the attic and attire you just fine. You'll feel divine in Prudence's sister's clothes."

"B ... But Prudence will know. Won't she?"

"Those girls will be debutantes. They're all little princesses. Allow them to rub off on you by wearing their clothes."

"But I'm afraid she'll see me and say something."

"Then take that as an opportunity to get to know her. Who did you meet today?"

Celeste hung her head. So far, she'd done nothing right. "No one."

"I thought so. You're like your mother. She was shy and tongue-tied. You and I are going to have some culture lessons. We will start tonight, but first, this heavy sack." Twisting around, Sylvie reached behind her chair. Taking some shoes out, she said, "These sporty old shoes are mine. I had them ready for the Mission. However, I thought to check the size of your shoes."

"Golf?" Celeste asked. Animated, she said, "You're going to take me golfing? That sounds like fun."

"Those are for weed picking in my mud garden. They are not golf shoes."

Sylvie left briefly and then reappeared with a small booklet. "Celeste, when I take you places, I want you to show well for my friends."

"You mean like a 4-H animal? I bet I'll be judged alongside other girls?" Laughing, Celeste did her rendition of a cow. "Moo. The judging sounds scary and—"

"For you, it will be scary."

Out of nowhere, Celeste thought of the little glass planter back home. It was shaped like a witch's hat. She wondered if Sylvie would grow in that planter if it had dirt. The hat would fit Sylvie's head.

"About manners," Sylvie said, "this booklet is called *Who Are the Cultured?* To start with, I will show you a picture with questions. Your job is to say what is wrong with the picture. The booklet is printed in New York City. It was written for girls seeking status. Let's see. Here's a picture of a man and two women. One is a college girl. Find the three social blunders in the picture." Sylvie waited.

Celeste knew one right away. She herself had the same problem. "The man with the hat is facing the pretty woman, but he's with the ugly one. The hideous one has her fingernail in her mouth, and he's ignoring her. That's cruel."

When Sylvie finished asking the questions, Celeste went back to her reading. She'd just turned the page when she heard voices. Looking into the hall, the voices were Sylvie's and Howie's. "Howard," Sylvie said, "you're picking up where he left off. That means college and law. You'll need to be ready for politics."

Celeste had no idea what Sylvie meant. Dumbfounded, she returning to reading.

*   *   *

It was March, and a month had passed since Celeste and Howie had come to live with Sylvie and Mack.

Where was everyone? Had they honestly forgotten her? The days were troublesome and long. She needed to ask Bonnie about Mom. Sylvie had told her that Mother was a thief as a teenager. She'd said how Shirley stole people's jewelry.

Celeste wanted to scream at her folks for dying and leaving her stuck in this life. Mostly, she hated herself. Even when the sun shone, the sky was dark and heavy and caving in on her. Her pencil thin limbs drug her worries around on a chain. Was there any way to escape her life? She imagined taking a shovel and digging as long as it took. She would dig a tunnel that came up in Bev's kitchen, magically joining the Temples for their meal, playing games in the evening, and cuddling with Ginny while sleeping. With her anxiety out of control, the world looked dim and despairing. The question was, how long could she hold on? She no longer liked the person she had become. Her smile was gone, her cheeks brittle. Where was that happy girl who never thought of murkiness and dread and dead ends? Where had she gone?

Celeste had been staying with the Soboris for three weeks when she opened her eyes and saw Sylvie's face directly above hers. Sylvie was ready for a second round with *Who Are the Cultured?* Once again showing Celeste a picture of a man and two women, Sylvie said, name the blunders.

Celeste, who was good at this social game, said, "Sylvie, people are so insensitive. The ugly one is clearly at his side. He's pulling the chair out for the pretty lady. I suppose it's a blunder, but that ugly one is slumping."

Sylvie closed the book. Part of her wanted to laugh. Celeste had her share of these problems, but that wasn't reason for sympathy. The girl needed to shape up.

Celeste leaned forward, asking to answer more questions; instead, Sylvie promptly left the room. She wasn't in the mood for her niece's fervent persistence.

*　　*　　*

Mack Sobori, drab and banal, gave Celeste a bit of cheer. During her first weeks in Lincoln, come Saturdays, Mack allowed Celeste go to the drugstore to help. She'd gone down to his O Street drugstore three times. He put her in charge of making ice cream floats, banana splits, and sundaes. She also did the cherry and chocolate cokes.

"A squirt of cherry," she'd say, enjoying making the sodas.

Claire, another helper, a young lady who was earning money for college, worked with her. She was responsible for teaching Celeste the art of being a soda jerk. Shapely and appealing, Claire was a fashion plate; she even offered to teach Celeste how to sew.

"I could teach you if Mack would pay me for the lessons." She'd winked at Mack, who was in agreement. Celeste figured that both she and Claire knew how awful she looked. Actually, that wasn't true at all. Claire couldn't figure out why Sylvie wasn't taking better care of a girl with so much potential. Celeste needed a timely cut, some agreeable clothes, and polish with her social skills. Claire thought that, if given these, the girl would turn into a knockout. Of course, she was still young and awkward, but with time, watch out. Another thing, Claire suspected that Celeste was lonely. Why wouldn't she be lonely? Only a twelve-year-old, she'd lost two parents and had made a comment about not seeing or hearing from her loved ones. Why wasn't Sylvie doing anything about it?

Less depressed, Celeste decided there had to be a reasonable explanation for her not having heard from those she loved such as Bonnie and Ginny. She'd hoped that Miss England would send a letter. Though intimidated, she decided to ask Sylvie if she could invite Ginny for a stay. Sylvie's response was that Bev couldn't bring Ginny. "Too much bother!" Coming would just amount to an extra visit with the countrywide depression going strong. Celeste knew that gas cost money but thought Sylvie used the gas excuse far too often. She was certain that, should she ask to walk next door, Sylvie would say that gas cost too much.

Then the hardest blow came along. Bev told her that Bonnie had called to say the baby wasn't doing so well, but she didn't have time to speak with Celeste.

"Bonnie didn't have time for me?" Celeste asked, dazed by Sylvie's words. "What's wrong with Carson?"

"Celeste, she told me because she wanted me to know. Had she wanted you to know, she would have asked for you? He'll live though; I guarantee you that much."

Celeste wanted to reach out and punch her. Sylvie was purposefully impossible. Ginny would have run away. Will would have been long gone, leaving her head stuck in the mud with a snake staring at her.

It turned out that the hurt involved more than Bonnie, the games included Howie. The problem jumped up like a well-watered weed in a garden. A week after Bonnie's call, Judge Hardy; his wife; and their son, Paul, Howie's friend, were invited for dinner on a Sunday evening. Afterward, the company all went to the living room to talk. About an hour later, when Howie and Paul returned to the living room, the Hardy's poodle came running in behind them. The nervous little dog, Weasels, was shaking Celeste's under pants in his mouth.

Howie began yelling at the top of his lungs, "Those panties are Celeste's. Look! They have holes in them. Eat them, Weasels." The boys continued to egg Weasels on while Mack and Sylvie snickered. Frantic, Celeste froze. Meanwhile, the boys cheered.

Then everything had gone quiet.

"Sylvie!" Mrs. Hardy had yelled. "Put a stop to this or we're going home. Why would you allow anyone to humiliate a girl that way?"

That said, she'd risen from her seat, and the Hardy's, as well as Weasels and the two boys walked out—leaving Celeste and her misery behind them. Celeste was already aware of Sylvie's tendency to egg Howie to tease her. She'd tried to pretend it wasn't happening. She knew she would lose Howie. She wondered if she had any family or friends left and why Sylvie held such disdain for her.

*   *   *

Later, on a Saturday morning at the end of March, a little over two months after Celeste had arrived to live with Sylvie, Sylvie awakened her with an invitation to the Country Club for a mother/daughter tea. She gave her niece new Mary Jane's shoes, a hairstylist, and an organza frock, the dress picked especially for the Celeste's striking auburn hair. Breathlessly, Celeste went about getting fashionable, although taking time to chastise herself for having judged Sylvie too soon. She added a personal self-scolding for expecting Sylvie to warm up before she was ready. After all, wasn't this only the start of her second month at Sylvie's? To have expected more any sooner had been totally selfish and unrealistic. Today was going to be their blissful beginning with each other. Celeste's low-wasted dress even boasted a ribbon with a bow about her narrow hips.

At eleven thirty, Celeste and Sylvie were out the door, motoring to the country club in the new Packard—this one a convertible. While Sylvie smoked, Celeste basked in her newfound joy—being Sylvie's invitee. Today, she'd become a special niece. While Sylvie sat gaily honking the horn at friendly pedestrians, Celeste waved and grinned. This filled a hole in her heart; until now, she had spent hours despairing over Sylvie's horrific put-downs and indifference. This was one of her gladdest days. Everyone needed Sylvie to care.

Arriving, Celeste and Sylvie were escorted inside and seated amid candles, flowers, and elegant ladies—women who made Celeste the center of attention. A piano player performed while they ate. Sylvie wanted Celeste to remember the day as one that had significant meaning, *which she would*. To Celeste, it was a coming out of sorts.

As an eighth-grader, the young girl knew nothing of this velvety kind of life. Union Aid at Bev's house and Bonnie's wedding were special but nothing like this. Enormous red feathers with sparkles had been mixed in with bouquets of crimson roses—no carnations for this place. The club's decorators had placed the flowers in leaded, cut glass vases. Celeste had never dreamed that carpet could be so luxurious and gorgeous in swirls of rich colors. Wiggling her shoes off, she exercised her toes, pushing them down into the fibers while the pianist played romantic jazz. It distressed Celeste to think that her mother would never know such delight. Surely, Sylvie, who was indulged and bathed in pleasantries, loved life. Celeste wondered what this would cost, believing it would take a whopping pile of nickels and a tall stack of dimes. She must remember to write her pals at Union School about this event. She'd written them once, but no one, not even Mrs. England answered.

A group of classmates were huddled together two tables over, looking like those gingerbread chains. Celeste was determined that she wouldn't agonize. She might have, if not for being the center of attention at her table. Pouting was a waste of time. She would no longer need to imagine swallowing arsenic in order to approach her peers. They finally knew she was Sylvie's property instead of a piece of fuzzy mold. The ladies were clamoring to meet her. What grade was she in? What did she enjoy doing? The boys would probably be ringing the phone off the wall.

Fortunately, Sylvie didn't hear that one, or the question about her having many nice, new friends.

The day was such a swell one—a kind of utopia.

Celeste was patting a bouquet of roses and noting her hands, for the first time, in that way an older girl studies the shape of her fingers. The manicure and deep red Hazel Bishop polish gave an edge of femininity.

As Celeste sat there, thinking her hands attractive, everything changed. Adorable Leslie Ann Huntington, the most popular girl in Celeste's class, came walking over in her shimmering dress. Celeste's heart flip-flopped. *At last, no more struggles.* In a moment, she would be sitting where the best girls sat! Leslie Ann had come to welcome and retrieve her.

Walking past Celeste, Leslie scorned her, making her feel as if a chilly breeze had passed through her. "Hi, Celeste," Leslie said coldly.

Then, of all things, the purple-eyed darling grasped Sylvie's arm. Bending down, she extended her flawless ivory cheek for a kiss! "Sylvie," she fussed, "It's nice to see my godmother." Then, sticking out her ring finger, she said, "I have this ring you got me. I also have that doll from France. She's in the glass case with my other European dolls."

Scooting her chair, so that she back was to Celeste, Sylvie cooed, "Leslie Ann, sweetheart..." To Celeste's dismay, Sylvie began listing off Leslie Ann's assets, saying she was future country club stock. Raving and giggling, Sylvie made over Leslie Ann. Watching them, Celeste's heaven disappeared. Pain and shame seared her heart. She was ready to go hide in the powder room. Or, better yet, why not flush her body down into the sewer, where the rats would devour her? She was preparing to take leave when she felt something warm on her arm.

Looking down, she saw a hand and a ring, the diamond bigger than Sylvie's diamond. Looking up, she saw the kindest face she remembered seeing since gazing into Mother's eyes. Celeste had no idea who this lady was. However, the other women and Sylvie obviously recognized this woman.

The lady was Grace Monroe, the real McCoy. Married to a successful manufacturer, a magnate, Grace had seen the whole thing. Pulling Celeste out of her chair, Grace curled her arm about Celeste's shoulders, leading her around the room, table by table.

Sylvie quickly lost interest in Leslie Ann Huntington, instead, making a beeline over to Grace. Every time Sylvie opened her mouth to talk, Grace put her finger to Sylvie's lips, shushing her. "Shhh," she said. "Mrs., uh, I guess I don't know who you are, but please allow these ladies a chance to meet this darling girl. You will have a chance to speak to her once we finish. I've heard so much about the girl. I understand her parents were killed." That was really the only thing that Grace knew, but it was plenty. Her heart was with Celeste.

Celeste sat reveling in the rightness of life, promising she'd remember this gesture. Grace was like a fairy Godmother. Having met this lovely woman, Celeste, soon to be thirteen was certain that somehow Sylvie was like Grace. After all, she was Sylvie's princess, living with the gorgeous socialite, in the loveliest castle, on A Street. No one in the crowd, even Celeste herself, was aware of the child who was peeking out that day—an anxious, lonely girl who cried herself to sleep at night.

*   *   *

Sylvie didn't feel quite the same effervescence. As with all she did, she'd convinced herself that her disdain for Celeste wasn't any fault of her own. Her highest goal was to reform Celeste. Moreover, this Grace woman caused Sylvie's lips to shake! What did Grace know about Celeste's character? Sylvie had sacrificed her time to make each decision with Celeste's well-being in mind. She alone had given the orphan a home when the rest of the world was content to allow the Temples to get by with kidnapping Celeste and Howard. And for this Grace to have said she didn't know Sylvie…Everyone knew Sylvie!

Thanks to Celeste and her mulish, stubborn, disposition, life was going awry. Normally when things didn't work, Sylvie made a practice of either putting them in the trash or having them fixed. The latter wasn't working with Celeste, and there would be talk if the trash man found Celeste in the trash.

Speaking of trash, how well she remembered the day her sister and Al died.

Mack had come to her with a sad face, as he'd taken the telegram and opened it before getting it to her. Both names were on it. He'd told her to sit down and that both Shirley and Al had died. Before she could stop herself, she's said, "Good." However, the *good* was just for Shirley.

As awful as it was to remember Shirley, Celeste possessed many of Shirley's annoying mannerisms and habits… Both fed strays and strangers, and each had those gooey smiles that made others feel all cottony and soft. Sylvie, however, knew the truth. Celeste's smile was superficial, and her praise was merely a jumble of false words. Who but Celeste told a scarecrow out in the flower garden how nice it looked? Who else would go and tell an old woman how nice her cracked false teeth looked? Who else would jump in someone's garbage can to hunt for a neighbor's glasses? Shirley had done stuff like that too—just for attention. In Sylvie's mind, Shirley had been a mess of scrambled eggs, unable to collect herself. She was one of those people who decorated half her yard and failed to finish the other half. Sylvie called these ladies "the half-baked women." This mattered because of Sylvie's need for the aesthetic.

Feeling silence around her, Sylvie lifted her eyes and looked about at the other ladies. Realizing how dour her thoughts made her appear, she smiled. This morning Howard had said to her, "When I grow up, I am going to be president." Sylvie knew that would never happen with Celeste in the picture. By nightfall, Howard would have Sylvie to himself in order to work on Sylvie's aspirations for him.

*   *   *

Celeste and Sylvie were riding home from the mother/daughter banquet at the club when Sylvie made the mistake of asking, "So, when is your birthday? It's the big one, huh? You'll turn thirteen." She no sooner had the question out than Celeste sat up in her seat, leaning in close.

Celeste couldn't believe her ears. Sylvie had thrown a wingding for Howie, whose birthday was February 28. Hers wasn't until October. But hey—if Sylvie wanted to make plans already, why shouldn't she? She hadn't thought Sylvie would be interested in having a gala for her big day.

Words began tumbling out. "I'll have a party? Thank you!" Celeste said. "I'll bake the cake. I'll do a vanilla cake, Ginny's favorite. We can go to O Street's fabric stores and buy some fabric for an outfit. Bonnie could teach me more of the sewing basics," she said, making stitching noises with her tongue, "sti-sti-sti-sti-..."

Squinting, Sylvie wrinkled her brow. This gesture stopped the stitching, but the talking went on.

"I'll be thirteen, and I'll have you to thank for my high school years."

My stars, Sylvie thought. Putting an end to this nonsense, she said, "When the economy decides to straighten out, we can do something." Staring straight ahead—"It depends on your behavior. I suppose you're going to tell me again that you just want ordinary friends and that the important girls don't need you."

"They don't. They have each other." Celeste fought back tears.

Sylvie couldn't stand such behaviors, or Celeste's white skin, for that matter—not an iota of sunbaked tan. Worse still, she stood picking and biting on her stubby nails, scratched, rough, and inflamed. Her ankles bore chap burns where snow had irritated her because of inefficient over boots. Sylvie, who'd caused these problems, couldn't stand the hideousness. Neither would she own up to the fact that these were her fault.

Swallowing her irritation, Sylvie ignited her plan into action. "Celeste, this is what I can't stand. You always have excuses. The very girls you refuse to approach are wonderful girls. You saw how nice Leslie Ann was to me today, and you didn't even bother to join the conversation."

Tears of shame and disappointment fell hot on Celeste's cheeks. She realized that the day wasn't what she'd thought after all. More criticisms were being hurled her way.

She heard Sylvie's disdain when Sylvie said, "Listen to you weep. Well I think you're going to have to cry some more, because I'm moving you to the guest cottage. Elvira will live with you as your sponsor. You'll no longer associate with Howard—except for when I say he can come over." Sylvie knew that even she would need breaks from the boy, who at times could be a real brat. "He's too dependent on you. Maybe at future birthdays, you'll have a list of age-appropriate Lincoln friends to invite."

*   *   *

Celeste packed her things for the second time. Detesting the idea of living with Elvira in the musty guest house, with four rooms, out behind the main house, left her unable to stop crying. Was she so bad that Sylvie had to move her elsewhere only weeks after coming here? As she packed, she was thinking of her twelfth birthday last year on the ranch.

For her party last year, Mom and Dad arranged for a hayrack ride and wonderfully decorated boxes holding sandwich suppers. Bev and Clark helped. They'd gone to a pasture and enjoyed a beautiful night. All the girls from school came—even the older girls. Mom let her make a chocolate cake and open her presents around a campfire. She held Howie when the girls sang "Happy Birthday." In her own way, she'd really been someone. Dad playfully spanked her as Mom stood there laughing. Bonnie made a yummy version of potato salad and brought Bob along.

Remembering this, Celeste used her twentieth Kleenex. She was crying so hard, she wasn't able to see. Then, of all things, Sylvie yelled, telling her to hurry. As far as she was concerned, Sylvie was sick and needed prayer, but she would not be the one to pray for the witch. If only Will Temple would come and save her from the candy cottage. She thought of Will, knowing she was nothing to him. Nevertheless, it comforted her to imagine him holding her hand and making her his girlfriend at school. That began the weeping again. No one liked her, and that included him. Where was everyone? They really had forgotten her. Bonnie and the Temples must think that she'd caused the car wreck. She wanted to scream so loud that those at home would hear her and get her, even if they hated her.

*   *   *

Celeste's fourth month in Lincoln, spent at the guest cottage, was eerily quiet. Living in the backyard, with only Elvira for company, could only be described as dreary. The old spinster and the orphan didn't exchange two words. Elvira's cooking was bland and colorless, consisting of an endless diet of rice and raisins with milk and a dash of cinnamon. They were two quiet figures, shuffling left and right of each other, looking like mummies.

Elvira reminded Celeste of a cranky shadow hovering over her. The cottage cramped. Celeste wasn't sure that Elvira's vocabulary went beyond, "Get out of there; I have to pee ... now," and, "Wash up the dishes. I cooked." From the window over the couch, Celeste could see into the kitchen of the main house. She watched Natasha's head as it moved about the kitchen. It was commonplace to see Howie and Sylvie take off in the car for places unknown. Celeste wasn't quite sure about why she'd been sent to live in the backyard. Was it because she hadn't made Lincoln friends or was it because she'd wanted a birthday party? *Why did Sylvie hate her?*

Although Celeste was not allowed to enter the house, Howie came over whenever he felt like it, making a nuisance of himself. Sylvie welcomed his absence. Without fail, Celeste found Howie irritating and distasteful. The boy, who had once been so sweet that the family joked, saying that he'd own a sweets bakery someday, had turned into a brat. Celeste thought him spoiled, lazy, and terribly mean. She was certain he despised her. He refused to acknowledge her as his sister— instead, saying she was a weirdo. If he wanted, he could come over and ransack things. She got in trouble if she disciplined him. She knew that he was under Sylvie's spell but had no idea how he could have changed so much in such a short time.

Grieved over the changes in the only family she'd known, Celeste asked herself, who Howard, her once-upon- a-time brother, had become? What was Sylvie using to poison his mind? On various occasions, he'd overheard Sylvie saying strange things. "Howard, you're not going to be like your father. You're going to Washington when you're older."

One evening, when Celeste was still living at the house; she'd heard Sylvie say, "Howard, you're nothing like Donnie. Thank goodness! He was supposed to be Howard's baby. Instead, he was a freak." Horrified, Celeste wondered if Donnie was the baby she'd lost.

Once when she'd gone to the linen chest, over at the house, to get pillowcases for Elvira, Celeste had found two pictures of a child in an attic dresser drawer. One was a minute baby who looked like the smallest baby she'd ever seen; the other was a boy around one and a half. The words "Eighteen months" were written on the back, along with the initials "D.S." The child had a wistful appearance as though there was nothing in his mind. His eyes had an empty stare. One evening, when Celeste still lived at the house; she'd heard Sylvie say, "Howard, you're nothing like Donnie. Thank goodness. He was supposed to be Howard's baby. Instead he was a freak."

Helpless to change the circumstances, Celeste became an avid reader, whenever possible. At least, some of her books came through Sylvie's library. It took audacity, but when she knew no one was there, Celeste snuck in and found two books at a time. One day, Natasha found her in there looking for something to read. Sweat poured from Celeste's pores. Seeing Natasha frightened and shocked the spit out of Celeste. Incredibly, Natasha had arranged to bring Celeste a basket of books every two weeks. Only then did Celeste know that there was one person who would befriend her.

Other activities included walking up and down A Street. It was on these walks that Mildred evolved. She and Mildred, an older lady, baked cookies on snowy days and threw snowballs. Soon they would do their spring cleaning with swinging on the porch come summer. When fall came, Mildred would teach her to make layer cakes—some with lemon sauce and others with jelly. Taking Mildred with her, anywhere she went, made life more bearable. Yet, as bad as it was, it was better than before.

*   *   *

Pastor and Sonnie King had moved to Lincoln three years before Celeste's arrival. The couple purchased a home two blocks from Sylvie's place. Before long, Sylvie was hearing comments about Sonnie—things like, "Sonnie's got money," or, "She's a crazy one," or, "There's nothing Sonnie King wouldn't do." One lady called Sonnie an exotic creature of wealth. Sylvie, who was bored, wanted a friend who would be something other than proper, someone who would take dares, such as going on a spur-of-the-moment cruise or flying to New York on impulse.

It was Elvira, a church member, who'd introduced Pastor and Sonnie to Sylvie, by telling the Kings of Sylvie's invitation—dinner at Sylvie's favorite downtown tearoom with the two of them as her guests. Later, Sylvie told Elvira, "Kiddo, it was love at first sight. Pastor is ... well he's okay, but Sonnie is the infusion I've needed socially. You know how the others bore me. Saturday mornings we agreed to meet for tea out on my screened porch. I have my Hoosier enamel table and the cooking set for making waffles. We'll heat my coffee on the porch. These folks will make the perfect guests. We will discuss art, music, and God. You know how important my faith is to me."

Celeste had first met the Kings right after moving to Sylvie's home. Sylvie had let Celeste go with her to the King's home while she and Sonnie visited. Celeste left thinking the pastor was somewhat irreverent. She'd witnessed him hurling beer cans in the trash, eight of them. He had no idea that Celeste was watching out the window. She wondered what his worshipers would think of that. Attendance at his church had grown 26 percent in the three years he'd been there, and the congregation continued to grow. Because Celeste had no place to go to church, after moving to the guest cottage, Sylvie told her to go to Pastor King's church with Elvira. (Sylvie went to one of the more affluent denominations).From the beginning Celeste found Pastor King left of normal.

Pastor, a large man, who slicked his hair back, wore pinstripe suits, spit shined shoes, and spoke with a drawl, was considered overwhelmingly handsome by his congregation. Celeste thought him decent appearing, not handsome like the others. She disagreed with the congregation's appraisal of the pastor in almost every way. To Celeste, Pastor was an enigma, a mystery. She could hear Dad saying, "That man is strange." One time, she caught Pastor pulling out ear hairs and then looking at them before dropping them on the floor. Another thing— he had a cheek grimace. His cheek twitched twice a minute. She'd timed it.

In Celeste's opinion, the church's success was because of Sonnie, who organized Southern meals, along with open houses and soup suppers. She also made unforgettable displays inside the church. She'd made a decoration, called "God's Treasures," using her grandmother's jewelry. To Celeste, this glittering sculpture was "Sonnie's Treasures." She found herself wondering why Sonnie had married Pastor in the first place, having noticed that Pastor and Sonnie seldom spoke to each other, thinking them distant. Another puzzle...no one knew where Pastor had come from. He'd say, "Goodness, y'all, I hail from here and there. Don't ask such tough questions unless you want a ten-minute answer." The congregation thought his answer cute, and since no one wanted that long of an answer, the members didn't persist. Unlike them, Celeste wondered if he was hiding something.

One evening when Elvira was talking to Sylvie on the phone, Celeste overheard Elvira, saying, "Sylvie, if anyone asks me why his credentials haven't come, I'll tell them that the day I have to call and check on a pastor is the day I'll give up on faith." While Celeste's personal observations made her wary of the pastor, she liked Sonnie who said things like, "Celeste, you are pencil thin, and you need clothes of your own. Let your hair grow out and tell Sylvie to get you a good stylist." One day Sonnie invited Celeste over for ice cream. She gave Celeste a little bag of makeup for home play and a set of paper dolls. Celeste kept them tucked away, except for when Elvira was gone

*   *   *

It was late spring when Celeste met the woman who was to become the flagstaffs to her sailboat in stormy seas. She was Miss Whippet, a teacher who was known for her sense of humor and compassion. Miss Whippet, the Home Economics teacher encouraged girls to try new things. An attractive woman, with honey hair and flair, she was with the high school. Each year, she taught the eighth grade class during the final six weeks of the year. Her first project was for her students to design a dream outfit, one that brought out the best of them. "If you're an intellect, choose colors that convey brains!" Miss Whippet said, making everyone laugh. "If you're a ball of energy, go with energy colors, like yellow!"

Celeste, uncertain about which colors would bring out the best in her, slunk into Miss Whippet's classroom one day after school. "Miss Whippet, who am I?" she asked. She'd meant to ask, "What color defines me?"

Miss Whippet jumped right in, leaving no time for embarrassment. "Celeste, how about we call you reserved with a few dashes of bashful? Then, we add some heavy shakes of sincere. We could bring out some boldness if you'd like. Perhaps some brave blue," she said, waltzing over to a swath of brilliant blue. "This would be dazzling with that stunning auburn hair of yours, which, incidentally, is just as gorgeous as your mother's was. And say, your father had that thick black hair… Oh, my."

Celeste stared wide-eyed at Miss Whippet. Upon digesting the new information, she giggled. Celeste had never considered that someone might have known her mom and dad or that her folks had attended this school.

"Celeste, I had a class with your dear mother. We were the same age. I watched your gallant father out on the court. He was quite the star.… We all thought he was a darling. We were relieved to learn that your father picked her, meaning your mother."

Celeste wiped her hair off her forehead and squinted. Picked? Of course, he'd picked Mother. She was his one and only. Furthermore, what was this about Dad being a star on the team? He'd always told Celeste that he was a fair player but nothing special. Mom would smile when he said this.

"And say," Miss Whippet dared say, "Sylvie has done exceedingly well. My goodness! It's nice when things work out. I'd wondered, but then I saw you and I thought, those two ended as friends. Your mother was lovely—sweet and gentle. I think you have those traits. Develop them, dear. I'll have you next year in ninth grade. That will be nice." With that, Miss Whippet left. Celeste had no idea what she was talking about.

*   *   *

Whenever things seemed moderately all right, Celeste found she'd been deluded by wishful thinking. —A distressing event occurred shortly after moving in with Elvira. Back when Celeste left the Temples' place, Bev had packed a small box of Celeste's most precious possessions, which she placed in Celeste's suitcase. Grateful to have these meaningful items, Celeste displayed them on a small shelf behind the cottage couch which served as her bed. One was the teddy bear that she held in her hands while falling asleep each night. Another was her Peter Rabbit china cup, a baby present. Believing herself too old for it, she didn't care. Along with the cup, she had an ABC baby rattle, a baby ball, and other mementoes, such as her piggy bank. Mom and Dad and Bonnie had given her the bank. On waking each morning, she set the bear back on the shelf before going to school.

One day, she'd come from school in want of a nickel she'd found and set on the shelf. Going to get the nickel, she immediately saw everything missing. The shelves were empty. Intuitively, she knew that it had to be Sylvie who'd removed them. Sylvie had commented on these keepsakes. "They're babyish," she'd said.

Propelled by a short moment of courage and fury, Celeste flew to the big house. Without asking if she could go inside, she found Sylvie in her office. Dashing in, Celeste yelled, "Where are my "babyish" things?"

Appearing bored, Sylvie sighed. "Honestly, Celeste, calm down. I gave them to a charity. You're too old two-year-old toys. Or aren't you? Most girls would be ashamed of displaying such things."

Panting with anger, Celeste screamed, "I hate you! I hate you. Those were mine!" Unable to stop, she yelled, "I hate living here with all your rules and silences and all the ways you tear me down. I want to go home, now!" Racing out, down the sidewalk, she collapsed in the park a good distance away. Sylvie, who'd followed her to the park in her car, found Celeste in a sobbing heap.

"Celeste, you look childish laying there. Besides, you'll damage the grass."

In that moment, Celeste ran out of light. "I despise your thoughtless world," she shrieked. "Those were the only things I had."

Sylvie walked over smiling. With a raised head, she announced that she had some work for Celeste to do. Taking Celeste back to the house, Sylvie disappeared. Ten minutes later she reappeared with Natasha. "Celeste," she said, "Natasha can't be here in the morning. You'll do her job. The Kings are coming in the morning for their weekly visit on the porch."

*   *   *

Sonnie, who sat beside Pastor, looked extra cute this morning. The sun shone down on her blond hair and her eyes were a sparkling blue. The wealthy daughter of a Southern plantation owner, Sonnie was telling one story after another about being a pastor's wife. She even joked, saying; she was the one who'd helped Pastor scoot past through the cracks of church doors. "'Why not counterfeit your way in as a pastor?' I asked him."

Sylvie, finding the story hilarious, laughed hysterically.

Pastor, who'd asked for more coffee, was graciously guiding Celeste's hand to his cup. "You're a tall one," he said. "How old are you, dear?"

His fruitiest cologne tingled Celeste's nose. "I'm twelve," Celeste answered.

Pastor's strong, blue-gray eyes followed Celeste's stick-like legs— his favorite kind of legs. He also found her height sensual. These were his thoughts as Celeste returned with four bowls of fruit. Looking at her carefully, Pastor wondered it those were tears. He hoped so. Once he began mentoring her, he would sit close while wiping her tears and gazing at her. She would be a fun one to look at in the basement of the church.

"Wouldn't she make a cute model?" Sonnie asked. "Celeste, darling, more coffee for me too."

"I modeled," Pastor said to Celeste

"Did you really model?" Celeste asked, concealing her excitement while watching to see if she believed him. If she became a model, Sylvie and the others would like her. She looked from him to Sylvie. "Sylvie, could I learn from him?" she asked, trying not to seem overly eager.

"Ha!" Sylvie cackled. "Celeste a model? You didn't bother to tell them about your fall down the stairs, did you?"

Her cheeks flushed, Celeste's eyes were begging.

"No," Sylvie retorted. "You can't practice modeling. You have no friends you can have as a mentor."

Horrified, Celeste stammered, "I...I just c...ame to Lincoln in February. F—riends take time."

"She's right, Sylvie. Shame on you," Sonnie chided, leaving for the powder room.

Watching her walk away, Pastor turned to Celeste. "Child, I don't think she's going to let you model. Instead, let's discuss your parent's passing and ways to meet kids."

Sylvie clucked, "Good idea. Celeste, you can mentor with Pastor. You earned the honors of needing his counsel. I hope he can help you make something of yourself, including appropriate friends."

"Sylvie, why don't you tell Celeste about that stuff I told you?" he said, rubbing his nose.

"Celeste, Pastor told me about some of the games girls play. Naturally, he would never play up to their advances. Consequently, they accuse him of forward, shamelessly corrupt behaviors. Two of his girls went to Wayward Home in the country— tattling and making up stories. The place that is new to me."

Celeste's eyes were the size of golf balls. "Did those girls go home?"

Unfeeling, Sylvie said, "I'm afraid girls who go there don't leave. Surgery is done on their brains. The part that thinks is removed."

"I think that's nasty stuff," Sonnie said, returning for her purse, which she'd forgotten.

"I'm afraid it's true. How about next Wednesday?" Pastor asked.

*   *   *

Elvira, whose self-importance rose on learning that Celeste would be going to her pastor, the man she'd introduced to the family, had a secret. One of the child workers had whispered something negative about Pastor King when she stopped in down at the old office. "Elvira," she'd said, "a pastor from Chicago called. A child was 'handled.' They asked about Pastor King."

Incensed, Elvira glowered at the worker. "Phooey! He lives two lawns away from the backside of Sylvie's yard. He and his wife have coffee at Sylvie's every Saturday morning. Does that tell you something about him?"

Rumors! Elvira readjusted her smeared magnifiers. Rumors! Was there any end to folks' fabrications? Besides, when he came to Sylvie's on Saturday mornings, Pastor discussed art and music. There was no way he fiddled with children. Pastor was different from her father. He'd raped her before going to prison. Elvira's mother had told Elvira that she'd caused it by showing her legs, which was why Elvira didn't shave. Either way, Celeste could take care of herself the way Elvira had done.

* * *

Celeste adored her teacher, Miss Whippet, who reached out, befriending her and asking questions about her parents. "Your father, did he still play basketball?"

"Dad used an old hoop for tossing the ball. He was a fair dribbler. Mom liked #15 because that's …"

"Because your father wore that number," Miss Whippet chuckled. "Say, Celeste dear, you've suffered a great loss. I'm here if you need an ear. I assist the school by listening to children. And while we are talking, you are a fabulous seamstress. I've never had a student learn so quickly."

"Miss Whippet, I'm really glad you're my teacher," Celeste said coyly.

* * *

It was nearing spring when Celeste began seeing Pastor. *She was still a young twelve.* Hours of nothingness had resulted in dulled senses. Not hearing from those at home had made her highly vulnerable and the perfect prey.

Escorted to the church by Elvira, Celeste started her first session on the last Tuesday in March. Pastor welcomed her into a small room in the basement— furthest to the back. As he shut the door, she feared screaming. In her imagination, she saw him choking her to death with no one learning about it. After all, she wasn't hearing from her family, Howie wouldn't miss her, and no one at school knew her. The worst was that Sylvie would gladly pay him to choke her. However stiff she might have been, she relaxed when he began with a Bible riddle. That helped her remember his sense of humor. Besides, checkers were next. Grinning, he urged her to join him.

Getting down on her knees–the game sat on a low table–Celeste noticed how Pastor seemed more normal in his casual clothes. After readying the checkers with her, he took her hand in his for several seconds, saying he hoped she didn't beat him too badly—which she did. For winning, he had a surprise. A red heart necklace just happened to be in his desk. He would like to put it on her if she would like to have it.

"Oh, yes! I would love it!" she said, finding this unbelievable. Would there be more things to come? It was special to have something from a man who everyone revered. Sylvie hadn't given her anything since she'd first arrived. Sylvie had taken away the pretty dress for the country club tea, saying it was meant for a friend's daughter–that the dress wouldn't have fit Celeste for long.

Slipping it around her neck, his hands caressed her upper arms, a pleasant sensation. Feeling his warm breath on her neck, she reared back shocked. What could she do but giggle? It was accidental, she told herself, aware that, oddly, his breath felt good.

He was saying that everything that took place in here had to be their secret.

"Oh, yes," she said; that would be fine. It would be how she and Ginny Temple had done it.

Pastor reached over with a bowl of candy. Setting it down, he took one. Then he put a piece of candy in the palm of her hand. What a nice, soft hand she had; maybe he would lotion it for her if she was good. That was it for tonight. He would see her next week when they would talk about her friendships and how she was feeling. Wasn't it nice of Sylvie to want this for her? And wasn't Sylvie a wonderful person? He said he had talked with Sylvie about all of the things they did in here. Good-bye and good night.

The second week, he had a second gift. This one was awaiting her, but when she reached for it, he said, "No, I was just kidding. You have to *prove* yourself, Miss. It's very expensive and the kind that Sonnie told me to get for you."

"Prove myself?" Celeste asked baffled.

He smiled sort of looking her over—a look that made her both happy and uneasy. It seemed a little scary or as if he was thinking of her like *that*. "Let's talk," he said. "I understand that things have been rough." He reached over and patted her.

She laughed thinking he sure was a *touchy* man.

"What are you laughing about?"

"Nothing." She giggled.

He got a very serious look. And then he gazed at her a long time. She blushed. He was pretending she was beautiful instead of a country tomboy. He reached with his hand and a deepening stare. "Talk," he said, still looking at her. "Honey, tell me what is happening with your parents' death?"

She lost it and began sobbing. No one had cared all of this time. She cried in big sobs.

Swiftly his arms were around her, and he was stroking her back. Was he stroking her back or her lower hips?

She felt funny. This wasn't right, was it? She wanted to back up and to tell him not to touch her anymore, but she had taken the necklace, and now he was going to offer the perfume. It wasn't about the gifts for her … It was about his generosity. Why hadn't she said she was prohibited from accepting gifts? This had the makings of a trap.

He was still caressing her back and buttocks. Wait. He was a pastor, for goodness sake. He wouldn't do anything wrong. Backing up, she laughed and sat down in the chair.

"That was nice, wasn't it?" he asked. "Did you like the rub?"

How could she say, no, it wasn't nice, when she'd let him rub her? "Thanks," she said. "That was nice."

"And, honey, here is the perfume. You enjoy it. Like I said, it's expensive, but I want you to have things that make you feel better. Remember? What we do in here is our secret."

That night, she wrote in a diary the kids made at school. Writing became a jungle of confusion. She didn't want any more gifts, but she had the perfume on. The next thing she knew, she was washing it off herself. But wait, it was from the pastor whom everyone loved. People said that he was the best in the city. He'd won an award from the governor for some work he'd done with the poor.

At her next mentoring session, he looked nicely wholesome in his corduroys. She had on some of the perfume, and when he asked, she said that yes, she was wearing it.

"Where did you spray it?" he asked.

To her, the question seemed wrong. "Thank you, Pastor." Celeste said. "I've really enjoyed wearing it." She planned to say, no more gifts, please, but before she could—and she couldn't have anyway—he reached over and patted her knee. He patted it more than once during their mentoring session, saying they would play a game to see who would answer a question about themselves and who had to ask the question. The winner asked; the loser answered.

He won. "Celeste, tell me about any friends here in Lincoln and what you think of them."

"I don't have any and ..." She was sobbing again.

Before she knew what was happening, he had pulled her into his lap. For as quiet as she was and as difficult as it was, she squealed and pulled free.

He looked hurt and then mad. "What was that about?" he asked, impatient and disgusted.

She was crying over the sound of his voice.

He reminded her that he was her only friend and that Sylvie would be furious if she didn't please him. "You aren't scared of me, are you, sweetheart? I would never do anything against God, and scaring you would make God very angry. Why are you afraid to sit in my lap?"

She choked. How would she tell him?

"Honey, we'll talk about your fear of being hurt." Right away, his arm was around her.

She wanted to scream for him to sit in his chair and talk to her. She was too overwhelmed and shocked to be properly scared. Unexpectedly, she remembered how often he'd touched her. She guessed he was just touchy as a means of affection.

"Now, now," Pastor said. "It's all right. Give me your hand, honey. Yes, that's it. Let me soothe you."

She cried, and he told her sweet things he'd noticed about her. At one point, she realized that her hand was on his thigh and was unsure of how it got there. He saw her looking and removed it, only to put his hand on her thigh. Surely, he was just being kind and wanting to father her ...

Thank goodness, it was time to go.

Then he was asking her about the doll she had mentioned the second time they'd met. She'd described it. Surely, he wouldn't. Would he? If so, he must really see her as being his little girl, which wasn't so bad. Here she was, twelve and going to school with girls who'd have a fit if given a doll, but she craved her old doll.

*　　*　　*

Another week, and he was saying, "I only see one girl at a time in here, and I chose you." Truthfully, he saw three or four a week—as many as were available. He'd even said how special she was to talk with. Tonight he was sharing some of his own frustrations and asking her advice. She felt older than ever before.

After they talked about the difficulties of making friends, he asked if she'd like to walk to the store around the corner for some pop.

"Sure," she said, proud to walk with a father like figure, who almost seemed more than a father? He was more like a boy in her class—a boy her own age.

They were returning with the pop when he interrupted Celeste's thoughts, "Come here," he said, leaning against the tree. Surprisingly, she found that this scared her. It was dark out, and they maybe shouldn't be standing like this.

"What would you most like right now?"

She answered, "I'd like to grow my hair out. Sylvie made me get it cut."

"Child," he said. "For a fatherly kiss, I think I could get someone to talk Sylvie into letting you have long hair."

Before Celeste could think about what he'd said, his lips were on hers. They felt wet and foreign. "You're like my little girl," he said. "Sonnie and I think you're adorable."

What could she say? Ick! It was a fatherly kiss, and she liked the idea of being someone's little girl again. Yes, that's all it was, and it was okay.

Next week, they were going to have their session in the country. They would wait until the next week for the picnic. He had a lady to see, and they would talk on the way. Only five more meetings until they would wait to pick up again in the fall. She still had no friends, and it didn't seem like pastor even talked about that. Was he going to mention modeling?

She was keeping her makeshift diary and writing their doings. "Finally, I've kissed a boy—Pastor! Not my first choice, but I'm glad he's in my life. I like him. There were times at first that I could hardly stand him. He's only trying to be my father. He is going to get my hair grown out."

They were on the way back from the country lady's house and talking when he abruptly pulled the car over. "Don't be afraid, Celeste. You're going to like this a lot, I think."

"What?" she asked, unsure of the look on his face?

"Remember what we talked about? It was something you liked but don't have here in Lincoln."

"A girl doll," she screeched. "A doll? I—"

"If it was, what would you give me?"

"I don't have anything to give back." Dumbfounded, Celeste looked at him and then away.

"What did we share last week that wasn't so bad?" He was fatherly.

Her stomach sank. "I shouldn't kiss anyone. I'm too young," she said even though she was afraid to tell him that. "I don't think we should do that," she said, hesitantly. She didn't want to share another kiss but didn't know how to stop him. Her dad hadn't done that. She sat quietly thinking. She turned, cheeks flushed, both excited over the doll and suffering awful feelings about the kiss. She really needed to stop after this. Instead, she put her face toward his, and in a second or two, it was over. How could women stand it? What would Sonnie think?

Her thoughts stopped when a beautiful doll from Madame Alexander, still in the box, was set in her lap.

"Oh!" She began to cry.

Pastor put his arms around her, working on desensitizing her to his touch. "Tell you what, Celeste. You can take the doll along next week. We'll do the picnic at our regular time."

*   *   *

She brought the doll on the picnic. They stopped by a stream to eat the bag lunches he'd brought with him. As they sat eating they discussed the kids in her class. "How does it feel to be rejected? Sonnie thinks you need clothes like the other girls."

She was saying how great that would be when she noticed his hand holding hers. He was warm that way. It wasn't so bad when he held her hand or kissed her. She hardly noticed—especially if she squeezed her mind into a ball and turned it inside out. The gifts were nice—the doll gifts that is. He had extra doll clothes today but needed payment he said. She said she didn't have money. Sylvie didn't pay her to do chores at the cottage.

He was laughing about something when he slipped his hands around her rib area and began tickling her. She was going crazy with laughter. Was there anyone as ticklish?

"Oh, please," she begged.

"What will you give me?"

"Take …" she cried, unable to say more and desperate for him to stop. She was going to get sick if he kept this up. His hands slid over her breast area.

She gasped. It felt good but wrong. "Stop," she pleaded.

Interrupting Celeste's thoughts, Pastor said, "We need to grill and swim. Doing our mentoring in the open air will be our reward. Now, once more and you can have those doll clothes." He reached out to caress her and his hands went to her ribs again.

She felt sickened as though his hands were relentless spiders, impossible to chase away. She was relieved to return home. Confusion swirled about in her that week, especially, as she wrote her in her diary. How could something as awful as his touch, feel so good? She was still a child, so why couldn't she get her mind off of him? Had all of his touches felt like this? Here she was playing dolls and thinking about *that*. She knew how babies came about because of Bonnie insisting she know. That happened back when life felt safe?

Well, where was Bonnie now? He wouldn't take this any further, would he? He was Sonnie's husband, and here she was a little bit flattered and a great deal confused. The thing was, how could she tell him no, knowing who he was? Would a pastor do wrong? Not him, not Sylvie's friend. Her thoughts went in circles, giving her headaches and making her exhausted.

They met for the next three weeks, and she was thankful when he didn't add anything else. That part was nice, but when was he going to mention modeling?

Today he was saying, "I've a surprise for you. Sonnie and I want you over once a week this summer. We'll have swimming parties, go to parades, and drive to Omaha for dinner. Next week, we'll meet at the house. I'm not sure Sonnie will be there, but either way, we'll swim. I can grill, and we can do your mentoring. Doing this in the open air will be our reward."

The rest of what he wanted would come later. Because he used his pool for initiating the ritual, he didn't have extra time for grooming Celeste. He needed the swimming pool, which would be drained for the winter when school began. The importance of the swimming pool lay in the big trees and the gates that locked tight and the water, which muted any cries for help should that be a problem. He'd designed his pool to accommodate his needs. Later, it was easy to take a girl elsewhere—once she'd been broken in, allowing him to lock the gates for carrying out the ritual.

*   *   *

Sometimes, Celeste had nightmares about Pastor. They were particularly bad when she'd seen him that day for a mentoring session.

They were frustration dreams, like not being able to find her classroom at school. Or one night, the Temples came to see her. She was so happy, but unexpectedly, they disappeared. Celeste began to feel like she was sinking and like she was dirty. She took two baths one night.

The way he was, she didn't want to be Pastor's friend, but how lonely when she was so alone anyway. Who would give her anything or say she was special? But what about the touches and kisses? They were sinful? She was sure he felt something physical around her. This week, as well as another week, she'd felt something hard; because of her farm upbringing, she knew what that was. She wanted to shout for someone to come save her.

Finally, it was next to the last week. Pastor of all things sat talking about Will—asking if she and Will had done anything. She laughed. "I can't even talk to him. I get too embarrassed. I'm only twelve."

Out of the blue, he asked, "If your mother was here, what you would say to her right now?"

. The thought of saying her mother's name out loud, as in "Mom, I need to talk to you," broke her heart. Celeste howled, and tears and sobs followed. Unable to catch her breath, he was asking her to do the same thing with her father. She was still bawling when she realized that he was holding her. His arms were around her, and his hands were where they shouldn't be. Here in the middle of her crying, he had his hands on her breasts. This time, she reacted. "No," she yelled, flying off of his lap. "Don't. Don't touch me. I'm afraid. Please."

Fierce-like, he said things to make her feel all this was her fault. "You liked being a little girl. What? Are you trying to confuse me? You know that I'm a man of God. "His face, deadpan, without a trace of warmth, he looked at her, asking, "What would you do if your brother turned up in the bottom of my pool?"

She looked away. Averting her eyes, she stared at the floor.

"Go! Disgusted, he said, "So, you don't want little brother in the bottom of the pool, huh?" Laughing, his laugh wasn't real... "We'll meet at my pool this coming week. Wayward House has four empty rooms. I'll call and schedule the last meeting with you. I'll tell Sylvie when."

Celeste thought they were done and had begun to walk away when she heard him.

"You'll need to come in your suit. Child, God came to me with a special message. He told me about your dream, the one you had the night before your parents died. God said that it was your words that killed them.

Because of you, they were hurrying and slid on the ice. In order for you to keep from burning in Hell, God ordered something. I imagine you have an idea what that is," he smirked. "Should you put up a fuss, God has Wayward House waiting for you…. Keep this God's secret," he said, pushing past her.

Overwhelmed with fear, too massive to absorb, Celeste grabbed the wall. Feint, she bent over gasping for air. Half an hour later, she tip toed out of the church. Death would be better than facing him again.

*   *   *

Later that afternoon, Celeste went to the park to walk. Instead of walking, she was pacing back and forth, when an image, from long ago, flew through her mind. There had been a rape in Lincoln County; and while Bonnie and Mother stood discussing what had happened to this teenage girl, Celeste accidentally walked into the room. Bonnie had grabbed her for a lesson on safety. "Any touch that doesn't feel right is a wrong touch," she'd drilled. When it came to her little sister, shaking hands was about all that was right. "If a man has bad things in mind, you'll know, either by his touch or by what you're feeling around that man," she'd said. "If the touch feels strange, run. If you have to ask questions, it's a bad touch. Run as fast as you can!"

Celeste stopped pacing long enough to wonder if this memory about touch had risen for a purpose. Lately, she'd been slipping. Her nightmares were awful; a man was chasing her. When she held up a mirror, she saw Pastor's face. Unable to get to safety, her fears caused her to lose her appetite, knowing what she would have to do in the ritual, or rather, what he would do to her. Now, with three s nights of dreams that left her paralyzed, Celeste set off to see her teacher. She knew what she wanted to ask her. Bonnie and Bev, who'd helped her with guilt back when her parents died, had promised her that she'd done nothing wrong. They'd said that her parents would have done well to listen to her warning. What was the truth? Oh, please, Miss Whippet! Celeste prayed, be there for me.

Turning to the person who would listen, Celeste was determined to visit with her favorite teacher. She almost collapsed when she saw Miss Whippet who had told her she'd be there working this summer and to drop in.

Maureen Whippet closed the door and told Celeste to have a seat. She gave her cold lemonade and made her eat a cookie. "You are far too thin," she said.

Celeste would have talked about her skimpy diet and constant hunger but was so anxious that, she was short of breath. "Miss Whippet," she said racing her words. "I have a friend who wrote me. She wants me to write back immediately. This is her problem. Her parents were going on a trip. The night before they left, my friend dreamed that they died in an accident. The next morning, she told her mother, 'If you go on that trip, and if you get killed on those slick highways and don't even care, I don't either. I can be a happy orphan.' Her parents left regardless of what she told them. She did not kiss them good-bye, because she was mad. My friend thinks that it was her fault that her parents died. There's that problem and then she has an even bigger problem. She knows a man who sort of wants to hurt her and … And she thinks he's punishing her because of what she said. God told this man that it was her fault. He even told him to punish her. She's pretty scared. He didn't actually say what he's going to do to her. Is her parent's death really her fault?"

Celeste broke the heart of this teacher who felt so bad for her.

"Celeste," Miss Whippet said. "There is a spirit who is a guide inside of each of us. It can be God, a wise man, an angel—whatever comes to each person." She explained that a child could call on this inner guide at any time. She said she herself did this. "Lean back, close your eyes, and ask your question. Of course, pretend that you are your friend." Miss Whippet was certain that Celeste was talking about herself. No one from this child's past had contacted her, making her doubt that a friend had written about such a frightening happening.

It took Celeste twenty minutes, but finally she opened her eyes. "I just met God," she said. "Wow, he knows an awful lot. He's the God I know. I'll tell my friend." Celeste felt relieved believing that none of this was her fault.

They stood a bit, neither speaking. Miss Whippet finally broke the silence. "Celeste, I think you were talking about yourself just now. Please tell me if you were. This sounds serious. The man is dangerous."

Celeste's heart sped up. How could she tell Miss Whippet? If Pastor or her aunt knew she'd talked, she would be sent to Wayward House for sure. And what about Howie on the bottom of the pool? Pastor had made it clear that this was a secret. She longed to be free of the man, but the stakes were too high. Putting her hand on her heart, as if she could slow the racing, her eyes flitted about the room, while she stood, answering Miss Whippet.

"It's not me. I would have told you. It's my friend for sure" Turning to face Miss Whippet, she offered an overly cheerful smile.

"Let me get us some more to drink before you walk back home, "Miss Whippet offered, leaving the room.

Celeste began leafing through the scrapbook her teacher had made as a senior. Her students liked the pictures of the outfits she'd sewn. Celeste turned another page and stopped cold. Number 15 had his arm around a young *Sylvie. She was wearing a cheering outfit. The caption said, "Marriage in June for Howard and Sylvie???"* She knew this; because of Mom and how she liked that number. All of a sudden she wondered if that could be him. The name, Howard, in the caption confused her.

Miss Whippet, who had returned with another cookie and more to drink, knew something big had happened. "What is it Celeste?"

"Miss Whippet, this man is my dad. Dad was number fifteen, and he greatly resembled this boy here in the picture, whose name is different. It's Dad, isn't it?" she asked, wide eyed, her skin whitish?

Not feeling like she could lie, her teacher hesitated, taking a drink of her lemonade to wet her dry mouth. "Your dad was called Howard when he was in high school."

"That was his middle name," Celeste said, hiding any emotion. He always liked it. It's in memory of his mother. Sylvie said that she dated a Howard. I didn't think about Dad at the time, but I bet he's the one she was talking about."

"So you didn't know?"

Celeste said, no, that she was, indeed, shocked but relieved. She smiled, and in the most pragmatic manner, said, "I finally know why Sylvie hated my mother and now me. And I now know why Howie is Howard." Smiling hugely, Celeste didn't feel the torrent of tears coming, but when they began, they were unstoppable.

Miss Whippet sat there with her arm around Shirley White's daughter, determined to weather this storm until the floodgates ran dry. For the first time, Miss Whippet didn't know what to say.

*   *   *

When Celeste got home, Sylvie, who was out working with her flowers, stopped Celeste, before she caught the sidewalk that led to the cottage.

"Pastor called a little bit ago and wants to mentor you tonight. You two will eat supper on the patio. Sonnie will be eating with you."

Celeste said she didn't feel good and wanted to go the bed.

Sylvie said that she was just making up excuses.

"Please don't make me go. I'm sorry, but I'm afraid of him. Something isn't right. Please, Sylvie," she begged, knowing Sylvie's mind was set.

Annoyed, Sylvie raised her voice. "You haven't made a single friend. You're not quitting until you have at least five friends. Listen to you talk. I'm not about to buy your lies. For goodness sake, Sonnie will be there. Good heavens, as if he'd harm you in front of her. Besides, he's a popular pastor. Nice try, girl. Go!" she ordered, mercilessly.

Setting off for Pastor's pool, Celeste chanted, "Sonnie be there. Please be there. Sonnie be there." She said this endlessly, under her breath, all the way to the Kings.

On arriving, Pastor unlocked the gate and let her into the pool area, saying Sonnie had a last-minute date with an old friend. He was working with the food and had decided to do the mentoring around the grilling and eating. The water would be last. "Did you hear from anyone at home yet?" he asked, laying steaks on the hot coals. In return, she was twelve and scared out of her mind. Her knees knocked with panic. The thought of Wayward made her feel as though she was about to black out. Looking at Pastor in his swim suit, he had the appearance of a giant. She saw him as a skyscraper hovering above while she was miniscule and powerless down below, a crack in the sidewalk.

"Child," he said. "Let me remind you that God condemns you for what you said. If you don't cooperate, God will take you into the fires of hell. Before that, however, you'll enter through doors that take you to Wayward's hell."

"Pastor," she pleaded. "Bonnie and Bev spent a whole week with me after the funeral. They said I didn't do anything bad, and that the car wreck had nothing to do with my dream. They also said the dream came in order to save my parents. It was more that my parents decided to drive, thinking—"

"Celeste, who is the trained man and God's disciple? Are you questioning me? It appears you question and lack trust in God. He came to me, not them. Shall we go talk to Sylvie?"

Knowing that would be her only possible escape, though unlikely, she nodded yes.

Pastor took on an enraged posture, his body stiffening, his glistening leg hairs standing up, his head hair, oily, his lips, taut and pouty... He sat that way staring at Celeste. Then the old smile was back. "Looks like we better have some fun and forget the ritual. I'm going to chase you into the water. Let's eat first. The meat here has been on low, and I brought this salad out. A member of our congregation brought it over, along with this pie. We'll need to play ball in order to get rid of that full feeling."

As they sat eating, her innocence took over, telling her that all he had wanted was to see how scared she'd get. Still, her intuition told her to avoid the water. "Pastor, I forgot. I'm not really supposed to swim. I just ate, and Sylvie told me not to swim after I eat. I have to go now."

She stood up, and so did he. All she was wearing was her suit and a blouse. She watched him, staring at her legs and then her face. His eyes were angry yet eager. Her sweat turned to chills, and her teeth chattered. She felt light-headed and nauseous, as though her heart was about to flutter out of her skinny chest.

He stood and began walking her way, each step taken with deliberation; she tried screaming, only to discover a mute voice. She watched in slow motion as his hands snuck in, gripping her around her teensy waist. Lifting Celeste, the weight of a feather, he tossed her into the water. Jumping in, he went after her, too excited and busy for talking. A hungry lion, eager for the kill, he yanked off her suit, tossing it, while cleverly removing his suit. If she screamed, so help him, he'd strangle her. The predator had lost his sense of reasoning, having gone out of control.

Pulling her fragile, bone thin body and her bucketful of dreams in front of him, he pushed her head beneath the water, keeping her there as long as he needed. Let her scream. Not a chance anyone was going to hear her.

Panicked, she locked her mouth, shutting it tight, as she became the feral cat trapped underwater without air. Helpless, she kicked, twisted, and shimmied, screaming to come up for air. In a fight for her life, her thin arms and fingers found themselves suffused with unrealized strength, grabbing at Pastor's giant hand, the one that held her under. Frantic, she pushed and pulled against his brick-like stature. Still kicking, twisting, and fighting for air and life, short of breath, she ran out of oxygen. Her eyes wild, she searched for a miracle. Instead, she saw Sylvie's deadly eyes, just as the water poured in, filling her mouth. By then, her movements had grown slow. Exhausted, and weak, Celeste succumbed. Death, dark and liquid, swam toward her, just short of victory.

She felt herself being yanked up to the surface … tossed down on the side of the pool. Struggling, as water and mucus poured from her mouth, she gasped, coughing and gagging, wanting to dash over for her suit. That's when she saw the blood swirling about in the pool and was struck by overwhelming pain. Her insides were split open, like a knife carving away at her flesh, her precious possession—not his for the taking. He'd taken regardless, having raped her.

She heard him yelling, "You dirtied the water… Here, take this towel," he said, tossing it and her suit. "You asked for this," he accused. "No one would ever believe you. Sylvie already knows about tonight. I'm disappointed in you. You let God down. Fighting the way you did is another sin for you to write down. God expects this to remain secret; it's his ritual and Wayward Home is waiting for you if you tell anyone. You are tarnished corruption; there will be no need to come over this summer. You are hopeless. God knows it is your fault."

*   *   *

Walking away, doubled over, Celeste felt numb and distanced. The man back there had raped a child, but the child was someone else. Instead, the Pastor had attacked a girl who looked like her while she stood at the edge of the pool watching.

If asked who the girl was, she knew. It just didn't seem like she had been there.

Pain—that was the other feeling—the pain of rape. Stinging, throbbing, the agonizing rips were unbearable. In a dazed state, her feet walked her to Sylvie's house. Surely, Sylvie would believe her and offer Celeste her help and comfort. She would remember what Celeste had told her earlier when she asked to stay home. However, her stomach said differently. Stopping, she threw up. Sickened, and smelly, and messy, Celeste was exhausted by the time she reached Sylvie's. Wanting to lie down in the yard, instead, she went to the back door. Sylvie was in the kitchen making tea.

The sight of arrogant Sylvie revolted her. Why hadn't Sylvie believed her? Crouched in pain, Celeste watched the lofty aunt turn to face her, walking towards her The woman's eyes, scornful and appraising, were like a spotlight, revealing Celeste's faults, blemishes, and imperfections. Wanting to hide the shame in her face, before Sylvie saw her, Celeste's thin fingers were too slow.

"You there!" Sylvie hissed, staring at Celeste. "You knew there were locks on the gates? Why did you go over there?"

"Y…You said I had to go, "Celeste stuttered.

"Oh!" Sylvie screamed. "I see. It's my fault. Well, as I said, your mother would have done what you just did. It's apparent what you wanted," she scoffed. "Did your hot little fire speak to him?" she said, pointing her long fingernails at Celeste's lower body.

"He … He did this to me. I didn't do anything. I thought I was going to d…die. He held my head under the water."

Ripe with fury, Sylvie hurled accusations at Celeste. Celeste seduced the Pastor. Celeste was her mother. Why had Celeste gone there if she believed Pastor would touch her?

Switching, Sylvie began harassing her. At least, Celeste was *baptized* in the water, which was more then she deserved. Celeste was stupid if she thought she would be having a baby to play with. Or had Celeste noticed that she wasn't equipped to have children just yet?

"You're bleeding on my carpet," Sylvie hissed, hopping backwards. "That's what you get for toying with a Pastor whose only purpose is to help you. Everyone will know about you. How does that feel? I suppose the pool is all bloody now. What will Sonnie do when she wants to swim tomorrow?"

Walking back to her cup, Sylvie added a tea bag. Taking a sip, she walked over to the open door. Sneering, she said, "Elvira doesn't need to live with the likes of you. She can stay at the cottage; you'll go elsewhere. Tomorrow, collect your things and take them up to the upper attic at the top of the house. It has everything you'll need. Come downstairs for food—nothing else. Natasha will leave your plate on the stove. There's no point in her waiting on you. For any other needs, ask Mack…. In my eyes, you're dead. Once you graduate, you're gone for good."

* * *

The next morning, isolated, her pain appalling, the twelve year old picked up her scattered paper dolls and left for the attic. The climb up the side steps, which led from the kitchen, was agonizing. With school starting soon and the pain tormenting her, Celeste was terrified. Would she would ever heal? Nearing the top of the steps, she broke down, weeping. Unbearable grief gripped at her, surrounded her, clung to her…. Where was Mother? She was twelve, alone, and raped. She needed a mom and dad to be with her, giving her a normal life and offering support. Instead, her parents were gone. She was abandoned by those she'd trusted. Giving into this heartache, she cried a long while before going up the last four steps and through the door that led to the attic proper.

A big open room with a bed and a bathroom off to the side, the attic had ten double windows, a small platform like stage, an old sewing machine behind a pile of boxes, and miscellaneous clutter. Once an apartment, there was an empty kitchen, a couch, and various pieces of furniture scattered around the floor. Lying down on a single bed, Celeste found it better than the couch at the cottage. Despite the cold fear of abandonment and total aloneness, she was relieved to be away from Elvira who smelled of evil. An infant in a foreign world, she closed her eyes and fell asleep.

*   *   *

Except for school and work at the drugstore and a few other structured events, Celeste spent her time in the attic. Howie was out of Celeste's life. He was the one person who made fun of her mercilessly. She knew he did this under the persuasion of Sylvie, who manipulated him. Living with the fear of judgment and ridicule, Celeste's life became one of avoidance.

Sometimes Celeste floated upwards not understanding that she was dissociating—removing herself from memories of the trauma. She still had no recollection of where she'd seen Sylvie's vile eyes.

Miss Whippet kept watch over Celeste. Something was wrong with the girl. She wondered if it had to do with what Celeste had said about that man. She'd known that Celeste was talking about her own situation. Worried about how remote and withdrawn Celeste had become, along with being grossly thin, Miss Whippet brought her special fruits and desserts. If Celeste wanted to talk, Miss Whippet assumed she would talk. Otherwise, her teacher would simply be there for her. One other person was doing what she could. That was Natasha. Celeste had begun to find little notes on her plate and occasional pieces of candy… The first note told her that the machine in the attic worked. Sylvie wouldn't know about her sewing if she waited until Sylvie was out and about. The next note said that she would leave some books in the kitchen drawer. And in which drawer she could find them. These kindnesses were like little bites of chocolate in the middle of a famine.

When Celeste wasn't sewing, she was sketching–rooms, flowers, birds, whatever caught her fancy. Though not trained in art, she was skilled, like her mother. It soothed her to imagine designing an apartment or home. Though interesting, Celeste's hobbies weren't enough to keep her going, to wipe away the darkness, or to cure her symptoms. She continually washed her hands and bathed. Pastor might be gone, but he rode in her skin. The washing was hard on her hands. Sometimes, she skipped lunch to buy lotion with the money for her school meals. She was to go to school and then come straight home to her room.

Pastor had intended for that night to be the beginning of a long-term relationship—one where he met his needs at a child's expense and ruination. What happened was that he grew scared. He'd taken it too far, had lost control…Though Pastor was sure Sylvie would accuse Celeste, he didn't want to answer her, on the off chance that she questioned him. He resigned before Sunday, saying he had a serious illness.

He and Sonnie were gone by morning two days later.

*   *   *

Midway through her freshman year, something awful happened. Celeste was devastated, and her anger ate at her. She had inadvertently seen aunt's financial ledger in the office when she went for a signature giving her permission to go on the school's field trip. Glancing from a distance at Sylvie's meticulous bookkeeping, she came across the name Bonnie. Moving forward for a closer look, she saw the name Bonnie Way. To the right of that she'd written $40.00. Completely confused, Celeste was leaving when she saw a purple envelope. It had Bonnie's name on it. Afraid of being caught with the letter, Celeste stealthily snuck it to the attic so she could read it. Dear Sylvie thanks for giving the kids a home. And thanks for the forty a month. That's a lot of money to pay me for letting you have the kids. For sure, I will stay out of your hair. I miss them horribly, but I do understand your point. From Bonnie, an admiring niece-

Celeste reread the lines a second time. Bonnie was getting money for giving siblings away? Celeste was too angry to cry. She never wanted to see Bonnie again. She finally knew why Bonnie didn't write or come to visit.

The letter was dated March 1932, the year Howie and Celeste had moved here. How much money had Sylvie sent to Bonnie? Celeste knew she could never have placed a price on a family member. Learning about this took her even lower. She struggled, searching for the will to live.

*   *   *

By now a sophomore, ice and bitter cold winds colored Mid-January.

Celeste was in the kitchen washing the evening dishes when Mack came along for another cup of coffee. Stopping for a moment, he asked Celeste if she would like to ride to the pharmacy with him. He needed to get something strong for Sylvie's migraine. "I hope this morphine helps with her migraine. I don't like doing this. She needs a prescription." Mack didn't like giving her the drug but gave it anyway, hoping to pacify Sylvie. Celeste had something she wanted to get at the drugstore, which meant being careful so that Mack didn't catch her in the act of stealing.

On their way to the store, Mack struggled to make conversation. He saw Celeste so seldom that he hardly knew her. Aware of her life in the attic, Mack kept the hideousness of what his wife was doing at bay. He'd learned long ago with Donnie to wear blinders, lest he see her repugnance, her greed, and her narcissism. Now having searched his mind, he found a question that seemed right for Celeste.

"Celeste, do you ever think of the farm back there in Lincoln County? The nation's poverty has got to be hurting folks bad."

"I never think back to then. That was then; this is now. I'd go back in a heartbeat, but since I can't, why think about it?"

*   *   *

Celeste and Mack were returning from the drugstore having gotten Sylvie her drug of choice. Unbeknownst to Mack, Celeste snuck what she needed and placed them in her pocket. There was one other thing. She wanted to see what was in her missing knapsack. Sylvie had promised she'd get the bag back the morning after she first arrived but changed her mind. "I changed my mind, dear. You can have your things when you graduate from high school." Now she wondered if Sylvie would have thrown away the bag.

Angry at the memory, Celeste clenched her fist. A moment later, as the house came into view, she turned towards Mack, asking if he would help her retrieve her bag. A cowardly man, at first he hesitated. "I suppose this one time I could join a conspiracy. First I need to go give Sylvie her medicine. The pills should knock her out. If, by chance, she gets up and comes out to the hall, hide in the attic space. I'll say I was hunting for an old chess set. I might have to close the steps back up."

Surprised at his courage, Celeste climbed the ladder that was attached to the ceiling of the second floor cubby hole, a storage spot, built into a gable. Disappearing, she entered a snug nine-by-nine space for storing documents, old games, Christmas wrap small indoor Christmas decorations.... She would be gone shortly and wanted to see her childhood things one last time. Loneliness, Sylvie's hostility, losing Howie, not hearing from those back home, no friends, her parents' death—these had taken their toll on her. Yet, thinking about the lost treasures in her bag, Celeste's breathing quickened, as sharp pins and needles pricked at her skull. Whatever was left of her in the knapsack would be tangible pieces of her identity.

Searching frantically, she looked through everything in sight. *It's gone*, she thought, despairing, doing one final, useless scan— pulling, dropping, feeling, seeking—Where was her bag?

Stretching as high as she could, she saw something on a top shelf. Checkered flannel fabric was peeking over a box? Reaching for the fabric she drew the bag into her hands. Goose bumps covered her body as a lump landed in her throat. Clasping her hands over her mouth, she stuffed her impulse to weep inside while chills zipped down her narrow, bony spine, her eyes absorbing the sight of the fabric bag. She clutched the knapsack, pressing it against her heart.

"It's time for bed, Celeste," Mack yelled, startling her back to normalcy.

It was early—eight forty-five. But so what? She could afford a careless attitude when it came to her bedtime. Why should she care? Where she was going, rules wouldn't be an issue. Besides, life wasn't fair—not under Sylvie's roof.

Looking down, she saw Mack frowning. "Celeste, you have to leave that behind. Sylvie's still in a grainy mood. You know what that means."

"I'll keep it veiled. Sylvie will never know. You said I could look at my things."

"It's too risky. She's awake and in a bad mood. Besides, I overheard her say you're too old for those things. Put them back."

"Please," she entreated, begging, needing to see and touch those things that had once held meaning for her. Maybe she would find answers to explain the black insanity that was coloring her world. She wanted to know, to understand, why those she loved had forgotten her. That way, when she returned, there would be no unknowns.

Also, she would be seeing her parents. Was there something in her bag that they needed to know? She would only be gone for a season or two. When things were right, she would return back to earth. The pills were temporary. In the meantime, she would rest, answer questions, and find solutions. Mom had been proficient at problem solving. She'd done it when her worries outweighed her. Celeste would turn to her as well as her masterful father. But only after her parents acknowledged the horrific misfortune that had come to her as a result of their secrets.

Determined that Mack keep his word, Celeste refused to give up. "Uncle Mack, if she sees these things, I'll say I found a way to open the cubby hole. I'm almost as tall as you are and could manage pulling down the ladder and come up here without help. Let's pretend I did this alone. Besides, I have a bag full of antiques. They're old and uninteresting. The exception is Mother's necklace. It's an heirloom, and I hope to wear it." This last statement wasn't true, but she thought this would make her sound credible. "Howie is staying overnight with the judge, so he'll never know. It's ridiculous for us to argue over childhood things?"

"Like I mentioned, I overheard her say you're too old for that stuff."

"Mack, you like your old toys, the one's you keep in your den. How come you bother with restoring them?"

"I guess you can bring the bag down. Sylvie doesn't go to the attic anyway. However, keep everything well concealed." Celeste scurried down the ladder, making her way around Mack and up the steps to her the third-floor attic. Remembering her plan, she impulsively reached into her jacket pocket, pulling out two of the thirty pills. She wasn't afraid or anxious; the weeks of trauma had dulled any possibilities for her life. Besides, she would return—an idea she'd created to escape the unbearable.

Diving inside the bag, she decided she needn't hurry. Heaven would be free of deadlines, curfews, false accusations… Her tears turned on and off like a leaky faucet, dripping down her cheeks in little streams, like tea pouring out of a narrow spout.

The first thing to come out was Ginny's favorite Nancy Anne story doll, the one with the red hearts on her dress—a Valentine doll. Dumbfounded by this act of generosity, Celeste sat stunned, stroking the soft, blond, mohair wig. After all these years, the doll was as pretty as ever. Ginny had loved her, or she wouldn't have sacrificed this particular doll, the most special in the collection. Carefully laying the Valentine doll aside, she reached in and pulled out a pink purse, the vinyl one the Temples had given her for Christmas, along with the pretty comb and brush set. "Precious," she whispered, running the brush through her chopped, stubbly hair and remembering the ponytail she'd worn that Christmas.

Next, the bracelet and necklace set from Ginny. How ironical it had been. The girls had each picked a silver-colored locket for the other and put their picture in it. Celeste had wanted Will to see hers. Twenty-five cents had gone a long ways at the dime store. They'd doubled up in laughter while Will made faces and funny noises. Reaching up now, she fastened the necklace around her neck, feeling a slight connection. She had been completely alone this entire year… No one said anything, but she felt as though the world knew. The few times she eyed Sylvie, she got the silent treatment. Furthermore, Sylvie's glares were worse than name-calling.

She'd all but emptied the bag, yet it still felt heavy. A few moments ago, scratchy stuff brushed against her fingers. She reached further down … Wait! There was still one thing down there, something fabric—probably her old petticoat. She had been so excited on her eleventh birthday when finding the petticoat; she'd wound up hopping up the old staircase on one foot. Finally, she had a hold of it. What was this in her hands?

It was her father's used Western shirts turned to rags in purples with reds, blues, tangerines, and greens. Celeste laughed. "Yes!" She'd once told Ginny how she'd like to have her dad's western shirts for wearing as the rag princess. Racing to the old machine, having learned more advanced sewing in home economics, she heard the wonderful stitching sounds…sti-sti-sti-sti-sti… She finished the gown two hours later. "Oh," she whispered holding it up. The gown she'd just made was beautiful, everything she'd imagined. *Oh my*, she thought. Racing back over to the mirror, behind the divider, she tried it on. Stepping forward for a look, she was shocked. Imagining, for a fleeting moment, that her hair was long, she saw a beautiful princess. Were these her legs and was this long figure hers? Laughing, about to enter *Cinderella's* ballroom, she said, "Pardon my vanity. This is me, Celeste."

For the first time she was seeing herself as sensual and desirable—a young lady. Shivers ran through her. Celeste hesitated before running her hands over her shapely, padded bones, her hands going from her shoulders to her feet. Her imaginary hair, long and swirling, she pretended how someday Will would be eyeing her. Taking the dress, she stepped into the opening. It fit! It really fit! Barefoot and beautiful, she was, all of a sudden, in the ballroom, the orchestra and Will, awaiting her as she whirled out in her beautiful new rag gown. She stopped when she'd gone half the distance to Will.

Dressed in a tuxedo, he stood gazing at Celeste. Her beauty was causing him tears. "Dance with me, now," he begged.

She, a lovely rose, nodded in a most curt manner. "Two waltzes, sir."

He gathered her in his arms, and they gracefully waltzed about the floor. They had just finished when he whispered, "Please, marry me now. I want the two of us joined together by these rings in my pocket. Please, my love, marry me."

Remembering her beauty and how she'd been enticed by the image of herself, she bowed. In a fleeting moment, she understood how he could love her with such intensity. However, why give in so easily? Long ago, just before coming here, she'd imagined being bored with Will as a means of repaying him... Tossing her head back, Celeste pointed her nose in the air. "Maybe someday, Will Temple. Not now." Laughing, she raced away. Putting on her old flannel nightie, the fantasy was over.

The tall beauty returned to her knapsack treasures, wondering if this was how it could be. It could, except ... except that ... Unable to picture the future, she balled up in a heap of suffocating sobs. Who would marry her once they knew her story? Inconsolable, she wept until she almost fell asleep.

Abruptly, she sat up! She had her answer with her. In fact, she'd made her answer that very night. "Yes," she whispered. "The man who can accept and love me in my rag gown will be the right one." At least he'd be a man who loved her unconditionally.

Who would he be? Whoever he was, he would know that love went deeper than skin deep. Love was unconditional. Her man would not be the cocky, arrogant Will Temple. Yet, what a letdown. Could she find a nice man who was like Will? Maybe a man a man who went to Banner, one who owned pigs and a space for a garden and a white farmhouse with a picket fence just for her. If she was lucky, this might be a possibility. Will would have no choice but to have to suffer the consequences of not choosing her. "Poor Will," she whispered, smiling for the first time in a long while.

Reaching deep, she found a chalk dog and two candlesticks. Dad had won the Scottie dog at the carnival for Mom. The candlesticks, red-etched European glass, were ones Mom had received as her Christmas gift from her Union Aid secret pal. Celeste had thought them the most beautiful she'd ever seen. Mom's pal had added white taper candles. Here, in the box, they were in perfect condition. Nellie had brought them over on the ship. Having loved them, she'd kept them put away. Now old, she'd given them to Mother. "Mom," Celeste had said to her mother. "Burn them on your anniversary." The anniversary had never materialized.

Unexpectedly, Celeste was laughing. God was good, she decided. He'd stepped in to save her, whereas she'd forgotten him. Without the knapsack, she would either be dead or unconscious. Apparently, he wanted her to live. Somewhere, a better life awaited her. Did he want her to have a family or was that out of the question?

It was midnight when she began putting her treasures back. The closet over in the corner would make an ideal hiding place. Busy putting the items away, she spotted a white envelope on the floor. How could she have forgotten the card that Ginny had said she was adding? Opening the envelope, she sat examining it, certain it wasn't a child's card. Instead, it was something you'd give to a teenager. How thoughtful of Ginny. She wished she'd done the same; the card served as proof that Ginny was the kind one. She read, fast, and then faster. It said, *"I can't stop my mind from finding you there all the time. It's the things you do—how you walk, talk, and smile. Valentine, I think you are the most worthwhile of girls. Let me be yours and do my part, 'cause you've won my heart. Be mine for all time.* Please go to the school dance with me. I think you're the cutest girl I'll ever see. Love, Will T."

"Will T.," she whispered. Unsure of whether to smile or cry, she did neither. Was it true? Was she cute like he'd said on the card?

Getting up, she giggled. Quickly slipping into the rag dress, she danced about the room. Once upon a time, a boy had loved her. Leaping her way to the full-length mirror, she stopped to look at her reflection, getting a clear view of her chopped hair and spaghetti-like, tall, thin figure. For a moment, the image was different. She nearly felt a full connection of whom she'd once been. Was it possible to make her way back to the self she'd lost?

That night, she slept for the first time since last summer—really slept. It would be rough, but she could do it. She could fight for a life as a nurse—maybe go overseas and have some kind of life while seeing Europe. She would be far away from all that had hurt. She clutched the new, blue hankie while she slept.

*　　*　　*

Now that Celeste was in her junior year, the attic was quite adorable. Her favorite place was a nook, two steps up, where she kept the machine. From a special window, she could see the skies and trees above. A bird had made a nest just outside the window, where she had watched the entire process, from the eggs to when the little birds flew away.

In her nook, she had material that three of her teachers gave her for sewing, as she was earning a special reputation as a tailor. People paid her for making outfits. She hoped to have her own shop someday. She kept paper for the sketching she did, sometimes adding embroidery designs to the clothing or stitching designs, such as flowers into them. Poppies were her favorite.

Sometimes, she asked Mother and Father why the secret, though she knew at some level that mother hadn't been able to trust that she could tell those things so private. She would have assumed that her daughters would leave her. That was Mother, yet Celeste would suffer moments of doubt and anger for some time to come.

Bonnie had become one enormous why. This same sister had made Christmas so special when Celeste was a child. Instead of big, unaffordable gifts, Bonnie had scraps of fabric to make the most amazing gifts. Her work was incredible. Talk about artistic! Now the two would never share their Christmas holidays or lives. Bonnie was the one who'd called Howie her sweet boy, saying that one day he would run a bakery. That is how sweet he had been.

Celeste's other purpose for this spot clear up here among the leaves and heavens, close to God, was to cry. She had wept many times over Howie turning against her. He could not remember the way she could. There would be no way Howie would dare reach out and accept his sister. How many times had she heard Sylvie talk to him about going to Washington like his father who hadn't gone? Celeste thought she might have pieced that one together. Sylvie had dreamed of going there. However, what about Howie? What was this doing to the little boy who called Celeste names, broke her things, and humiliated her? Somewhere, she still cared about him. Sylvie was lecherous, a woman who made Celeste feel that she was an ugly and evil thing. If she could do that, what could she do to Howie?

One bright light was that she continued to work as a soda jerk, a job she did very well. On Saturdays, ordinary kids from her class came in, ordering only from her. Celeste had a reputation for giving them extra squirts of cherry and chocolate. In return, they gave her extra big smiles. Of course, she blushed. Unfortunately, with the used clothes she wore and her silly haircuts, they had no idea what she could look like. She was blossoming into a girl with gorgeous inquisitive eyes. When it came to boys, she turned away, but Will Temple shone clearly in her bright mind.

*   *   *

When spring came, Miss Whippet was still keeping an eye on her and worried about the dear girl. However, she wanted Celeste to take over and manage the sewing for the operetta that the music department put on each year. This one would be bigger than usual. They were doing a musical version of *Cinderella, next year,* the autumn of Celeste's senior year, and Celeste would have a chance to begin her sewing and designing this coming summer. She would begin extra early because of the extensive amount of costumes to make. Stella and Lou, two classmates, would assist her over the long hours of arduous work. Celeste wanted this opportunity but worried about her abilities. Amazingly, this was not a problem. As soon as she touched the first pattern, she and Miss Whippet were on the way to the fabric store and Celeste was redesigning the dresses. *Cinderella* had its head seamstress and designer. Celeste's biggest concern was that Sylvie would learn of her new position and stop her by saying she couldn't participate. Celeste vowed to keep her work a secret from her aunt.

*   *   *.

Celeste spent her summer making *Cinderella's* detailed gown. Due to the number of gowns, the other two girls started their sewing as soon as the senior year began. Celeste, Stella, and Lou designed and sewed eight new gowns and remade the men's costumes. They even renovated the carriage to be used by *Cinderella's* prince. The final task was to revamp the umbrellas. The job of covering them with satin and bows was glorious but endless. The girls were finished with their work by mid-November, a week before the play was scheduled for the public to watch. Not seeing her anyway, Celeste avoided telling Sylvie about the play, knowing that if she did, Sylvie would cancel her sewing. Fortunately her aunt was always busy. In fact, Sylvie's busy ways, took Sylvie out of town the nights the play was performed. She and Mack were at a convention. It was a pharmaceutical convention, but Sylvie always went along for the shopping. Howie stayed at the judge's home. Thank goodness for miracles this time!

The final night of the play, the girls received two stage calls. Miss Whippet presented Celeste with roses. Stella and Lou received carnations. They even got an invitation to the cast party. Celeste felt shy with her short hair—Sylvie's silly rule was still in place. A friend of Sylvie's had chopped it to within an inch and a half of her head?

Nevertheless, the three girls wandered about the party, watching and observing. They had a wonderful time.

*   *   *

It was February, a little over two years since Celeste had opened the knapsack. Now a senior, mid-evening spoke to her eyes through the glass window, allowing her to smell the fresh, cold air. She was home alone; Sylvie had gone to bridge. Mack was downtown doing inventory. Howie was staying over at the judge's house. Celeste was restless, wanting to take a walk in the fresh air. Little had changed, except that Sylvie offered cool greetings upon seeing Celeste.

As far as the attic, Celeste liked this uppermost room. It was a perfect place for dreaming.

Restless, she checked the time, deciding on a walk in the snow. Sylvie wouldn't be home until later.

Celeste's mind went to nurses' training. She was bright, and there was no question about getting the scholarship. What would it be like if not for Miss Whippet and Miss England, the latter who'd told her to study? Where was Miss England? Her fiancé's folks lived here. Surely, Miss England was still at Union School. Celeste wondered if she ever thought of her.

Miss Hattie England, always Miss England to her students, young and single, a woman with bright red hair and freckles...From the first, Celeste had a crush on her. School became an exciting and safe place, a world that buzzed with activity. When it was too cold to go outside, Miss England taught the kids things that had to do with thread or yarn. During her first year Celeste embroidered a sunflower on a square of cotton, then, because of prolonged storms, she added batting, made from an old blanket, and turned her piece into a potholder. She gave it to Mom for her birthday in April. Ginny made a bleeding heart potholder for her mom. The next winter they had to learned paper Mache, making puppets and doing skits with their characters. They even did some darning, which would have been horrible, except that Mrs. England read them Black Beauty.

Twice a year, Miss England, planned a day away from the schoolhouse such as a field trip. One year she'd arranged for the children to have a day of roller skating and picnicking at Lafayette Park at the Lake in Gothenburg. The mothers packed the children's lunches and away they went in cars up to the park by the lake. Skates were brought from home or borrowed and around and around the children went laughing, falling, and circling about the inside pavilion. Another day she made plans with a friend whose parents lived up near a disappearing town, a town in the Sandhills called Buffalo. There along a creek sat a beautiful meadow, fully resembling the prairie in all its glory. The kids played games, walked along the creek which ran through a gulch, ate their lunches, and sat listening to their teacher read a story…a wonderful way to have another view of the prairie. Other places were Scout's Rest Ranch with Buffalo Bill and the House of Yesterday, a museum in Hastings, and the beautiful, hilly, Halsey Forest, all in Nebraska.

Noticing a steeple, lighting the night sky, she thought of Banner Church in the country. It had been her heaven back then. *She'd liked the oak pews and songs, the stained glass windows, the cattle just outside in the snowy fields; she'd liked leaning against Dad's woolen coat, Mom handing her hard candy, Bonnie smiling. She and Bonnie had always been close, even after Howie's birth when they were at odds. Maybe Banner would be in heaven with the church all lit up, having the Christmas program on Christmas Eve, white snow covering the roads. Sitting in the pew, she'd smell Dad's cologne and Mom's perfume. Her own dress, all frilly and little, would touch Bonnie's dress.* She had to reach for her dream, to fight for the things she loved, to once again see them as she had as a child. She would turn to prayer. Her God wasn't the same one Pastor had blabbered about knowing. Her God was beautiful and good.

Passing one of the big old homes, she saw a lady closing the curtains. What would it feel like to be free like that woman? Freedom included being able to close curtains or go safely to bed or bake a dessert for the next day. Since getting Will's valentine, she'd had fantasies of being married and free. Smiling she wondered what Will would think if he knew she'd planned their entire family. They had six kids, including a set of twins, and she'd named them all. Likewise, they had a garden, horses, and cows. In August, they picked berries and made jam. For breakfast, Celeste fixed waffles served with raspberry sauce. Her family would have lots of unlimited love, safety, and freedom.

Freedom and safety? Love? For the past four years, she'd been in a box with a big lid that kept her inside its walls. Why? Had she done something to deserve losing her family, having no friends, being a girl up in the attic, having her hair cut off? What had she done to feel like she lived in a box?

Boxed ... Something was coming to her. It had to do with a box—the box ... She stopped. Yes! Like a flower unfolding in slow motion, she remembered.

Celeste recalled a day, long ago. She had taken it on herself to help when the family had first started packing to move. She'd assigned herself the task of unloading Mom and Dad's closet shelf. Only an eight year old, she'd climbed up the ladder and was almost finished when she spotted a pretty hatbox pushed clear back on the shelf. Barely reaching it, she'd climbed down with it in her hands. Inside, she found a picture of Dad's father and another picture of her parents 'getting married. The wedding picture and a picture of Dad, at age eight, were the only two photographs the family had of him. After looking at them, Celeste came upon another picture. "Sylvie" was written on the backside. Sylvie was standing with a boy her age, a high school kid, who vaguely reminded Celeste of Dad. However, it was Sylvie's eyes that kept Celeste's attention. She was trying to get a closer look when Mother, swept into the bedroom, unannounced. On seeing Celeste, who was holding the picture, Mother flew at her, the same way Orbit, the Dustys' mad rooster, flew at people. Going to pieces, Mother grabbed at the picture and the box of miscellany, which also had a letters that were in *lavender* envelopes. Sylvie" had written her name on them. Mother tucked these letters deep into her apron pocket, unaware that in her frenzy, she'd scratched Celeste. Instead of offering comfort, she paddled Celeste.

Unsure why the memory was emerging ,Celeste remembered how aunt's angry eyes scared her. A strong sense of disaster *floated* over her that day. She'd felt an unexplainable kind of fear that bordered on terror.

Pausing from her own feelings, Celeste wondered if she'd been too afraid to remember all of this until now. As opposed to when she'd arrived four years ago, she was older and about ready to leave her prison.

Celeste had told her dad about what had happened the next day. She'd told him several things, but in his nervousness, all he'd been able to say was, "Err-uh ... Sounds like Mom was in need of a nap." Celeste had gone on to say that the boy in the picture wearing the number 15 jersey rather looked like him. "You dribbled some ball." She'd asked. "Did you know him?" Instead of answering her, he'd left, saying he had work to do.

Now Celeste recalled that, just before Mother had entered the room, Celeste had been looking into Sylvie's eyes in the picture. Though she'd thought Sylvie was pretty, her aunt's eyes scared her. A strong sense of doom had floated over her. She didn't finish because of Mother rushing in. The eyes, which seemed both angry and hollow, had frightened Celeste for a few days. After that, she'd forgotten the whole thing

She stood on the snowy sidewalk, feeling the emergence of anger while spiraling down inside. Why was she the one paying for those things that happened between her parents and Sylvie? She'd had nothing to do with any of it. It wasn't her fault that she looked like her mother, a fact that infuriated Sylvie. Besides, her parents had no reason to keep Sylvie a secret. Who would have cared that Mother married Sylvie's boyfriend? It served Sylvie right.

Celeste thought about a day recently when she went in after school to ask Miss Whippet if she knew anything about Donnie. Because of where the conversation led, Miss Whippet eventually shared something huge— Mom and Dad had married the day after the dance. "Fortunately, even though they weren't at the graduation ceremony, they graduated," Miss Whippet had laughed. She'd also said she knew that Donnie wasn't Dad's baby. Miss Whippet's old high school boyfriend, had been a good buddy of Al's, someone he had confided in about the situation.

"Celeste," Miss Whippet had said, "I would never tell you this except that, under the right circumstances, you might have learned false rumors. If so, you would have lived wondering if the boy she gave birth to was a half-brother. I'm among the few that know the truth."

"I will never say you told me Miss Whippet," Celeste had assured her teacher, "but thanks for telling me. It must have taken courage for you to give the information. Knowing this helps me make sense of all that's happened." Older and ready to graduate, Celeste didn't cry over the new information.

Now as she thought about it, Celeste would bet that Sylvie had set the entire thing up so Dad would have to marry her. Celeste shook her head, her pale cheeks growing moist. Tears dripped down onto the freezing sidewalk. It was Sylvie's eyes she'd seen underwater when Pastor had held her under. Was Sylvie's hatred so strong as to reach her victims from a distance? What had Mother thought Celeste would find in the hat box?

Celeste had been too young to know that the boy standing with Sylvie was her father. She'd seen Sylvie's name on the lavender envelope, the one that mother had stuffed in her pocket that day.

Celeste didn't think there had been any reason for it to come to her. Instead, she realized that very sensitive people could feel the vibration of Sylvie's hatred. What else would she have experienced if not for Mom interrupting what was happening? What had Mother thought Celeste would find?

What had happened to Donnie? she wondered. That poor, dear boy. Someday she would try to find out exactly how he'd died. Sylvie obviously hadn't wanted him. There were those awful things she told Howie about Donnie while making others feel sorry for her loss. Unwilling to let her emotions turn to anger, she walked on, forcing herself to think of good things. Nevertheless, the tears fell slowly.

She remembered how the sun had streamed in on the kitchen table. Was it possible to be Mrs. Will Temple with kids about the kitchen table?

Snow continued to fall as she wandered home.

Later on that night, deciding it was bedtime, Celeste pulled down the covers. Living alone as she did, cut off from the family, she read before sleep. Sometimes, she'd slip down for an apple. Natasha dared to leave Celeste this treat, knowing she was underfed. Feeling hungry, she readied herself to dash down to the kitchen.

Just then, Sylvie came flying in, unannounced. Shocked, Celeste watched the madwoman work herself into a quick fury. Strands of her bun had come lose, and she was livid. Her eyes—they were what Celeste noticed. They were the same livid eyes she'd seen long ago in that picture.

Sylvie began to scream. "You little sneak! I became a fool because of you. We were on our third hand of bridge when Betty Holden asked what I thought of the costumes. Gloria Danes worth said, 'I didn't see you at the operetta, Sylvie. Were you sick?' Ruth Havoc said, 'Ladies, it went for two nights. You must have attended on opposite nights.' Lucille Ivory said, 'I compared with Anne Jorgen's, who didn't see her either night. I went on Friday.' Maria asked what night I went. I said, 'Ladies, what are you discussing?' One woman gasped, and then the room went silent. I said, 'Well? I'm waiting.' Jean Hargrove said, "*Cinderella*. Celeste sewed for *Cinderella*." Stupefied and unprepared, a frightened Celeste said, "I didn't think you'd care or be interested."

"How do you think I felt? And how can you say I don't care? I give you a warm roof, food, clothes, your bed … I give all this. You are just like your crazy mother. I gave and gave and not once did she mention it," she said, her voice rising, her arms flailing out of control. Infuriated, she steadied herself on the pole of the floor lamp, listening as Celeste began her own tirade.

"Why? Because you hated her for marrying my father? You were jealous. She was everything you're not. She was kind, thoughtful, giving, gentle, beautiful, tall and slender—"

"Shut up! You're invisible in my presence." Sylvie's bun was coming down in strands, falling apart from the violent headshaking. "Nothing about you is right!"

"The only thing that's wrong with me is you're isolating me. I've been lonely. That's not a sin."

"Lonely! I had my boy alone because of your mother. That's lonely. I had no one because of her running off to marry your father, a dirt worker. He was Donnie's father. I had Donnie alone on this floor right over there." She pointed. "I went into labor all alone up here. I felt so bad for my precious baby. He was your father's boy, Missy."

That was when the controls broke. Celeste knew where Donnie was born. She'd overheard Elvira and Sylvie discuss this. "I hate you," Celeste yelled. "My father was a wonderful person, and so was my mother. So was baby Howie." Celeste couldn't shut up. "You're a batterer, a hypocrite, an intimidator, a persecutor, evil, and a liar. You're selfish and cruel. You wanted to marry my father. I saw his picture at school. He was your boyfriend, Howard Anderson. He married my mother, whom you hated. I don't know who Donnie belonged to, but it wasn't my father. Dad would never leave his children. He took care of his offspring. Did you? What else are you going to accuse my parents of doing?"

Sylvie's mouth was twitching so badly she couldn't talk for a moment. "Did you know your mother wrote and gave you kids to me?" she snarled.

"Right, like all the other lies you've told about my mother and dad."

Sylvie fled out of the room returning with a lavender envelope. Tossing it at Celeste, she quipped, "Read it! Here take it. I said, read it!"

"I don't need to," Celeste said, recognizing the lavender on the envelope. Taking the letter from Sylvie, Celeste ripped the paper, leaving it in stringy wads. "The way you manipulate, you could have written this letter. Mom's love was much greater than purposefully handing us over to you. My mother lived for us. You won't make me hate her. You should have tried to be more like her. Because of her kind ways, Mom tried to protect you by saying you were nice. Dad was different. He made no pretense about you. Neither Bonnie nor Mom dared bring you up when he was around. I didn't understand it, but now I do. He despised you."

"Like I tell people, your mother was a loser. You're just like her."

"No! Dad married her instead of you. You were jealous of Mother. My father adored my mother."

Sylvie's eyes were hot with hate—hardened with fury and rage. Not moving, she stood staring at Celeste. It was when Celeste turned to walk away that Sylvie made her move. Balling her fist, she punched Celeste twice, finishing with two cracking slaps to her face. Without looking back, Sylvie ran down the stairs, leaving Celeste hunched down, rocking on her two feet, hands plastered to her cheeks, gritting her teeth, and moaning. She felt hopeless. All of her good feelings had just abandoned her.

This time she knew better than to swallow pills. If she did, there would be no coming back to earth. She had to find something to live for. First, before finding that one illusive thing—that miracle in the midst of the dark, she would take a bath, hoping it would lessen her anguish. There would be time for grieving later. For now, she would light the candles while bathing in the dimness. She wanted to watch the flames. Because of such a terrible fight, she felt worthless—uncertain of which hurt worse, her face or her soul.

Despite Celeste denying that her mother would give her children to Sylvie, Celeste figured there must have been something to it. On the other hand, Mother loved her children with such fervency. Celeste doubted she would ever know the details as to why Mom would give Howie and her to Sylvie. Nothing made any sense.

Still throbbing with pain, she undressed, removing the candles and holders from the drawer. Filling the tub, Celeste quickly flushed the pills. Next came lighting the candles and turning the lights off. Crawling into the water, she lay back and watched the flames as they burned and glowed, the flickering carrying her back to the Temple place and then back to here in the attic. The glass that made up the holders was old and European, etched with snowflakes. Presently it glimmered in the candle glow, easing the hurt and scars. The flames flickered and then flickered again. What was happening? A message? Were they saying something? It almost seemed as though they were speaking to her. Candles didn't dance like that—not without a breeze.

Was someone there? First, she felt a presence; next, she saw his face, tender and loving. He moved closer. She bent forward for a better look. Will? It was him. He was there in the candlelight smiling at her. Was she losing her mind? She closed her eyes tightly and then opened them. She thought so. His hands were touching her swollen cheeks. He was on the edge of the tub, his feet in the water. He'd made a cold water compress and was rubbing it ever so gently on her cheek. She was naked, with lots of bubble bath but it wasn't like that. To her, it seemed like her body was neutral rather than sexual. Instead, this moment was like being with an old friend. Maybe she was in heaven. But why was he lifting her from the tub drying her? She groaned.

He chuckled. "Cripes, Celeste, you're a mess. Let's pick you up and put you to bed."

He laid her down tenderly, placing her on her back, his lips brushing hers. "It's going to be all right," he said. "Wait for me. Don't go. Wait and I'll return—not today or tomorrow, but I promise, I'll return."

She'd opened her eyes. He was disappearing right where he stood. Could it be true? Had Will been there? Or had it been a dream? Had an angel brought him to her? Something was different. She felt stronger, as though infused with greater courage. An inner joy was filling her up, a new spirit—a light, hope.

Strangely, the next morning, she clearly remembered the night before. The candles had burned down, and a bottle of lotion was beside the bed. She felt strangely wonderful.

She hadn't thought of Will much, not since the night she got his valentine. Now she thought about him most of the time. She would never see him again, not really, and if she did, he would be married. His presence filled her with something she couldn't name. His coming hadn't been a dream. He'd been there with her, either him or his spirit. His essence was like an aura. Yet, it had felt surreal, like a candle glow dream.

After that, every time she lit her candles, Celeste got that same feeling. It was funny how strangely the flames flickered on and off, ever so softly— proof his presence was there in the candle's glow. In time, this would fade, but it was enough to carry her forth to a new world—to nursing college. Her scholarship application was looking good.

She could never trust the woman again. Sylvie said that she and Mack would cover her schooling just to get her out of the house for good. She called it "a last gift." Celeste wasn't so certain. Celeste had seen enough that she knew Sylvie could change her mind any minute. She had the power to ruin everything.

Though she could be sure that Sylvie was ruthless, she was uncertain about herself and her goodness. Mother would never have understood or approved of her yelling at Sylvie. Mother claimed to have liked Sylvie. But had she liked her? Or could it be that Mother was deluding herself, having no love for Sylvie? The wise man inside of Celeste thought the latter true. Sylvie had abused Mom. Celeste was sure of it. She wished Mother would have come out and talked about Sylvie. Had she or Dad just been willing to do that, she and Howie would have spent these last four years of her life with the Temples instead of in this horrible place. If not for Will's visit, Celeste would have felt trapped inside the box.

She wrote the final entrance in her diary the day after Sylvie slapped her.

March 1, 1936

Sylvie slapped me last night after I finally stood up to her. She came home livid about *Cinderella*. I embarrassed her by not telling her I was sewing. I told her she wouldn't have allowed me to sew if she knew. No one will ever touch me like that again. I think she knew that the pastor was at fault when that terrifying thing happened. I decided to live and was looking for a reason to justify my decision. Life is always the better choice. I tell myself to hang on. I can never marry, and I regret that. However, there will be something to enjoy.

All I am going to say is that Will came along. We were in the Candlelight. Rather, he was a spirit that came in the flames. He talked to me and looked at my face. He talked to me while putting ice packs gently upon my cheeks and holding them there. He had me lie down while he sat on the edge of the bed, checking the bruises every few minutes. Before he left, he told me to wait for him. "I'll be back, I promise. It might not be for a few years. Just be patient and wait for me," Will said. Ready to go, he carried me to bed.

Just seeing him gave me the strength to deal with life until I'm out of here. Before he left, he bent and brushed his lips against mine. It's the sweetest memory I have to date. His lips actually touched my lips. I can still taste him.

*   *   *

Miss Whippet planned a party for Celeste who skipped telling her about Bonnie and the money.

First, she called Bonnie Way. After chatting for some time, Miss Whippet brought up Celeste, saying that Celeste would want to see her sister on graduation night.

Bonnie, believing that Celeste knew nothing about what she'd done, was eager to see her sister. At the same time, Bonnie spoke of Sally, her daughter who'd been born deaf. Who would watch Sally and Carson? She concluded that she would stay with the kids, during the ceremony, but come for the after-graduation celebration. Miss Whippet informed her that the Soboris, even little Howard, would be gone on a trip come graduation. "I know this, "she said," because my very social sister plays bridge with Sylvie. I'd like you to cut the cake and surprise her. It will just be the two of you alone at my home. I thought maybe you could use some time together. It might be best to keep this reunion quiet."

Celeste had spoken of Bonnie, telling Miss Whippet little vignettes—the good things. She'd told Miss Whippet that she didn't see Bonnie as she was too poor to drive to Lincoln during the depression. Though she doubted that, Miss Whippet wondered what the truth was.

Following the ceremony, Celeste almost didn't go. It would be more comfortable to drop in alone sometime. Perhaps nursing school would be a good time to visit. Her hair would be long and trendy, and she'd be wearing nicer clothes. Fortunately, hunger won out. She was the first guest and went on inside as Miss Whippet instructed her to do. Someone would be there tending the cake.

Celeste wanted to laugh at the word "cake cutter." It reminded her of a wood chopper.

Upon arriving, one person was there—the cake cutter, who had her back to Celeste and was busy cutting pieces. Celeste, who felt too inhibited to start a conversation, sat quietly on the foyer bench, waiting for her piece. Finally, too hungry to do nothing another minute, she walked around and in front of the cutter.

Bonnie, who turned to see her sister standing there, was speechless.

Celeste stared at Bonnie with searching eyes.

Bonnie was looking at a wide-eyed skeleton, a girl whose beautiful hair was gone and whose clothes hung loose. Known as stoic, Bonnie couldn't pull herself together this time.

Celeste, who was numb with years of pent-up anger, precipitously shot forth like a volcano spewing lava. She had given a lot of thought to what Bonnie's actions might be. Yelling, she told Bonnie what a cheap thing she'd done. "You're a hypocrite as a sister. "I don't acknowledge you as my sister anymore. First Mom and then you. Mom was understandable. Your betrayal was worse." She was hoarse by the time she collapsed into tears.

By then, Bonnie was leaning down holding her. "Celeste, I took two checks and returned them. We went back to the trailer where we are today. I didn't go to school. Later on, I had Sally, a deaf baby. Until recently, she's taken all my time. I want to work with deaf children when the Depression ends. She's incredible.

"Celeste, I wrote you every week, but I never heard back. Part of why I turned the money down was so that I could write you. I asked to come visit, but she always had a reason for why I couldn't come. Not to hear from you though… That wasn't like you and I worried about you."

"I wrote you," Celeste cried out, "but you never answered me." The room went silent. Catching her breath, a questioning look coming over her face as Celeste choked, "Sylvie didn't send them? "Before Bonnie could respond, Celeste was crying before getting angry all over again.

It took time for Celeste to become rational. "She withheld our letters!"

Bonnie apologized profusely for having been thoughtless. She explained where she'd been coming from when making her decision, saying she was so sorry for all the fantasies she'd built about Sylvie. She also spoke of the guilt she'd felt over having her parents visit that fateful day. "I felt I'd stolen your parents and wanted to give you financial freedom. I thought she'd love you. I never dreamed she would be so monstrous. Please forgive me."

"It's going to take time," Celeste said with greater understanding. "I am never coming back here once I leave for nurse's training," she said, avoiding any mention of the pastor. Instead, she wanted to know about Bonnie's children. "Tell me all about Sally and Carson."

Bonnie said she felt bad about the Temples and what she'd done. "I haven't heard from Bev in all these years. I'm too ashamed to call her. They were such good people." To that, Celeste said she wondered where they'd been during her abandonment.

About Howie, the sisters made a pact that they would watch Howie from a distance, acting if necessary.

*   *   *

Anxious to be gone from Sylvie's for good, Celeste felt both overwhelmed with insecurities and delighted when the day came to leave. Early that morning, as soon as Celeste finished packing her last outfit, she whispered, "Good-bye, Pastor. Good-bye, Sylvie."

Her most important job was to find out who she was. Did the girl she'd been still exist? She wanted to heal as a way of honoring the brave girl who had worn the little dresses in the trunk—including the Valentine Party outfit. Along with those, she packed the Rag Princess gown, doubting she would ever need it. As for marriage, a future husband was out of the picture. In her eyes, marriage wasn't a viable alternative. Any man she loved would leave once he knew about her past. Sylvie had done an adequate job of teaching her who and what she was.

Scooting her long body into her graduation gift from Mack, an old car, Celeste looked back one final time. As strange as it seemed, the attic had become a friend, and she wanted to thank the space for the gift of sheltering her. Then, facing forward, Celeste drove into an uncertain future. Again, she wondered about that twelve-year-old child of long ago. "Where are you?" she whispered.

Book Three

Healing the Rag Princess

September 1941

A recent nursing graduate, Celeste performed a final check on her patients, before leaving the children's hospital on South Street in Lincoln. She and Sandra, her roommate, shared a small home eight blocks north on Washington Street. Sandra was at a wedding at home in Fullerton, Nebraska, and wouldn't be back before Monday. Celeste was looking forward to the fair. Sandra's being gone wasn't going to stop her. Arriving home to an empty house, Celeste changed into a stylish yellow sundress. After grabbing a banana, she drove her faithful 1928 Ford to the fairgrounds. With luck, she parked outside the ticket gate, fighting her way through the throngs of people. She'd come here once during nursing school and was looking forward to her favorites, the pigs. Before going to the hog barn, Celeste bought her yearly treat—a huge glob of sticky, pink cotton candy.

The long narrow hog shed held endless rows of fat, squealing pigs. Watchful sows were in pens with their babies while others stood alone or lay blissfully in the cool dirt. Celeste was almost to the final row when she spotted a black-and-white sow with six piglets. Something felt familiar. Looking closer, she realized they looked like the babies she'd played with as a child at the Temples. Kneeling, she began talking to the mother. "Just look at you and those beautiful babies. A good mommy, aren't you, sweetheart? Can I visit your little ones?" She was only vaguely aware of a man stopping beside the pen.

"Do you like these pigs?" he asked. "Reach in and take one. Who's going to know? I'm not planning to tell on you."

Annoyed at his banter, Celeste gritted her teeth, wishing he'd be quiet.

"So," he blurted, "do you still play marbles up in the attic? I remember beating you," he chuckled.

"I'm trying to talk to this little fellow and ..." She was about to say she wished he would be quiet. Instead, something clicked. Glancing up, she saw that face and those fabulous blue eyes.

"Do you remember my beating you and Ginny? I'm thinking it was a rainy Saturday."

"Will, Will Temple! These are your pigs!" she exclaimed. Forgetting her manners, she dashed over, hugging Will. Realizing what she'd done, she stepped back, embarrassed.

"I didn't plan on seeing a Temple," she said self-conscious. "Is your family here?"

"It's just me and the kids," he offered, pointing to the sow and her babies.

Her first thought was that a good-looking guy like him either had a girlfriend or was married. That reminded her of the vow she'd made, years ago, when she was twelve, and they were doing the marbles. Looking back, she wondered where such confidence had come from. Over time, she'd run out of any such thing. Having it the day she left the farm had probably sustained her, she thought. Besides, she wondered how she could have hugged a Temple, considering their abandonment of her

Celeste hadn't thought much about Will since leaving Sylvie's home. She didn't think either Will or Ginny had played a part in her being abandoned while she lived with Sylvie.

Fortunately, she and Sylvie had nothing to do with each other... Bonnie knew that part, but she didn't know anything about what the pastor had done. Pastor's assault had been years before, but the effects hadn't left Celeste. She still wondered if she was good or evil. On one level, she knew the answer, but on another, she was a little girl listening to Sylvie say that what had happened was her fault.

Celeste's eyes had a faraway look, making it apparent that she was lost in thought. She was remembering Will as a cocky, egocentric boy, but he appeared to have greatly matured over the years.

"You've changed," he said. "You seemed afraid of me back on the farm. You impressed me as being wispy and self-conscious. Now you seem confident. I'll just bet that you're unattainable."

Daring herself, she asked, "What's happened to all the Temples?"

"Well, let's see. That may take some time to explain. Could I escort you to dinner tomorrow night? That's providing there isn't another guy."

His grin was the same mischievous grin. The face— wholesome and wonderfully handsome, unlike the cute boy she'd remembered.

Their dinner reunion was set. However, why was Will so friendly? And why had she carried one of his hankies with her for all these years? Neither made any sense—nor did looking forward to tomorrow night. Sometime during dinner, she would ask about the family and Ginny. If given a chance, she would tell him how she thought his parents could have done something to help in her perilous situation. At least she adored the pigs as much as ever. The pigs couldn't hurt her.

"By the way," Will said, "ordinarily, I don't risk asking women who have someone. I about lost my eye doing that. Is there someone else?"

"Do I have another guy?" With her hands on her hips, Celeste was buying thinking time. She didn't date—had never been on a date. She wondered what he'd think if he knew that no one had ever kissed her. "I date around. Don't worry. You'll keep your eyes. And since that takes care of my side, I should tell you, I don't care to lose either of my eyes. They're unique. When I cry, my tears come out of one side or the other, not both at once."

"Fascinating, although it's not my intent to make you cry. Ginny's still a bawl-baby. She cries and runs to tattle every chance she gets, but I'll take it easy on you—at least until we finish eating," he winked.

Celeste was confused about the wink.

"Anyway, there's no girl just now. It's a shock to my system. I'm a little hungry," he said, playfully wiggling his eyebrows and laughing, penetrating her with his blue as the sky eyes, alluring and so joyful that she wanted to crawl inside them and stay for a good long while. Standing there, she thought of the blue green ponds of summer and the wild flowers with lacey leaves that grew near the water.

"If you're hungry, why don't you go eat?" she asked. Celeste thought it silly to be hungry with all the food around. There were hamburgers, hot dogs, snow cones, waffles—anything and everything. "I don't let men in the house, but if you're terribly hungry, I could fix you something. I guess you're not exactly a stranger."

"Well, thanks." Wanting to howl with laughter, Will took on a grateful expression. She looked so serious and caring that he could hardly continue teasing. "I thought I'd have a hot dog, but gee, thanks anyway." Apparently, she didn't know other meanings for hungry. Of course, he was only kidding. At home, they called it teasing. What was with her? Then again, she looked quite tasty in her yellow dress.

"What time?" she asked.

"Do you mind going out on the town in my pickup? Kind of awkward to climb up inside."

"I can manage to crawl in. I'm citified but country at heart. Why else would I be looking at the pigs?" *Really,* she thought exasperated. Did she look *that* old?

*   *   *

Celeste called Bonnie first thing and gave her the details. Over time, Celeste had fully forgiven Bonnie. They were as close as ever. Bonnie, a tease, was delighted. "I smell romance in the air," she laughed, joking about Will finding her sister down wooing the pigs. "I bet he wished he was one of the pigs. Wow! You really do have a dinner date with Will? Interesting. As I recall, you couldn't stand him."

"He isn't that cocky boy anymore. Besides, we became friends before I left. It might seem unbelievable, but I've always had one of those hankies with me. I darned the other hankie. I had a horrible cold and rather blew too much in public one day. Only one is left untouched; it's still in the box. As far as calling this a date, you're wrong. We want to catch up on what our families are doing. I'd like to hear about Ginny and the rest of them."

"So you had a blowout with the old hankies?"

"Why did I bother calling?"

"Honey, just know that I'm here for you day and night. You do know that, don't you? Seeing Will for an evening could bring up old anxieties. You already know this, but I haven't talked to Bev since that day we got into a tither. She has a right to be disgusted with me. If Will says anything, understand where he's coming from."

"Thanks, but I'm O.K. I'd bet anything that Sylvie hid or threw Ginny's letters away. I can't say that I understand why Clark and Bev didn't pursue this more closely. That's no fault of Will's though. I've got to go now. I'll call again as soon as I can afford it— sometime around Christmas."

"Wait, honey. Where are you eating?"

"Chuckles. Have you been there?"

"On our salary? We don't eat out. Instead, we go where it's free. Look for us at church potlucks, funerals, wedding receptions, and family reunions. We never know the people at any of these events. I scour the newspaper and make a weekly list of freebies. Now and then, I goof up. There's a couple living here. First of all, we went to her mother's funeral. Next was the parents' wedding anniversary. The husband smiled at us while giving us strange looks. Eventually, he asked which side we were on. I said, 'My husband is in on the grocery store.' That took care of the problem. He didn't know which store, but it worked. Everyone knows the grocer. On occasion, we go on one of my famous picnics, but those aren't free—not unless Bob's uncle gives us his expired food. And even then, it's not free. He charges us half of the regular price."

"Stop, Bonnie," Celeste begged. "I hurt from laughing at your tall tales. I'm hanging up. Tell the kiddies that Celeste loves them. Tell the kids hello for me."

As for her Sally and her boy, Bonnie was incredible. In time, she wanted to earn a degree, allowing her to work with deaf children.

Celeste thought about Bonnie's prediction for her. Shaking her head, she put it out of her mind. She wasn't going to let Romeo hurt her.

* * *

Nervous about tonight, Celeste stood at the screen door watching. She didn't want to keep Will waiting. When he drove up, she already had the door unlocked and quickly walked to the car half-skipping. Getting in, she slammed the door, turned to say hi, and saw an empty seat. Will was just outside her car door, laughing. Celeste's cheeks turned scarlet over her mistake. Sandra had called the house. Wanting to give advice to an insecure Celeste, she'd told her to imitate her, saying that if she did, everything would be all right! Ha! Sandra, the ultra-sophisticate, a tiny, knows everything, soon to be doctor's wife...

Will scooted back inside the car. He still enjoyed what had happened. "So you city girls really go for independence, huh?"

"Well," she said. What could she tell him? Then it came to her—the perfect answer. "Actually, it began with the girls who were attending college. They liked to set independent trends to outdo the guys down on campus. Eventually, it made its way all over town. We all do it. If I seem strange to you, blame it on those girls." There, she thought.

Will didn't believe a word of it. What was making her so darned nervous? he wondered. She should have a lot of experience, with her beauty, those legs, and that hair. "Gee," he said, "Know who you remind me of an awful lot?"

"Ginny?" she said. She would love to remind him of beautiful Ginny. As a grade school girl, she'd been adorable.

"No. My mom."

For heaven's sake, Celeste thought. Bev had reminded young Celeste of one of those large farm fertilizer trucks. Big boned with strawberry hair, Bev had been a female steam-roller—the take-charge woman. Celeste groaned, realizing too late that Will heard the groan.

"What's wrong with you reminding me of my mom? I heard that groan," Will said, poker-faced.

"You're taking me wrong," Celeste stammered. "My groan was my way of empathizing with her for being like me."

Will just grinned.

Celeste wondered if he always teased or if she really reminded him of Bev.

Driving on west to Chuckle's Chicken, they kept up the small talk. Will explained that, when he came to the fair, he stayed with a friend from Brady. This friend had lent him his car for tonight. Celeste asked Will about the crowd at the fair and his pigs. Will answered and said how the evenings cooled down. He complimented her again on the outfit she was wearing. By then, they were turning into the packed parking lot.

"Do you want me to drop you at the door?"

She shook her head, saying she liked to walk. This impressed Will, who found a parking stall at the north end. "Celeste, you stay put. This time let me get the car door," he said.

Looking at each other, they laughed in unison.

As the pair walked inside, a whir of moving air from large ceiling fans hit them. The cooler air left Celeste feeling better about the evening ahead. A bubbly waitress led the two of them to a booth. Before accepting it, Will asked, "Is this spot all right with you? I want tonight to be special for you."

"This is a good booth," Celeste said, her insecurity causing her to start rambling. "It's especially nice with the fan overhead. It's very pleasing. I think it will be fine," she answered.

Confused, she cocked her head to one side. Why would Will want to please her? She did the pleasing. Until leaving the Temple place, she hadn't given these things a thought. Her new life had changed this. It was all about satisfying Sylvie. In nursing school, when the girls rubbed her back or brushed her hair, they sensed her discomfort. "We're not trying to torture you, sweetie." *Sweetie.* That word still brought her nightmares. Sweetie fit girls who were demure and dainty.

"I'm glad this pleases you, Celeste," Will said, winking.

In response, her cheeks turned red.

Bending toward her, his hand brushed hers while his cologne breezed her way.

"This meal is for you. Order whatever sounds appealing," he said, his twinkling eyes looking at Celeste. Her history with Pastor would have caused her fear around anyone but Will. Instead, he turned her legs weak. She'd felt her heartbeat, before tonight, but not this hard.

"I enjoy Chuckle's," she managed. "Having their chicken is a real treat."

Thump ... Thump. Was she out of her mind? Why, after all these years was she dreaming of being his bride? That was a silly childhood fantasy. He was her first crush. This was now—not back then. And Will probably had not changed that much. Thankfully, she saw through him.

"You're pretty," Will said. "This candle lights up your auburn hair."

"You're still a tease." She wasn't falling for his nonsensical flattery. What did he want from her anyway?

"I'm not teasing." His eyes reflected hurt, maybe even that he was a little offended. "I'm saying what's in my heart; I'm not that kid who knew Ginny and you. I'm a man. Accept the truth about yourself." The sparkles in his eyes touched something way down inside her, like when she was twelve. She felt like crying; he was touching emotions she couldn't name and places she didn't want to go.

"Can I ask you about your family? I thought so much of them." She'd wanted to say I used to think a lot of them. Her wise person stopped her short, redirecting her.

"Who should I start with?"

"How is Bev?"

"Not much has changed with Mom." Will shook his head, pretending he was disgusted with his mom. "She's still the take-charge woman she always was. She's in two clubs, and she talked Dad into taking square dance lessons, so she drags him to a dance at least twice a month. In fact, she is busy planning a barn dance for next month."

"That's fantastic," Celeste said, joyous. "That sounds colorful and so like Bev. I can only imagine. I missed farm life so much when I left your place."

Will looked confused when she mentioned missing the farm but bounced back fast.

"And Clark? My father never had a kinder boss than your dad."

"He's still the same. He lives for the family, the farm, and the church."

"You mean Banner, the country church?" Celeste said, remembering how she'd loved going there.

"Yes, Banner, the white church sitting on a corner there in the country. It's the same. We still have Lord's Acre Day and our other traditions."

"I'm going to go back to that church someday," Celeste said in a dreamy voice, picturing herself in a long white dress with a veil.

"I could see you as a bride. With your tall elegance and beautiful face, people would look at you and wonder if they were dreaming."

"Will Temple, you embarrass me." She blushed. Bending over, Celeste put her hands over her face. Sitting like that, she looked like a ten-year-old.

Forcing herself back to a sitting position, she peeked between her fingers.

"Let me finish." Reaching, with large, well-cared-for hands, he graciously took her fingers from her face, laying them on the table, while giving them a pat that almost blew her out of the chair. "The groom would be a bit taller with blond hair. He'd be unable to take his eyes off you. A large white candle would sit burning. The kiss at the end would be soft and tender. Is that close to how you'd want it?"

Tingling, her mouth open, she answered, "What would you want?"

Will grinned, offering nothing more. He knew of no one even vaguely like this girl. He thought he liked her. He loved her hair and liked how she reacted without pretense.

Celeste was at a loss for words. He'd just described their wedding as if he too had been planning it. She choked on a swallow of water, grateful to see Lucille, a tall, skinny bean with a smile. Celeste questioned if waitresses, in busy paces, even saw the people at whom they smiled. She wondered what Christmas had been like for Lucille growing up. Had the woman gotten a doll? It was hard to see grown-ups as kids. Her life at that age had been cut off early?

"Here's your chicken, kids. Where are you two from? You look like you're a match made in heaven if you don't mind my saying so. Make sure you hear our piano player. Enjoy your meal."

Clearing her throat, Celeste said, "I like her a lot, but why ask questions about where someone is from if you don't stay to listen?" Thinking about what she'd just asked made her feel foolish. Even a question showed her insides. She wanted to hide herself but couldn't. To keep herself occupied, she ate twice as much and twice as fast as Will. She was too nervous to do nothing.

"I like your question," Will said, looking earnest.

"You did? Why?" Celeste was trying to hide her smile. "I felt silly asking that."

"It shines above any question the girls I know ask. The deepest they go is they want to know who was in the car you just met or if you can buy them a root beer float. It's really mindless."

"I suppose you're right. I had never thought about that."

"That waitress is the chatty kind. Remember the Brady Café?" Will asked

"We were too poor," she said, remembering too late that his dad had paid her dad. "Oh, Will, how could I forget that Dad worked for your dad."

"Don't get frenzied," he said. "I feel bad that hired help doesn't earn more. If I hire men to assist, their salary will be a good one. I'm going to see to that."

Still, she wondered if she could say anything right. How good it would be to feel adequate and not question every word that came from her mouth—to not ask herself how she was doing or to feel she had to shut up. Her self-criticism was a constant dialogue. In that way, she preferred being alone, but it wasn't how she wanted to be. She was nothing like Sandra who was outspoken, extroverted, and loaded with confidence.

Will filled the uncomfortable silence. "Ginny loves to come here. Incidentally, she teaches at Union School."

"I can't believe it!" Celeste said excitedly, drawing the eyes of the two closest couples. She was chewing, and a piece of chicken flew from her mouth over onto Will's plate.

He roared with laughter. "Girl, when you share, you share."

Celeste only heard the last part. She was on her way to the ladies' to flush herself down the toilet.

Carrying Sylvie in her head, she raced to the ladies' room. Tears were rushing down her cheeks. Gritting her teeth, she tried not to imagine what he was thinking. She would crawl out the window and take a taxi home. Unfortunately, that was not a viable choice.

This sort of thing didn't happen to girls who were popular. She was standing at the sink when the tears came. Ten minutes passed. Someone else needed the bathroom. Filled with insecurity, she splashed water over her eyes, pasted a huge grin on her face, and charged back to the table.

She couldn't believe it when Will stood and pulled her chair out. "Glad you're all right," he said with genuine concern and relief on his face. "Don't worry about the funny things in life. Sometime I'll tell you about what I did in front of the whole school."

"What?" she asked.

He only smiled before going a different direction. "I'm curious, Celeste." he said. "Ginny wrote you several times but never heard back. She didn't think you cared anymore, so she quit writing. Mom told her Sylvie might not be giving the letters to you. Think that's possible? His eyes were unusually serious and searching. I hope that wasn't the case. It broke Ginny's heart."

"Ginny wrote me? I didn't know that." Celeste had already guessed that to be the situation. Then why were tears threatening? She didn't want Will to know about the abuse. He'd think her deserving of what she'd gotten.

Will offered her his handkerchief.

Celeste dabbed at her eyes. Her voice trembling, she said, "It makes me sad. Sylvie was so good to me. We grew too close to each other and decided to take a break. I told her that I needed some independence. Howie is too busy to see me," Celeste laughed, choking on swallowed teardrops, gripping her fingers to keep them from shaking. "Anyway, Sylvie's mail was a different story. It was her maid's fault." So Ginny had written, after all.

"Yeah?" Changing the subject, Will said, "You should see Mike. He's a senior now—at the top of his class. He's close to a genius in math and science. He'll get a good scholarship, but I don't know which college he'll choose."

"I'd like to see him. Going back a moment, what about Miss England?"

"She's married. She and Frank left the farm. They moved to Montana where his brother lives."

"Really?' Celeste asked, disappointed. "I still miss her and hope to see her again. What about you, Will? What are you doing now?"

"Wait. Tell me about Bonnie."

Gripping her glass with cold fingers … taking a sip, Celeste told Will about Bonnie, adding that Bob still worked in the grocery store in York. "Their little girl is deaf."

"I'm so sorry. I hadn't heard that. Mom and Bonnie…"

"I'll tell you all about her later. Bonnie is a wonderful mother. How about you, Will?" Celeste asked, wanting to avoid the awkwardness of Bonnie and the entire mess.

"Ranching. Also roping. I rope with Wind, my quarter horse. She's a real beauty. We travel to Gothenburg, North Platte, and up to Broken Bow. Add Thedford to the list. Its hard work but rewarding."

"Have you won any ribbons?"

Will laughed. "I can't say I've seen any ribbons being handed out to the winners. However, my earnings haven't been too shabby. I also have a collection of belt buckles to go with the money." Pushing his chair back, he said, "This has been good. Do you suppose those pigs are surviving now that they saw you and realize you're gone?"

Surprised to see her face crinkle up, Will bent over, looking at her, as though studying her thoughts. "Don't you feel good? You look awful."

"I was just thinking how much I miss farm life and the freedom to wander. I won't have kids, because I won't marry, but if I did, they would be farm through and through, and they would know every neighbor. They'd get home from school, and I'd have treats for them—peanut butter and chunks of meat and apples." Her hands came up to hide her face. She played with the corner of her eyes. She could have been pushing her tears back in, hoping they wouldn't run out. Bending as far down as she could, she began sobbing. Now what should she do?

He asked if she was okay, and had he said something? Sounds were escaping her and people were looking. Reaching over, he patted her, a gesture that escalated the sobs.

It almost seemed like Lucille had been waiting for this. Taking Celeste's arm, she bent and whispered to Will. "I'll take her to the restroom! I have a lull in work just now. We'll get this taken care of. She's not going to talk with you sitting there." Lucille smiled.

They returned fifteen minutes later. This time, Lucille was patting him. "How nice of you," she said quickly and quietly in his ear. "Keep up the good work."

Will nodded, completely confused.

Celeste, who normally would have been too embarrassed to return and who would definitely not have been all right, was quiet but composed. Will was counting in his mind the number of times she'd been teary eyed or cried this evening. He didn't get far. Lucille was wheeling a dessert cart around. She stopped at their table and looked at Will. "Having something?"

"I'm a big dessert man," he said, "but—"

Celeste, discombobulated by the fifty different kinds of desserts, did something she never did. She ordered pie with ice cream, realizing too late that Will wasn't ordering any more to eat. "Oh," she said in a dither, feeling exactly the way she had when Sylvie had become the rat-eating farm cat. "I can't have dessert if you aren't. I'll tell Lucille. I don't eat sweets anyway. I don't normally stuff; I never eat pie out. I guess I'm a little nervous."

"You need it. You're so thin. Sit," he said. She was beautiful but such a flit, he thought. She fascinated him in a sort of perverse way. It was possible that folks back home would call her eccentric. Surely she wasn't on drugs from the medicine vault at the hospital.

Lucille brought her pie back— a la mode. Will looked over just in time for Celeste to feed his chin a mouthful. Instead of letting him clean his face off, she was grabbing at napkins and was wiping him off. It seemed the audience couldn't take their eyes off her. No one was much interested in him.

She ate her final bite and licked around her lips. Will wished he was licking the pie from around her mouth. He was wondering if she was normally this talkative, a bit like a noisy squirrel.

On her behalf, she didn't want to look like a woman who dreaded going home. "Will, I feel full and quite nice with energy for doing my work this evening. I have to wash clothes, scrub the floor, call Bonnie, and clean the blinds."

Why were they leaving here so early? The loneliness was returning. He was taking her home, and the thought of never seeing him again caused her to ache terribly.

"You remind me of Ginny. She goes on rampages when things don't go her way. She dated this jerk who never asked her out until she was sure she wouldn't hear from him again."

"That's too bad. Playing hard to get can backfire on you. However, take me. I don't care whether they call again. I plan to go overseas as a nurse. I prefer one-evening encounters like this—a meal and a chat and then home."

"Really? I had planned to ask you to go for a ride. I guess that's out."

"Not really," she said too quickly. "I'll still have time to clean."

They started out on their ride. The land was beautiful, going up and down, over pine-covered hills that wound round one curve after another. Some of the hills were higher than other hills. None of what they were seeing was steep. Traveling along, they saw ferns and vines, and several kinds of flowers—pink roses on wild rosebushes, bleeding hearts, wild poppies, wild daisies, and little violet flowers that Celeste didn't recognize. It had been forever since Celeste had been to a place that was either serene or bucolic. This woodsy place brought out a longing for her roots.

In time, they came to a roadside area— dainty and charming. There were empty picnic tables set about, a reminder that summer, with its family outings and folks playing softball, horseshoe, or football, had come to an end. There would be no more kids chasing each other from tree to tree with squirt guns and water balloons —not until next year.

Will, who wanted to drive to see the edge of the area, asked Celeste if she minded. She didn't mind, so Will guided the car over a well-worn dirt road but only for a short distance.

"Look, a pond," Celeste said, surprised to see a circle of water just ahead of them. It was lovely, with several pine trees around the edge. "I didn't expect to see anything this enchanting," Celeste said.

Will nodded, pleased to have come upon something so unexpected and appealing to the girl who sat beside the opposite front window, albeit, he would have preferred to have her sitting next to him. He was used to having a girl crowding his space. Most of them used needing to look in the middle mirror as an excuse; he had never argued against the idea. It was apparent that Celeste wasn't like *anyone* he'd dated.

"Celeste, look! Deer, and there's a buck in with them. Mind if I jump out and take a look?"

"Go right ahead," Celeste said, chuckling. *You'd think he'd seen an elephant or giraffe*, she thought. Honestly. Men turned into boys when it came to deer and hunting. He was acting as if they didn't have deer back where he lived. Back at Chuckles, he'd told her about the deer he'd gotten the winter before. Getting it had required that he duck, tiptoe, crawl on his belly, wiggle under a fence, shake, whistle, squirm like a snake, and what all else. She hadn't wanted to listen in the first place. She hated hearing about anyone killing an animal. If they ever got married, she'd end hunting. What? She was doing it again. "Stop it," she scolded herself. "You are not marrying," she said aloud.

Celeste was sitting in the car, looking out and humming "Amazing Grace," and feeling astounded at how relaxed she felt when a full-blown panic attack struck. Thoughts of Will and kissing him flooded her brain, but unlike the exuberant feelings she'd had thirty minutes ago, this time terror filled her. A grown woman at twenty-one, no one had ever bothered to kiss her. What would she do if her lips refused to work? Would they feel hard and rough? Would they feel like the trunk of a tree, and what if her breath smelled like dead fish lying in the sun? What if Will was about to kiss her and she impulsively yelled out something profane, like, "Damn you?" Why hadn't she practiced kissing herself in the mirror? At the very worst, she could have asked Bonnie to be her pretend partner, embarrassing but possible. No! Not possible!

If anyone ever found out she'd learned to kiss by kissing her sister, her life, at least the life she had now, would be over. She'd have to move far away where no one had ever heard of her—a punishment worse than death. The only thing worse had been Sylvie's treatment of her. Her years at the Sobori home had seemed endless.

Waiting for Will, she didn't want the past to overcome her with the blackness that sometimes infiltrated her emotions. Being with Will tonight very possibly could begin a cycle of depression. Will was tied to every person and placed and thing she'd missed for all of these years. Even tonight there were times when she ached, listening to him talk of family. Well fine! That was then and this was now. There was no way she would fall for Will Temple. She had her plans, which included becoming nurse turned seamstress over in Europe. Men didn't exactly want women who'd had her experiences. Needing to blow her nose, she picked up the old yellow hankie. Seeing it, she smiled remembering her attic fantasies while at Sylvie's.

She had decided that Will secretly loved her and was plotting to return to save her someday. He would see her worn and outdated clothes, insisting on buying her a new outfit. Then he would ask for her hand in marriage. She would return home, a rag princess, with her prince beside her. She would have Ginny for her sister-in-law and together they'd raise kids, do their housework, and have picnics with their families. In time, these fantasies had all but faded. Yet, somehow, a small flame of hope had burned eternal.

She heard the car door open. Will slipped inside, looking like a grade-school boy on his way to a birthday party. "I never saw the buck again but counted five does and two fawn. The darn mosquitoes herded me back to the car. It's getting dark anyway. I suppose we should head back toward Lincoln. I imagine my pigs are getting lonely."

"What happens when they are lonesome?"

"They make crying sounds, and their eyes run. It becomes impossible for them to eat or sleep."

"That's the saddest thing ... I can't talk about it." Celeste dabbed at her eyes and sniffed.

"Hey, I made that up. I'm sorry. I didn't know you were that fond of pigs."

"I am. Ginny and I used to play with the baby piglets at your place."

Will yawned. "Whew! Tired"

This was it. She was going home now; she'd never see or hear from Will again. Her anxiety had come way down the minute Will scooted in beside her. There was something about his smell. She felt safe. Was it the dill, Tide, or saddle leather that moved her? It might be a mixture of all three. "Does your mom still do dill pickles and wash with Tide?" Celeste asked.

Will gave her a funny look and then laughed. "You still remember those little things? Pretty amazing."

Why had she asked him? He probably thought she was crazy instead of amazing.

What was wrong with her? Celeste wondered. When he wasn't there, she was afraid she'd make a fool of herself. Then when he was there with her, she wanted to be closer. All of this and it had only been yesterday that they'd had a brief encounter.

After all these years, she was still tied to her roots and the past and all of the Temples. She had to face it. She wasn't going to see him again. Normally she could think of something to say in most any situation. Obviously, this wasn't *normally*. Her mind was as blank as a brand-new blackboard still in its box. Her mouth felt parched, like when she was little and had played outside on a hundred-degree day when the first available drinking water was at least a mile away. Why, she wondered, was she as lonely as she'd been in kindergarten when she'd played with a motherless, homeless, stray—her only playmate? She knew the answer. In five short minutes, he was going to dump her off at home.

She turned to look at Will. She was sure he had just glanced at her.

"You seem tired, Celeste. I guess tonight's been a disappointment for you. You're probably used to doing more downtown. I could have planned more of what you do in the city."

This time, she caught his glance out of the side of her eye. What could a loser like her say to make him want to keep her out a little longer tonight?

"No. The city is noisy. I'm quiet. I'm never ever loud. I had a great time. Thank you. Thanks a lot," Celeste said, fighting a wave of anxiety.

Will's frequent glances—glances directed at her—left her tongue-tied. "I ah … like seeing the … land. I like the country. Outdoors, nature and, uh, picnics.

"Pigs! Why didn't I say pigs first thing? And … let me think awhile." Panic! She couldn't think. She was sounding like a nitwit. "Oh, yes, I know. I like big tumbleweeds. The country tumbleweeds always have stickers. It's fun to count and see how many there are," she fibbed, buying time. Where had her mind gone? "Uh, gardens. Gardens make me happy. I was thinking about all the things we saw on our drive. I saw the barbed wire fences. They're fun unless the barbs on the wire catch you. I need to get out and see the countryside more often."

What was going on in her? Will wondered. She wasn't the vivacious girl who'd run over to give him a hug at the fair last night. He knew he wasn't the best at targeting in on what people were feeling, but something told him Celeste was lonely. Maybe she wasn't ready to go home and be alone. He'd take a gamble on this premise. She was so darned lovely but so … unsure of herself. Was *unsure* the right word. She almost sounded a little goofy, like when his mom had been on strong pain medication following a surgery. She'd come home sounding weird, even though she'd been in the hospital recuperating for several days.

"Do I need to take you home? Honest, it's all right."

"Will, you think I'm tired. Really, I'm not tired," she said, trying to sound as convincing and normal as possible. "Sometimes I'm someone who gets tongue-tied. I don't want to admit this, but I'm somewhat shy at times. I'm sorry. I'm having fun. I really am," she said, looking over at him so she could see how he reacted. Would he look bored, yawn, or perhaps appear disbelieving? He did look rather bored, she thought. Feeling like a wilted flower, she decided to show him she didn't need him, that she had a big important life. "I'm very busy tonight. I use Saturday nights to clean so that I have Sundays free for socializing. As I said earlier, I'm going to clean tonight."

"I had planned to ask you if you wanted to help with the pigs, and then I decided you were too dressy. I thought we'd swing by your place and you could change. I can see it was a bad idea since you're so busy. Too bad." Will became silent, pretending to study the road ahead, although there wasn't so much as a car behind or ahead.

Her voice was childlike and slight. "Well," she blinked, "I haven't fully decided on overseas and can clean Monday night. If it's the pigs that need me, I'm thinking I should say yes."

"You're sure? I don't want to interfere. However, the pigs are a different story. They can take the blame if you wake up to a dirty house."

The night ended at eleven thirty with the hogs sleeping soundly under Celeste's amazing devotion. She was sitting in her good dress with three of the babies snuggled against her.

Will didn't kiss her. Instead, he suggested something for the next weekend. She forgot about needing to turn him down. Standing on her landing, she heard him come to a halt before he got back in his car.

"Celeste," he said, turning her way, "You really are beautiful inside and out. I'm a swine judge; however, that carries over to women. You get the first-place ribbon."

Rushing inside, Celeste went to the bedroom mirror. She had one of those tall swinging mirrors, the old-fashioned kind. She knew that her nursing friends used false flattery to enhance her self-esteem. Was Will doing the same thing? But why would he deceive her? She smiled. There was no reason he would deceive her—at least none that she was able to drum up.

Wouldn't Sylvie have liked setting Will straight tonight? She would have used subtle knife-stabbing hints like, "Celeste's nose has the same hook as a witch's nose. The beautician said Celeste's reddish hair matches a coleus plant. Celeste's legs are just short of touching the clouds."

Will's opinion held weight with Celeste. His words were powerful and real and had a permanent place in her heart. Life was like that. When certain people spoke, others listened and believed. She was about to turn away from her reflection when she saw something that drew her closer to the mirror. She saw her mother's bone structure. Celeste had the same high cheekbones, big and round eyes, full lips, long neck, and brown eyes with magenta tints. This was the first time she'd seen it. A tear rolled from her left eye and then her right and then both. Grabbing her pillow tightly, she fell on the bed, weeping.

Later, she took her mother's picture from the dresser and studied it up closely. What drew her was mother's honesty. She needn't ask anyone about Mother stealing. That was another of Sylvie's lies.

But what about her? Was she good or bad? Was she blameless? Who was at fault for her treatment? Should she accept the blame? Without a doubt, she saw herself as flawed—marked for life. What was the truth about her? That was the true confusion. Celeste couldn't ask anyone if what had happened was her fault. How would they know? Or why would they even believe such a crazy story? In her befuddlement, how could she expect a clear view of reality? Fear kept her locked in a spider web that continued to weave her tighter between the strings. She had to stop seeing Will.

Once again, Celeste studied mother's picture, discovering more similarities—full lips, slender nose, and a perfectly oval face. She'd been a child when her dad and Miss England had told her she looked like her mother. She drew Mom's tinted photograph in close. Tonight she could see the resemblance.

She felt her mother's arms around her as she fell into a deep sleep. She'd just taken a step toward reclaiming herself. Mother had been afflicted with worries from time to time. On the other hand, most of the time, she'd been well. During those times, Mother had offered incredible nurturing, especially considering that Sylvie had most likely shunned her throughout their childhood. As far as Miss Whippet knew, no one knew back then that Sylvie and Mom were sisters. Sylvie Lord would have feared Shirley White, thinking that others would guess that they were sisters. Having White for a last name meant that one was trash. Even today, Sylvie avoided admitting the truth about who she was.

*   *   *

Will had just picked her up. This time, she waited inside. He was taking her to a surprise place. Hearing her squeal like a baby pig, he chuckled. "You remind me of a kid who's never been to the circus and thinks they'll never get to go. Incredibly, someone invites them along, and they can't wait. You're funny and a joy to be around."

"I'm getting over my shyness," she chirped. "Shy people need time to warm up."

She found herself unusually content and relaxed. How would she tell him she couldn't see him again? More than likely, he wouldn't want to see her after tonight anyway. His eyes, a playful blue, made it hard to feel serious around him. She had no idea where they were going.

"Like surprises?" he'd asked when she opened the door to greet him.

No one had surprised her like this for years. Unexpectedly, she said, "When I was growing up, a surprise was Lords Acre Day, a surprise was deciding it was time to pick my pumpkin from the garden or getting to go to Brady for the Thursday night movie. A surprise was the Ringling Brother's Circus; a surprise was the RCA mother won, a surprise ..." She named ten more, including a weed patch she'd found and watered for the entire summer when she was seven, with the hope that the weeds would turn to flowers if loved. She claimed one did—a sunflower.

"How did Sylvie surprise you?"

"She didn't care for surprises," Celeste lied, thinking about the things that Sylvie had done to her: Sylvie's first big surprise had come on the first day when Celeste learned that she wasn't to snack. The next surprise was wearing used clothing from Henrietta's attic. The next one had been the day Sylvie moved her to the guesthouse to live with Elvira. Sylvie had sent her there because she'd gotten mad over not getting a birthday party. These surprises had an evil ring to them. Not wanting Will to know anything about her past life at Sylvie's, Celeste said, "Though Sylvie wasn't big on surprises, she had a big heart."

Swallowing, she remembered Christmas while her parents were living. Her parents' gifts had been small but rich in content. Celeste got socks, pants, and one toy, but the fun made up for all the toys she didn't get. Some of the good things became group activities. A puzzle had been a gift that everyone put together. Another year Dad made a small mantle size manger and Mother laid out scraps of all kinds. People made whatever they wanted to contribute. Bonnie did Joseph, Mary, and the baby. They were so very believable. Celeste's donkey became lumps of crumbling clay. Once they went caroling along with the Temples and covered the entire countryside. Another Christmas, they'd gone with the Temples to decorate a wild tree before skating on the pasture pond. Bev had provided the hot chocolate. Her last present from Sylvie was a set of curlers for her hair. The strands of her hair were too short for rolling in the hard brown curlers.

They were close to their destination. "So you're surprising me?" she wiggled and giggled. Sylvie's treats had been for Howard. Actually, it made Celeste uncomfortable to have something planned for her. "Will, next time let me earn the treat by feeding you." What? She'd said next time and hadn't a clue if there would be a third time. She wanted to run the rest of the way in order to get the pink off her flushed cheeks. Was dating always a series of goofing up?

"Relax," he said, patting her leg. "Are you always so stiff and rushed?" He looked over at her long, lean, arms and fingers, busily fanning herself, her skirt sliding just above that bony, sexy knee. Did she ever eat? He'd thought of taking her for a late- night dinner but then decided against it.

He wondered about free beef from the farm but figured her frig/freezer would be too small to accommodate half of a cow.

He'd found himself thinking of her a lot this past week, and though he was drawn to her like one of Mom's crocheted magnets was drawn to anything metal, she was simply too far away for dating— darn it! The drive back and forth was too far. Tonight would be their last date.

As soon as he drove into view of the Sunken Gardens, a place that Celeste had wanted to see since coming to Lincoln, she clasped her hands together, eyes dancing. "Will, I'm thrilled. I've never come here. The people living the closest are the last to visit the sights, or so they say. I'm so glad we're here; I'm so appreciative that this was on the agenda tonight."

He smiled, nodding the way his animals do. He found a great parking spot. "I'm glad you like the idea," he said.

Walking around the car, he was reminded of how unspoiled she was. The girls he'd dated wouldn't be happy in a quiet atmosphere like this.

Located at Twenty-Seventh and Calvary in Lincoln, the gardens were considered by many to be the most beautiful spot in Lincoln. Celeste and Will meandered about the rock ledges, ponds, and hundreds of flowers and well-tended plants. Will talked about the history behind the gardens.

"My friend's uncle worked on these ten years ago. These gardens were a public works project that gave men employment. They got paid six dollars and some cents per week. This place cost a little over two thousand dollars. If I remember right, it sits on about one and a half acres. The masses of plants and foliage came from other places, along with the huge variety of trees. Pretty impressive, isn't it?" He reached over to give Celeste's hand a quick squeeze.

Celeste felt shivery and broke out everywhere with goose bumps. Will's touch had been purposeful; it was no accidental brush but titillating and enticing.

They strolled down to the large pool of water, where a geyser was shooting up into the air. The water had a sheen that glittered like diamonds in the sun. Continuing with his small talk, Will spoke of the experiments at the gardens that had met with failure.

"It was hoped that pictures and movies could be shown on the water, using it as a movie screen. So far, technology hasn't caught up with the plans. But who knows? Maybe folks will be coming here to watch movies someday. About as likely as a man walking on the moon."

"Will, this is fascinating. Excuse me, but do you smell the grass and flowers and the scent that accompanies early autumn? I hear crickets."

"Yeah, I do, now that you bring it to my attention. It's like hearing water from a hose in summer or the smell of dill when Mom is canning."

"Mm. Sounds of home. I am dying to hear the rest."

A large statue of Rebecca at the Well was out in the center of the pool; a beautiful waterfall cascaded down around her, alluring and tempting.

"Shall we?" Will asked, pretending he was about to grab Celeste and throw her in.

"Will Temple, don't you dare. I'm not jumping in—not in these clothes."

"You don't have to wear them. Take them off. I won't look. I promise." He chuckled. Then looking her in the eye, he winked for the second time that night.

At his remark, Celeste stiffened, her jaw set, her muscles rigid. His comment had shocked and confused her. Was undressing what tonight was about? Had he just been biding his time, thinking she was a cheap floozy? "Will, you'd best take me home. I'm not the kind of girl you think I am."

Will continued his teasing. "Darn it, I had you pegged all wrong. My friend said that city girls were different than girls back home."

He turned to look at her face. Her lips drawn tight, she began walking away from him. gee whiz, had she taken him seriously? Maybe she believed everything he said, but he'd joked with other girls about such things.

"Celeste, wait up." Running to catch up with her, he reached for her arm. Instead of letting him touch her, she jerked it away, glaring at him with a look that could've cut steel.

With the palms of his hand up, he said, ""Honest, I didn't mean what I said. I wouldn't like it if you disrobed. Sure, we fellows have our fantasies, but we don't get serious with girls who, uh … undress on a second date. I'm glad you aren't like that."

"You'll never get that from me. I was meant to stay like this."

Realizing that what she'd said meant she couldn't marry(married women undressed), she said, "Someday, if I meet the man I plan to marry …"

The incomplete sentence dangled in the air as Will waited, barely breathing, for her to finish it.

Finally, she said, "I am who I am."

By now, Will was totally confused. In his estimation, Celeste seemed vulnerable, delicate, and drawn into herself, like a mistreated animal.

Walking on, Will spotted an intriguing sign on the east side, good for bailing them out of their awkward silence.

"Let's go have a look."

He didn't dare to reach for her hand, so they walked, at arm's length, in the silence of the night air, a chorus of crickets playing a symphony. When they got close to the reflecting pool, the darkness prevented them from seeing themselves. Will almost lost his balance trying to catch his reflection. Celeste caught him just in time, both sputtering with laughter.

"Will, I wanted to give you a little push."

"Yeah, I wondered if you were going to catch me or push me. Watch out!" he yelled. Will chased her as if they were playful puppies.

She ran from him, laughing. The tension loosening, they went round and round until they were both exhausted.

"We could sit on the bench and enjoy the quiet, or I could take you to one more spot."

Her face lit up like sparklers on the 4th of July.

"Let's go. Why not? You know your way around Lincoln."

"You surely know more than me. You live here."

She didn't answer immediately; she barely knew the city.

Thinking of happy times kept her mood high. Celeste unbuckled her shoes, spun, and whirled across the grass, sandals in her hand. She'd had so few good surprises and now another. She was a child riding the merry-go-round repeatedly. Maybe she would see him one more time.

"Careful! You'll get dizzy," Will warned.

"Dizzy on fun," she teased, almost losing her balance. Feeling slightly queasy, she slowed to a stop, her chattering flowing like the waterfall in the pool.

Back in Will's car, they headed north. Passing through downtown and then driving a bit further, they came to the far edge of the university's campus. Will parked in front of several tall cement pillars. "Let's go sit. I'll protect you from the boogey man."

"Good. Sometimes the dark scares me."

They sat on a ledge, Celeste leaning against the stone column, Will close beside her. She wondered how he'd happened to find this place. It was quiet, away from the noise and bustle of the nighttime world. She wondered if he had brought other girls here but reminded herself that, regardless, he wasn't with them now. He was with her, living, breathing and close enough to kiss her.

The night was one of those magical ones, the stars almost singing. The air was warm but not too warm, typical of Nebraska this time of year, and it was just the two of them, friends from long ago reunited again at last. "This is so peaceful," she murmured.

"I like that about you, Celeste Dusty. You can enjoy the quiet. This is how it is out in the hills where it's the cattle and me—solitary and calm."

Something spiderlike touched her on her head. Startled, she jumped, squealing.

"You're safe. I'm the culprit. I couldn't resist playing with that exquisite auburn hair."

In contrast to the old-fashioned haircuts she'd had at Sylvie's, her hair was long with waves pulled back on one side, feminine and sensuous, a perfect complement to her beautiful face. She wanted to cry and hug him close. She wanted Will to know how he moved her, how he held her ever-fragile heart in his marvelously constructed hands. A game of marbles in the attic seemed like yesterday.

She welcomed his hand, the one that was massaging her neck, rubbing the nape lightly with his fingertips. The strands of her hair were weightless feathers sliding through his hand. Unexpectedly, everything was blurring. She was aware but powerless against a rush of tingling, melting, swirling, flying, and swooping. It was like entering a secret passage in her mind that she hadn't known existed.

He was kissing her ear, skimming over it, both nibbles and kisses. She not only heard the quickened pace of his breathing but also felt its delicious warmth reaching down, running clear to her toes. She could hardly bear the exhilaration, hoping it would never end. She heard a low moan and realized it was from her own mouth. Her ear was on fire.

"Can I kiss you?" he asked in a breathy whisper.

"Yes," she gasped as he placed his lips against hers, parting them just a bit, and her lips knowing just what to do. The holiday sparklers, she'd thought of earlier, were there between their lips. The kiss was more glorious than a butterfly winging its way to heaven; it took her to heights that even the eagles couldn't reach. She was at the top of snowy mountains going higher, reaching for the clouds, white and magnificent. He was kissing her again and then once more.

She rested her head on Will's shoulder while he held and stroked her. All of this seemed surreal, as though, before his kiss, she'd been delicate and precious, a dried flower in an old book that might shatter if touched wrong; after his kiss, her flower was stunning and indescribable, beyond compare.

Before that night, she'd never been touched, except by Pastor or for practical purposes. Then there was Sandra's touching. During the first week of nursing classes, Sandra had insisted on cutting Celeste's hair, saying it was the worst mess she'd ever seen, a memory that elicited old hurts.

Sensing her pain, Will whispered, "It's going to be okay."

Reaching over, he began rubbing her spine rhythmically. It was how he soothed Wind, his rodeo mare. His caring released more of the pain from the past, and from time to time, he dried her eyes with his handkerchief, saying nothing. He was there, offering support, listening, being a friend. The animals had taught him how to comfort those he loved. He had learned well.

Sitting in the silent dark another ten minutes, Will yawned. "It's late. We had better get you home. I have a bunch of paperwork to have ready for Lexington early tomorrow morning. Let me help you up and back to the car. By the way, Ginny said to tell you hi. She can't hear enough about you."

"Fine," she said, swallowing. A long yo-yo string was quickly taking her down to the hot center core of the earth. She could hear it in Will's voice. If he would only ask for another date, she would say, "Yes," no matter what. Instead, she knew he wasn't going to return. After driving her to her house, Will walked her to the door where she heard him saying, "Wish it wasn't so far to Lincoln. We could do some dating, but the price of gas and all …"

Quieting her inner screams the best she could, she replied, "It is best this way." Saving her pride, she added, "A lawyer has been after me to go to a big law conference dinner in Omaha. I designed a gown and said I could escort him. He's quite a VIP and a nice fellow. That's next weekend, and then the following weekend—"

"I'm surprised you opened your own car door. Still, I like independent women. Farm ladies are like that, the salt of the earth. I thought that maybe another kiss would be nice, but sounds like you're getting your share. Bye, pretty lady."

She saw herself running after him, saying it was all a lie, but pride blocked the idea. Besides, what good would it do? Gas was expensive, but if he'd really wanted her, he'd find a way. He'd ride his horse if needed. Blinking back her despair, she realized that, just when he'd come back into her life, he'd left it. Wiping her eyes, she watched him drive around the corner and disappear. The Temples, they did that. They always disappeared from her.

*   *   *

Unlocking the door, she went to the bedroom, still riding the invisible yo-yo down even further. She'd just had the best time of her life tonight, along with her first kiss, less than an hour ago. What was the real reason for his not asking to see her again. Earlier that evening when they took a break and sat to rest at the Sunken Gardens, something happened to make her think there might be something between the two of them. First he'd told her how nice she looked. Next, Will told her about especially liking her dress. In that moment she remembered something about a dream. This caused her head to fly up. At the same time, her eyes grew rounder, and her mouth dropped open. How could she have forgotten? Will was the man in the dream.

It was about a month ago, during early summer, when she'd awakened with this unreal feeling. She'd had a dream where she met a guy who astounded her. It was crazy the way dreams are, but she knew she was going to meet him. Her dream was like a prophetic message. Be ready, it said, leaving her both skeptical and euphoric. She wasn't planning on having a man in her life because of her trust and a man's judging her. Needing to be prepared, she'd gone shopping downtown at Gold's department store, where she bought a dress and shoes for the occasion. She'd even looked at two styles of flowers, a huge gardenia and a tiny daisy, worn as hair clips. Sadly, the man from her dream didn't come, and she put the clothes away.

She wondered what Will would say if she told him everything about her dream, along with her other dreams. She wouldn't divulge the parts that had come true like the car accident and orphan ladies. If she did, she'd sound like a fortune teller at a carnival. Instead, she said, "I got this dress on a Saturday when Sandra and I went downtown. Sandra's in Omaha tonight. She's five feet and weighs one-hundred pounds soaking wet. We've been roommates since nursing school. She's engaged to Thomas Tryon from Genoa. Thomas is three inches taller. He'll soon be done

with medical school. He's getting his degree from Creighton; he'll be…
a surgeon." Skipping onto another topic," she felt it best not to reveal
Sandra's idiosyncrasies.

*   *   *

Walking over to the mirror in her bedroom, she studied her reflection.
Seeing how forlorn she felt, Celeste broke down, weeping. She wanted to
embrace something intangible in Will, who was gone for good. Knowing
it unwise, to be leaving her house this late, alone, she didn't care. Going
out to her car, she flew down the dark streets and headed north to the
fairgrounds. It was after midnight when she entered the hog barn.

Celeste was visiting the sleeping babies when Will, holding a cold, lime
slush, walked up to her. "Why don't you take that one? No one will notice."

Celeste looked up at him. The only reason he was here was to check on
the pigs a final time. She wanted to run the other way. Will would know
that she was here as a way of touching him through his hogs." "Will,"
she said, with flushed cheeks. "I couldn't sleep. The pigs were the only
ones who would visit with me this late at night and… Too much coffee I
suppose. Now, where did I see the ladies?"

Will, wanting to laugh, purposely frowned. "I didn't know that city
women went out alone so late at night."

"W…ill, it's ah; it's the independent country g…irl. I used to check your
pigs late at night, back on the farm. Really though, I've never been alone in
public late at night. I…I'm not like that." She sat there looking "caught."

Hit with compassion, Will said, "I'm a tease. I called your place to see
if you could go have breakfast and meet me next weekend, but you didn't
answer. I was sort of lonesome for you, but all I had were these pigs. I
came out her to scratch their ears." The last part was a fib. Gotta needed
some medical attention. Deciding to skip over the date with a lawyer,
whom he doubted, existed, he was propelled towards her again . Seldom
impetuous, despite his carefree attitude—instead, a man who gave thought
and consideration to his actions, he knew there was more to come between
them. "I don't do things spur of the moment, but it seems I also drank a
little too much coffee. How about some sausage and biscuits?"

Springing up off the ground, her hands ironed the wrinkles out of
her dress, her mood changing to playful. "You mean you want to have
breakfast with me?"

"Celeste Dusty, can you think of a better way to end a second date?" My papers for the courthouse can wait another day or two.

That night had been the beginning of something that was worth lasting. Their relationship had the feeling of a rich bond. Celeste, who wished there could be more, was not accustomed to this kind of happiness, the kind where life was a wonderful adventure. She knew it wouldn't last, but she couldn't stop saying yes. Each time, she'd tell herself, just one more date.

Will started coming to Lincoln almost every weekend. For now, he'd found an answer to the gas situation. Will was getting up extra early each day so he could also do the morning chores for a sick neighbor who paid him to help. Those times when Celeste worked the late shift at the hospital, they got together around 1:00 a.m. They would go for coffee and end up talking the night away. Will would drop her off and come back to her place for breakfast and to read the paper. Whenever Celeste had Sunday off, the two went to church, followed by dinner and a picture show. They took long drives and explored stimulating places. Will loved the State Capitol building, known as one of the Seven Wonders of the World. He talked Celeste into going up to the gold-domed top, not just once but five times. From that height, they'd look down at the fabulous Catholic Cathedral or try to guess the stores in the distance or just watch the miniature cars far below.

"What is this love you have for heights?" Celeste asked.

"I have something I need to tell you. I'm about to get my pilot's license. Bill Elliott, a neighbor, is letting me use his plane. I love to fly, and it's handy for checking the hills and cattle. Next to you, of course, flying is my greatest passion; I hope to own my own plane someday."

"You never mentioned your flying."

"First, I wanted to make sure I could learn."

"I know nothing about planes. How many people can go up at one time?"

"It's a Cessna 120 single engine. It only holds two people."

"Will, please be careful. I don't want you to get hurt."

"Don't worry about me. Bill's the daredevil. He loves to do aerobatic flying."

"You don't need to learn those skills. People get killed showing off like that."

"Back before we met," he added, "I enlisted with the Army Air Corps, just in case we go to war. Before I signed my John Henry, I made them guarantee that my flying experience would hold weight. I'd like to be a fighter pilot. It's a longing that's in this aggressive blood of mine. Goes hand in hand with the way I played football."

"Will! Shooting at other men isn't shooting the ball to your friends in order to score. Granted you were good at sports but..."

"Hold it, Celeste." Now, he was doing the interrupting. "America hasn't joined the fighting overseas and even if they do, I'd still be stuck at home helping," he said, knowing he would go overseas. "Mike will get a fantastic scholarship. And I want him to go to college. That's his dream. Still, I can't lie to you."

"Not at war," Celeste didn't attempt to mask her fright. "I'm already worried that the United States will become entangled in the war overseas."

"Okay, Celeste. Say we did get involved. The truth is that I'd be as scared as the next fellow would. But look at it this way. Why shouldn't I be there doing what I like to do? I'm a good pilot. Besides, I like to be up high in order to see what's blowing around. Look out there at the clouds. See any you know?"

"Well, that one over there might be a stratus?" She paused, seeing a horizontal steak in front of her eyes. "Will there's a banner in front of us. What on earth is it?"

'What's it say? Read it. The letters look big."

"It says, The Temples Want Celeste at Their Thanksgiving Dinner!

"Will, please don't joke with me. You wouldn't would you?" her face begged, unsure of him. "Is this a joke?"

"Have I done something to make you think I'm a tease?" he smiled. "This is for real. If I didn't bring you, Ginny and Mom would throw me out. I looked at your schedule on the calendar. You have Thanksgiving and the next day off."

"It's about time," she giggled. "It's my homecoming."

"I should have my license by then. I'll fly you from Lincoln to the farm."

"So if we crash, I'll use my nursing skills to save us, huh?"

"Of course," Will said, putting his arms around her.

* * *

Celeste pretended that she and Will could continue dating for the rest of their lives. She wouldn't have to call off the relationship. Most of the time, this imaginary game worked but not always. She pictured herself marrying him just as she had years ago as a girl. Unfortunately, Sylvie's dour chin would float in, ruining her fantasy. Will's bride would need to be lily white and pure. Celeste was at her best when her nursing kept her busy. She preferred it that way. Time to sit and dwell allowed her insecurities to rule. If left to her own devices, she didn't see herself as "Will Temple material." He was a rich, successful rancher, she a girl who'd never had much financially. Living in a wealthy environment had left her in shreds. Over time, she'd gained in security, but now the past was like an obsession, especially what happened with Pastor and telling Will. It was still difficult not to blame herself, thanks to Sylvie.

On a Thursday morning, two weeks later, watching down below, Celeste could see the farmhouses, along with the barns and animals—minute dots in the snow. Celeste had never been happier; she felt free as a bird here in the sky with Will at the controls.

"This is wonderful," she exclaimed. "Any worrying I did was a waste of time. The ground below would make a wonderful crossword puzzle or checker board."

Will grinned. "We'll be home in a wink. You're coming has the family all thrilled."

After all these years, she was about to see the Temples again. She tried not to ask herself why Bev and Clark hadn't rescued her by having the police come take her away from Sylvie. Thinking about that caused her horrible pain and it also aroused anger that was directed at them. She wondered what Ginny was like and would Ginny even like her? What about the others? Stopping her worries, she made a conscious decision to let her anxieties evaporate. She would lose herself to the clouds, hoping not to miss this wondrous flight with the man she loved. Would she ever have this chance again?

They passed over numerous towns, and the cars below looked smaller than ladybugs, the fields like neat squares of ribbed fabric. The most awesome was the icy Platte River, its water running about and around sandbars, winding its way across the prairie while massive trees grew on either side. Women would be basting crispy, brown turkeys, those delectable birds they'd slipped in the oven well before dawn. This thought reminded Celeste of waking as a child on Thanksgiving morning to smell the enchanting aroma of pumpkin pie spices, turkey, dressing, steaming corn and oysters, green beans from the garden, and homemade rolls. Other goods were sticky yams, Waldorf salad, mashed potatoes and gravy, pies, whip cream, and mother's currant jelly. Much of the meal came directly from the garden, from picking berries, or milking the cows.

Will sat calling out the names of towns and the sites. "Look! Kearney is below us." He did the same thing with Wood River, Lexington, Cozad, and other towns. "Some good-looking horses down on that farm," he hollered. "Gothenburg coming up. See, there's the school. There's the water tower. See the power plant."

Turning the plane south and then west, he headed for the Temple place.

"There's Banner Church," he yelled over the engine's noise. "They *celebrated Lo*rd's Acre Day not long ago. We're flying over the home of the man who lent me this plane. We're about home. We'll land down there on that flat dirt strip by the grain bin."

The ground rose up to greet them, and in what felt like the passing of a moment, they were down and the plane was bouncing along the frozen, hard as rock, dirt, out by the grain bin, the snowy hills behind them, the corn stalks frozen and fallen.

Celeste's stomach lurched. It wasn't the landing's fault. She would be seeing the family in what promised to be an emotional greeting. She would finally be doing what she had longed to do for so many years. It hardly seemed real.

The prop was still winding down as Will jumped out to help Celeste to the ground.

"I don't want that tasteful wine suit of yours to get dirty. You look wonderful." His lips were a breath away from hers when Ginny came whizzing in, burrowing her head against Celeste's shoulder.

"I can't believe it's you. It's really you. Celeste, do you remember me?"

"Ginny," Will scolded. "Give her a chance to breathe and see that it's you," Will scolded, thinking Ginny would scare Celeste away. A second look told him that wouldn't be a problem. Celeste was hugging her back while they both cried. They stood that way, locked together, Ginny pulling Celeste closer than Celeste had allowed Will to get.

However, wasn't that the way it went? He supposed it impossible to have Celeste to him the entire time she was here.

The long ago friends stood back, giggling like schoolgirls, carefully studying one another, both surprised at how the other had "grown up."

Ginny, as adorable and peppy as ever, still wore her hair in pigtails and still had the same freckles on her cute nose.

In comparison, Celeste was tall and poised—a delicate beauty with her hair in a permanent wave. It was obvious they were still best friends, whose bond had never been broken.

"Guess what?" Ginny said. "You and I get the upstairs to ourselves tonight. Mom thought we'd be too noisy."

Will interrupted, saying they should head for the house. Reaching inside the plane, he grabbed Celeste's suitcase. They could talk inside where it was warm. No sense in waiting in the cold air.

"The walk isn't bad if we don't dally," he said, as a black car flew up, skidding to a stop.

"That's Mike showing off." Will stood shaking his head and then yelling, "Mike, get out and say hi to Celeste. You're always asking about her; here she is."

"Will, you never told me that. I'm touched," Celeste said.

"Mike's' crazy about you. He still remembers everything you and Ginny did with him."

Celeste flew to Mike with open arms. A bit embarrassed now that Celeste was right in front of him, Mike stepped aside, just in time to see Celeste whizzing past him, hitting the ice, falling hard. Glowering, Mike shook his purple face at Will.

"Ma'am, I'm sorry. Here, let me pull you up."

"Looks like you and I need to get even with your brother," Celeste smiled. Brushing her coat off, her pride was briefly hurt. Soon they were off in Mike's car.

From Will's comments, his parents thought her life had been quite happy. Bonnie was the only one who knew the truth, and even she didn't know about the Pastor. Celeste had told no one. She couldn't share that part of her life with anyone, fearing that whoever found out would blame her. At times, she still blamed herself, so why wouldn't they?

Celeste had just stepped inside the oak foyer when Bev padded in from the kitchen.

"Let me hug you, girl." Drawing Celeste against her weighty stomach, her heavy bosom became a soft pillow. "Look at you. You're so thin. Pretty, but thin. I guess they haven't been feeding you at that hospital in Lincoln."

"Clark, come in here and see who we've got."

Timeless and gentle, Clark came in from doing some chores.

"Celeste, we're so happy to see you," he said as he clasped her hand and held it with honest emotion.

"Told you they missed you," Will teased.

Celeste excused herself to wash her hands and "fix up a bit." Then realizing she didn't know if the bathroom was still outside, she acted nonchalant.

"Could I use the bedroom mirror?"

"I knew that was going to happen," Will hooted. "We're like city folks now that we have a bathroom upstairs. I'll set your luggage in my old room."

Going upstairs brought back emotions and sensations of that day so long ago when Ginny had packed her things. Determined not to let old demons grab hold and ruin her time here, she tossed those evil feelings out the window. Now wasn't the time to wonder about Bev and Clark and where they'd been during her time at her aunt's. Returning to the dining room, she took a seat, enjoying the sight of the holiday table. A lovely cornucopia, overflowing with vines, pumpkins, gourds, and autumn flowers, sat between, with candles on either side.

"I fixed that just for you, Celeste," Ginny said, dashing through the room.

"What's it been now?" Clark asked in his pragmatic farming voice. "Nine, maybe ten years? Whatever the number, you can be assured, we've never forgotten you."

"Isn't she lovely?" Bev chimed in from the kitchen. "Still looks like her mother." Then, sealing her hands around her mouth, she bellowed hog-calling style, "Five minutes, everyone. We're eating in five minutes. Wash up." Bev was still the same confident, no-nonsense lady.

All was well on this most blessed Thanksgiving Day. In fact, the walnut table was too crowded to hold food, so instead, Bev had loaded the sideboard with turkey, dressing, mashed potatoes, gravy, candied sweet potatoes, molded lime Jell-O, strawberry salad, cheesy corn, baked lima beans, rolls with marmalade and real butter, and of course, cranberry sauce. Celeste's stomach growled loudly, and she hoped no one else heard it. She was so ready to eat, but Bev and Ginny were holding things up. Bev was methodically fixing six glasses of water while Ginny was walking back and forth, from the kitchen, in search of the "right" serving spoons.

"Hungry?" Will asked, leaning toward Celeste.

"Starved," Celeste said, speaking in a whisper.

"Mom, sit down. Celeste wants to eat," Will yelled. "She's starved."

"Will! I'm not either," Celeste muttered as she slapped his thigh.

"Well, I hope you're famished," Bev said as she and Ginny finally sat down. "I want all of you to be good and hungry. We need to clean up this food."

Celeste reached for her fork interpreting that as the go-ahead. Noticing five bowed heads, she all but threw her fork down. Catching Will's grin, she blushed.

"I should have reminded everyone," Bev said. "First we'll join hands and pray."

Everyone joined hands, making a chain around the oblong table. After a prolonged silence, Clark began, "Lord, we invite you to our table today. We thank you for our many blessings. This family is as healthy as last year, and we ask your blessings upon our doctors. We thank you that our guest, Celeste, is with us today. Lord, you bring her here for a visit, and we know that her presence today is part of your heavenly plan for those of us who currently dwell on this earth. Bless and be with Will, our pilot, that both may return home safely. We pray for the well-being of our livestock and, if it is your will, may our farm grow and prosper with the blessed rain that you send down from heaven."

For Celeste, this was unfolding, just as she had pictured one of Bev's Thanksgivings; it was the opposite of Sylvie's. With Sylvie in command of the day, instead of enjoying a family meal prepared and infused with love, Sylvie's clan celebrated Thanksgiving at hotel restaurants, eating food prepared and served by strangers. Sylvie would make reservations well ahead of time, requesting a family-style liver dinner with the fixings. Dessert was black walnut pie. The fact that no one, but Sylvie, wanted liver didn't bother her. If anyone complained, she yelled, "Make like you like it!"

Celeste's attention returned to the moment! Clark had been praying for close to five minutes and was still going strong. What if she married Will and he prayed for this long? She and the kids would starve to death. Although she'd never seen Will stop long enough to give thanks, giving a long-winded blessing might be in his genes. Feeling his hand let go of her hand, the next thing she knew, his fingers were playing with her thigh. Honestly! Not at the table during the prayer. In the most lady-like manner, she could manage, she reached under the table. Taking ahold of his hand, she forced him to join the circle of hands. She hoped his audacity had gone unnoticed by closed eyes.

Clark continued, "And dearest Lord, we give thanks for our country church. We most earnestly ask that you guide and watch over our pastor. Lord, this prayer would be remiss if I didn't mention Union School, Ginny, and the children. Keep them safe and guide their minds in Christian ideals and beliefs."

Will, Ginny, Mike, and even Bev were squirming by now. When would he stop?

Bev, deciding that enough was enough, declared, "Lord, thank you for everything, everywhere. Amen!" she yelled, her fist coming down on the table, like a gavel. Shocking everyone, she began passing the dishes of food.

"Take a helping and pass it on. No need to hold us up," she said, tossing her blond bangs in Clark's direction. Not ready to forgive him for cooling the steaming hot food, she gave him a piece of her mind. "Clark, prayer is a wonderful and powerful thing, but not ten minutes worth and not at the expense of turning my food to ice. The older you get, the longer you pray. In two minutes, you could have said everything that's worthy of prayer. Next year, you'll rehearse, using the stove timer."

Reaching for Bev's hand, Clark said, "Food looks as delicious as ever. And so do you."

Clucking, Bev blushed at her lover's compliment. The only sounds now were forks striking plates, chewing, swallowing, and slurping. Momentarily, the hunger lowered.

"Celeste," Bev asked. "Do you do any cooking or baking?"

"I'm experimenting; call me a beginner because—"

Will's eyes lit up at a chance to praise his mother and seem helpful to Celeste. "Mom's a great cook. She'll be glad to teach you everything."

"Will," Ginny admonished, "that's not something you say to a girl who you really like."

"That's not necessarily true," Bev joined in. "Celeste, we'll do some cooking together on your trips back."

Celeste's face turned a deep scarlet. Will had said nothing about a return trip. How was she supposed to respond? She couldn't say, "Oh, sure, I'll be back for cooking lessons. Teach me how to make chicken and dumplings."

Mike, the "quiet one" was determined to have his turn too. "As soon as they get married, Mom can be her teacher."

"Hold it," Clark said. "You all keep this up, and Celeste won't return. She'll think we are a family of busybodies. Besides that, you're making her blush."

"Time for dessert," Bev said, loud enough to get everyone to stop talking. "We have delicious pies. I did five kinds—pumpkin pie, which is Clark's favorite; cherry Ginny; Will's favorite, lemon meringue; and blueberry for little Mike. I almost forgot mincemeat for me. Celeste, your favorite is?"

"I like all of them," Celeste said. Hers was strawberry, which wasn't on the menu today.

"It's strawberry, Mom. Can you make her one?"

"Will, I just happen to have one waiting for her!"

Celeste, not hearing her and embarrassed because he hadn't said anything about her returning, said, "Really no, please don't ..." Her cheeks were burning hot. She didn't know what worried her most. Was it being fawned over or the fact that she and Will might not be together next Thanksgiving?

That's when Bev sat her piece of pie in front of her.

Celeste grabbed Will's hankie out of his pants pocket. "Oh, thank you, Bev," she said, wiping her eyes with the hankie while pretending to be blowing her nose.

Seeing this, Will grinned as he nudged her.

When the meal was over, Will asked if she would like to walk over and see his bachelor pad. Stepping inside the old place, Celeste was shocked to find that the house, where she had once lived, was scratched, cracked, and musty. "Like my decorating touches?" Will wanted to know.

"It has potential," she said, wondering where the potential was hiding.

"This lady helped me. It's going to be my first home when I marry. Be sure to go up and see the bathroom. Thanks to my helper, it's feminine looking."

She tried to act as if the "feminine touch" didn't matter. This was his way of safely breaking the news, letting her know he had someone else. She became overly talkative to prove she didn't care—but boy, it mattered. Under her cheery veneer, she suffered a seething kind of ache. Why care, when she couldn't marry him anyway? she asked herself.

Before long, Bev and Ginny came for coffee. Drinking it oily black, from four cracked cups, Bev talked about helping with the hammer and nails. Celeste wondered if she'd used them to make the chips and dents in the wall when she heard Bev say, "I did most of the bathroom."

Celeste glared at Will. How dare he put her through this agony? His mother was the decorator! Will grinned, winking at Celeste.

Interrupting the moment of comedy, Bev grew serious. "Celeste, I am so glad that all turned out well for you. Will and Ginny don't know this, but Clark and I went to a lawyer after you left. I was real suspicious. Mr. Wright, the man we saw, said that most likely, we didn't stand a chance. He assured us that Sylvie would be a fine woman. Regardless of what he said. I worried. Ginny wrote but didn't hear. Will explained and told us what happened. I'm sorry about that. Personally, after what she did with Bonnie, I can't say I could ever befriend the woman. With Bonnie it's different. I'd like to see her and those kiddies of hers again someday. Will told me about her having a deaf one along with that boy."

Sweating, Celeste nodded, relieved to pieces, thinking that Bev must still have suspicions about Sylvie. Celeste was overjoyed that they didn't blame Bonnie.

*   *   *

Evening was spent nibbling and stuffing full stomachs with leftovers, building a fire, and playing pinochle. Quiet Mike was the winner at everything. He wanted Celeste to have his girlish prizes—a potholder in the shape of Nebraska, a plastic spatula with a long handle for stirring candy or jam, pink pillar candles, and laundry soap that smelled like a spring breeze on the prairie. Acting envious, Ginny, playfully, tried to snatch them away. Refusing to let Ginny have them, Celeste hit her with the spatula, saying, "Bad girl," while Ginny yelped and whined.

Finally, on Bev's orders, the young people took their energy outdoors. First thing, Will grabbed Ginny and tossed her into a snow pile. That prompted a snowball fight, everyone creaming each other several times. Celeste promised herself, that someday she would have more nights just like tonight.

After the others retired indoors, Will said he wanted to check on Wind and the other animals and invited Celeste along. The walk was romantic, with Will holding her gloved hand; he said that having her there was a blessing for the entire family. "You know, I never told you this, but we weren't the same family without you and Howie. You two were like the missing pieces that complete a jigsaw puzzle. Maybe he'll come out someday. Sylvie and your uncle could come with him."

Will's talk of asking Howie for a visit, set Celeste on edge. Will still didn't know the real reason she didn't see them. All he knew was what she'd said on their first date. Maybe she would tell him someday soon.

Unexpectedly, he stopped her just before they reached the corral gate. Not saying a word, he turned her toward him. Putting his mouth on hers, he pulled her against him, slipping his hands inside her coat, brushing them against her breasts and moaning.

She gasped as electricity shot through her, wishing they were married and free to join together. Pulling him closer for a split moment, she thought she'd never forget how badly she wanted him. Pressed against each other in the moonlight, she let him hold her a few more seconds. Then lightly laughing, she pushed him away, knowing she mustn't go any further. Still, she ached for him and wanted him—more than she'd ever wanted anything.

Even so, she was plagued by insecurities about her body and the fears she'd endured with Pastor. If she was going to take a gamble, she wanted that man to be Will when they married. Who else could she trust? Unfortunately, he'd never said he loved her. How could she imagine Will marrying her?

Running his hand through her hair, he smiled and gritted his teeth, groaning. Taking her hand, he walked on with her beside him. *Dang it!*

The couple went on into the barn, where they talked to Wind and two other horses, rubbing their noses and giving them Thanksgiving apples. Will stepped away to get some oats. When he returned, he put his arms around Celeste from the back. His surprise move tweaked her frayed nerves straight into a flashback.

Screaming, she blindly hit out at him, yelling for him to keep his hands off her. Shaking and white with fear, she took off running toward the house. He caught her, but she kicked hard, striking him on his ankle. Angry and limping, Will told her to go on inside, that he would see her the next day. Celeste slipped quietly into the foyer, where she just stood, not moving, until she heard Bev walk by. She was beside herself with shame.

Later, she woke Ginny. She had never shared her story with anyone, and she couldn't bear it any longer. Ginny wanted to go to the bathroom first. She needed to put her hair in rollers for tomorrow. When she returned, Celeste, who was emotionally exhausted, had fallen asleep. Ginny was gone when Celeste woke the next morning. Her new boyfriend had invited her to his home for the day. But she'd left a note: "You fell asleep. I love you, best friend. We'll talk more another time."

Breakfast was miserable. Will didn't say a word. He sat there messing with the food on his plate, reminding her of a two-year-old who refuses to eat. He even ignored his mother, who asked him if he wanted more pancakes, further asking him if he felt well. Instead of answering, he left for the bathroom.

Celeste was dumbfounded—certain their relationship was over. She felt dark. Shame swam about, coloring her emotions. She forced a smile while chattering away, certain the others noticed her exaggerated mood opposed to his silence.

The flight home proved even worse than breakfast. Will didn't say one word to her the entire time. Did Will think she had rejected him or that she was troubled? She bet the latter. She wanted to talk and explain what had really happened. This time, she knew that if she told Will her secrets, she'd never stop crying.

At last, the flight was over. He rolled the plane to a stop on one of Lincoln's landing strips and went around. Opening her side, he helped her down, handing her the old tapestry suitcase. Not daring to look him in the eye, she headed for the airport door. She was reaching for the handle when something grabbed her elbow. That's when she noticed how pale he looked. Had he been that white this morning? "Will? You look pale. Are you sick?"

"Flu," he said, running for the bathroom.

So that was why he hadn't talked to her? When he returned he told her he felt better.

"But are you able to fly?" she asked concerned. "I'm fine. I'll call you soon." Turning, he headed back to the plane.

At least she knew why he'd acted distant. Relieved, she felt the warm sun on her face, as she danced along to her car. Before driving away, she watched the red plane as it rose, going through the clouds, until it disappeared. She would call tonight to make sure he made it home safely. Celeste wondered what Will thought of her terrified behavior the night before? She felt immense shame and fear. Though he was sick, she'd obviously upset him.

*   *   *

A massive statewide blizzard struck Tuesday. Everything shorter than three feet was covered up with snow, including her car. The hospital provided rides to work. With phone lines out of commission and Sandra working the evening shift, Celeste was alone with her radio for news. Deep in despair but not understanding why, she couldn't eat or sleep. Her worries about the flashback and her reaction concerned her. Will would never be back again.

She'd called his home and talked to his mother about Will's flight home but hadn't spoken to Will since the airport parting and wondered why he hadn't called. She fretted despite a good explanation. *He was ill with the flu,* a statewide epidemic. She tried baking but tossed the cookies away, tried hemming, got half-done, and quit. Much of the time, she was in tears

Howie came to mind as she remembered how much she'd once loved him. She and Bonnie had tried, without success, to figure out what they should do. Miss Whippet, who had made a point of getting to know Howie, reported that he appeared to be doing fine.

The following weekend, December 6, seemed like an eternity away. Remembering the saying about how absence makes the heart grow fonder, Celeste disagreed. Longing for Will only intensified her misery. She had a recurring nightmare that they were at the altar, and he was reaching to slip the ring on her finger; instead, he threw it to the guests before running out of the church and disappearing. Confined to the house with few chances to interact, Celeste sank further into dejection.

When the phone finally rang again, Friday evening, Celeste lost hold of the tight control she was trying to maintain over herself. She was a dam breaking–a river overflowing and flooding the prairie. Her restraints were gone. She never wanted to be without him again. Acting on impulse, rather than contemplating what she would say, words ran out of her like a tributary running wild. In her mind, Will was calling to make up, to say he was sorry for being short.

As soon as she heard his voice on the other end of the line, she blurted out, "Will, let's get married," immediately feeling like a fool.

"Will, are you still there? I don't hear you."

"I'm here," Will said as his mind reeled. He felt half-dead from fatigue and battling nature to keep the cattle and other livestock alive. He was calling to see how she was doing, because he had worried about her. However, the frozen cattle and calves put him in another world. Seeing the livestock like that, knowing they'd suffered, helpless to change their plight, hurt bad. Four of them, two cows and two calves, found frozen in the canyon. "Look, Celeste, it was a hard week."

"Will, what I meant to say was, 'Let's get together.' I just got my words mixed up due to exhaustion. Please forget it," she pleaded. "Everything's gone wrong lately. No phone, snowed-in, my car stuck, home alone, lonely and wishing you were here."

Will sat in his kitchen, fingering a diamond in a red velvet box. It had been his grandmother's—Dad's mom. The ring was a rare beauty. He'd been planning to propose come Christmas.

A form of disgust overcame Celeste. Why wasn't he saying anything? "You just said you had a hard week. So talk about it." Celeste's voice was sharp. She knew he hadn't called to make it right. Somehow, she knew. It was the tone in his voice

"I'll call back another time," he said, showing no emotion.

"No," she said, sensing abandonment, while going to pieces. "It's been a long, hard week for me too. My car remains under snow. The hospital arranged for the police to drive us to work. I stood waiting. When one of the policemen arrived, he asked if I was a married to "Frosty the Snowman." Otherwise, Sandra and I worked opposite hours, so I was all alone."

"Lucky you. We only slept a few hours a day. This isn't the time to talk. I'll call back." He'd planned to say more but just couldn't talk; instead, all he wanted was sleep. "We'll talk later."

"Will don't hang up."

Silence met her on the other end.

*   *   *

"Bonnie, I am terrible." Celeste could see that her lies were growing like the links of a chain. One lie led to another. Did she owe Will the truth? Would Bonnie or Will, either one, listen? If they acknowledged what she'd said, it would help.

"Sister, you always feel guilty," Bonnie replied. "You two should have listened to each other, but guilt isn't the answer. Anyway, why do you feel guilty? You were honest. He should have understood; instead, his week had him in a bad mood. Please, stop blaming yourself for everything. The cattle and losing some of them might have been the entire problem."

"I'd better go. This costs a bunch."

"I understand. My little girl wants to meet Bev."

"Hopefully, she will," Celeste said, hanging up.

Will didn't call back that week. She still had faith that he would. If he did, she was going to apologize.

*　　*　　*

Saturday when the phone rang, it was Will. He sounded normal, as though nothing had happened between the two! "Celeste, I'll be down next Saturday if that's okay with you."

"Will," she said, trying to stay calm.

"Mom found some of your Mom's Christmas decorations after you went to Sylvie's. I'll bring them with me. Another thing—Are you having Christmas dinner over there with the family? I sure do want to see Howie again."

Thank goodness, she'd thought of something. It came to her because of Sandra doing a holiday meal, for Thomas, a week later. Jumping in, "I would like to have you over for Christmas dinner. I'll cook and decorate things up in holiday fashion. It will be my first time. I'm not doing a turkey. Wait a little longer for Howie."

Will chuckled. "I'm the first one, huh? You're making me the guinea pig for your future dinners. By the way, I'll tell Mom to write and tell you how to do the turkey."

"Will, this is hard enough for me as it is. Please don't ruin this with jokes. I'm serious about wanting to treat you." Another idea came along. "I have a surprise for later, and it doesn't involve us taking off our clothes, so don't say it." Celeste had tickets for the movie, *Citizen Cane*, a huge success at the box office.

Feeling both thrilled and scared about the upcoming event, she wanted her cooking to top Bev's. She'd do her mother's special—sauerkraut and a pork roast.

She was back to pretending she would marry Will. It had been close to five years since she and Sylvie had last seen each other. Celeste had moments where she wondered if anything bad had actually happened. Maybe she'd dreamed it all up in her mind. Of course, she knew better.

*　　*　　*

Christmas decorations filled the halls of the hospital. It was there that Celeste and Sandra crossed paths. Sandra was filling in for a nurse who'd gone home sick. Tomorrow she'd be going to a funeral back in Fullerton. Her cousin's child had died at age five. The little girl had finally succumbed to a long battle with polio.

"I'll get up early, in the morning, and fix coffee for you," Celeste said. "You leave for Fullerton at seven. Right?"

"The funeral is at two in the afternoon. I'll have to be on the road by six o'clock. I want to have time to go home. That way, I can freshen up before going to the church. By the way, get me two rolls. Pick out the biggest ones, and make sure they're caramel pecan. Get them at Ideal."

Celeste shook her head. "God gave it all to you—blonde hair and brains, a doctor for a fiancé, and the metabolism to eat like a grown man. Add to that the fact that you're stacked."

"Poor pitiful Celeste. All you have are those long, curvy legs and a face that makes you Susan Hayward's twin. And then there's playboy Will, that cowboy fellow you've got wrapped around your little finger."

"Sandra, he isn't a playboy, and I don't have him wrapped around my little finger. You're the one who has a guy spun around your fourth finger. What about Thomas, the about-to-graduate doctor. He's going to make you fabulously rich. I hope the poor guy knows about your spending habits and tastes."

"You'd better keep that to yourself. One word and I'll tell Will about your addiction. I heard they only have one store out there on the prairie. It's Woolworths! You'll be in good shape when you marry. It's Will's checkbook that'll fall apart."

"Sandra! We aren't going to marry, and Will doesn't live on the prairie. He lives in paradise."

They both heard a ruckus down the hall. A nurse was yelling, "Sandra! We have some beds to wash."

Celeste left, heading east for Ideal Groceries in south Lincoln. Sandra bought everything there. An excellent cook, she'd won a trip to New York to meet Marjorie Husted, the originator of Betty Crocker.

*   *   *

The car was nice and snug by the time she reached South Street, the street on which the hospital sat. They would indeed have a white

Christmas. Huge soft flakes had begun falling, adding to the snow that was already covering the lawns. People—including her—were forever out scooping the stuff. Sandra inevitably constructed elaborate excuses to get out of helping with the shoveling.

Celeste felt dreamy and relaxed as she headed toward 27th Street. When she reached that intersection, there was so much oncoming traffic she decided she had plenty of time to go on a scenic ride to a part of town she loved. As she turned onto Sheridan Boulevard. A group of carolers were out, which surprised her as it seemed too early in December. "Silent night, holy night," they sang, in voices that were soft and melodious, as the dusk shaded into dark and snow came faster.

The homes in the area were as beautiful as a picture postcard — stately pine trees jutted upwards, meeting the clear white stars overhead. Pulling to the side of the street and parking, Celeste thought of the Temple ranch with its big hills. She wanted to be standing at the top with Will's arms around her. She imagined the two of them alone there with God and the owls in the cedar trees, an eagle hidden away, watching for prey and a coyote's howl echoing for miles in the crisp, and cold air. So much of her heart was still back there, having stayed behind with the girl who'd gone to Union School. Perhaps that younger Celeste was waiting for this older Celeste to return home.

The huge older houses where Lincoln's high-society families lived, with pinecone wreaths and velvet ribbons tacked to thick doors, crackling fires, and sparkling trees that tickled the high ceilings—each as awesome as the next. One featured a white wicker sleigh, Santa sitting on the seat, two wicker deer pulling it along. The display was sitting under the breezeway of a long, sprawling ranch house, and Santa had a pile of wrapped packages on both sides of him. The house beside it had a merry-go-round that turned, bit by bit, showing off the lights, playing Christmas songs and giving rides to storybook characters. The mansion across the street boasted a party. Dapper gentlemen, driving the finest of cars, escorted ladies draped in long, satin dresses.

As fascinating as it was, she didn't want this for herself. Like the Temples, she belonged to the small towns and their parks, to Union school, to the prairie and the people who lived there, to the hills with the cattle grazing and a group of horses chewing grass and whinnying into the clear, cold air. She belonged to the magpies and bald eagles, the prairie dog towns, the mossy, snail-filled tanks, and to windmills whirring out their songs to nearby ponds. She belonged to farms with barns for playhouses and ditches to swim in, to fruit trees that caught warm breezes, to gardens with scarecrows, chicken coops, and pigpens.

She belonged to Banner Church, to Union Aid Society, and to Ginny. Most importantly, she belonged to Will, who was succeeding in finding and drawing her out—returning her to a smidgeon of the girl they'd both known. "Will!" she cried through rolled up windows. "You and I belong together." And tomorrow night, in a blink and a wink, Celeste was going to knock Will off his feet. Her arsenal would be her home-cooked dinner, but sadly, there was no way he would still want her, once he knew about her past.

*   *   *

The next morning Celeste scurried over with Sandra's first cup of coffee as Sandra sat gobbling a roll. Sandra had chosen a light gray suit and a lacey white blouse, accentuated by the pearl necklace, a gift from Thomas. Her long nails were deep "lipstick" red. Would "cover girl Sandra" be a distraction for the mourners, Celeste wondered, considering the tragic nature of the funeral? Celeste looked over at Sandra, who'd begun her purposeful blink, the one that told Celeste to listen up to what she was about to say.

"Celeste, I snooped through some of your groceries last night while I was eating my snack. I had an apple and chocolate milk. I had to add a fourth of a can of chocolate to get the stuff to taste chocolaty."

"You had milk and an apple? That sounds good." Ugh, she thought.

"What's the sauerkraut...?" Sandra asked, wiggling her tiny nostrils.

Celeste jumped in. "You don't need to make a big deal out of it, Sandra." Celeste didn't want to listen to Sandra's histrionics. "The kraut is dumped over the roast as well as the cut-up vegetables."

"Sauerkraut is stinky," Sandra said, squeezing her tiny aristocratic nostrils together. Pewee! You don't want your lover to walk into an acerbic smell like that. His maleness will go as flat as a tire."

Needing to convince herself she was tough, Celeste folded her fingers into a hard ball. "Sandra, unplug your nose. You sound like those nasal ten-year-olds who wear those ugly nose plugs and bob up and down in the swimming pool, spitting out water. Real men love sauerkraut, and Will happens to be a real man. However, Will isn't my lover. We've been over and over that. I cringe when you say *lover*. Keep your labels to yourself. I will never ever do 'that thing' that couples do outside of marriage. And since I don't plan to marry, I won't do it."

"I'm sorry, but please, can I say something?"

"Say it," Celeste's said apprehensively.

"You know, I won't be here tonight. If you and Will would ...Well, it's like this. No one would ever know if Will stayed overnight. My sheets that you like, the ones with the cranberries, are all washed, and you could put..."

"Sandra, stop! You're incorrigible, just like Mrs. Willis said." (Mrs. Willis was their nursing instructor.)

Sandra ignored her but not for long. Sandra got this zoomed-in look before she came in for the kill. She was planning something. "Have you looked at this old gray kitchen? You don't want to wine and dine Will in this ugly room. You could use our small living room ell, and turn it into the Christmas Cafe. The archways on each side of the kitchen will serve as open doorways for entering and exiting. The space isn't roomy, but it's big enough for my Duncan Phyfe. I suppose I could let you use it."

"That would be wonderful, but it was your grandma's gift for getting your nurse's diploma."

"Grandma will never know. Her ashes are happily blowing about. Please excuse me while I make a little list. We need to make our place here beautiful, to doll it up. I have a few things for you to get today."

"What? I'm too busy as it is."

"Celeste, I need for you to listen. Make sure you get a dozen roses. Thomas likes nothing less than a dozen. And for goodness sakes, stay out of Woolworths and other five-and-dime stores. Use jewelry stores for your finer items. When you and Will marry, show the people some culture."

"Sandra, I'm insulted. We have libraries, plays, theaters, factories, gorgeous clothing, airplanes, cars, jewelry stores, clubs, drugstores, and more."

Seemingly ignoring Celeste's retort, Sandra slipped into her long, black coat. "Here's the list I wrote. Remember, get everything on the list." Halfway out the door, Sandra returned with open arms. She hugged Celeste, her body warm and tingly, almost vibrating with emotion. Celeste hugged her back, her earlier frustration, at least, temporarily forgotten.

"Bye, doll. Have a wonderful weekend. I'll be anxious to come back and see the house, the Christmas Palace."

As Celeste closed the door behind her roommate, her thoughts opened. She realized that any favor Sandra had done for her was a payback for things Celeste had done for Sandra. But the ledger seemed out of balance to Celeste. She raked, scooped, and mowed. And another thing, Celeste drove Sandra to work and picked her up. That way she didn't have to get into a cold car. On top of that, Celeste did Sandra's grocery shopping, mailed her letters, hung her sheets out on the line, fixed her coffee, and made an extra run after dark to get her roommate's favorite rolls. She cleaned the house and on and on. Even Will had noticed. He didn't like it one bit.

She decided to put her foot down now. Wearing only her robe and slippers, she rushed out to Sandra's car, still warming in the driveway.

"This is your list and your wishes. You buy them. I have my own list. Here," she said, tossing the money into Sandra's lap. Turning on her heel, she returned to the house to get ready for shopping.

Sandra laughed and then giggled, saving her hoot until last. "Yahoo and cheers!" she yelled. It was high time; five years had passed. Sandra had tried to annoy Celeste into stopping her habit of letting others use her.

Dang it! Celeste thought. Too bad this would happen during a funeral, but for the first time, she would be buying what she could afford and what she wanted. For the first time, she was going to please herself, Celeste Dusty. She would see if Woolworths had what she wanted in stock. She made a list—roses at a floral shop, two red candles, garland, and the china tree. Maybe she would purchase a tablecloth if it wasn't too expensive.

In the past, Sandra would tell Celeste what to buy, saying she'd pay for her part of the bill once they knew the amount. Celeste never received reimbursement. So why had Celeste stuck with her throughout the years? Why? Sandra had gone to bat for her in ways that people didn't understand. Celeste's appearance, her style, her desire to grow and know who she was— Sandra wanted this for her. It was something Celeste felt in her heart but couldn't put into words.

*   *   *

The Temples had just finished Bev's Saturday morning breakfast. Like usual, Will and Mike were giving each other a hard time. Bev was fussing but secretly loved the commotion, proof that all five were there.

It was about time for Will to head for Lincoln. He jumped to his feet and then gave her an annoying hug and kiss.

"Go! Get out of here. Save your kisses for Celeste." She laughed.

"And you cut down on those chores. Got to save you for Dad." Will laughed, thinking it high time she quit pretending her grown kids knew nothing about sex.

For once, Bev had no comeback, just a ruby face.

"Will." Ginny caught his arm as he was walking out the door. "I got some pictures together for Celeste. They're from my Halloween party. Some are of the Thanksgiving art projects. Here's a note for her. Tell her how much I enjoy our letters and miss her. And by the way, has she ever mentioned a valentine?"

Will shook his head no. He followed this with a questioning look. "She and I haven't been together for Valentine's Day. Knowing Celeste, I'm sure it will come up."

"I'll walk you to the barn and explain on the way," she said, her face full of the impishness she was known for. Ginny walked beside him, pausing every now and then to explain. "Will, she had a crush on you. Looking back, I'm ashamed. I didn't like it. The morning of the day she left, I saw a card from you to Mary, that girl you liked who moved away. I slipped it out and read what you'd written." Ginny was relieved when Will began to smile. "I could just see what was going to happen. Celeste would open it, and I'd grab it away. When I saw that it was from you, I'd run and tease you. Later that day, when Sylvie came to get her, I put it in her knapsack so that she would be happy when she opened it."

"You were pretty busy with that card that day." Will stopped to laugh.

"I felt awful about all of it. After years of kicking me for what I did, here she winds up with you anyway."

Will hooted. "I went to get it to take to school, and when it was gone; I figured Mom had found it. I didn't say anything, hoping she'd forget the whole thing. Mom didn't forget; she never even saw it."

"If Celeste ever brings it up, pretend it was for her."

He could see Wind's mane streaking in the breeze, and if he wasn't mistaken, she was looking over the corral boards at him. He loved Wind more than he'd ever loved any other horse. Wind reminded him of how 'Black Beauty' should have looked. Will took a bite of the apple from the fruit dish and then played peak-a-boo, a daily routine. "Be a good girl," he said. "I'll be back soon." Will whistled, knowing he was the luckiest guy on earth.

*   *   *

Celeste was sweating some decisions too. She was finished with the decorating, peeling carrots and potatoes, and cutting up vegetables for her chef's salad. She would make her special dressing in a moment. She also had apples on hand and brown sugar and real butter. According to Sandra, who apparently could call the Betty Crocker test kitchen, apples were more appropriate and would offer her sauerkraut a gourmet touch. However, what about the kraut? Sandra might be right. Allowing Will to walk into a stink would throw a damper onto the whole affair. She'd better call and ask Bev.

While the operator put the call through, a realization came to Celeste. She didn't want to ask Bev about Will's taste in food. How childlike to ask his mother. Instead, she would consult with her peer …Ginny.

Bev answered. "Hello? Hello!"

"Just me, Celeste."

"Hi, Celeste. I recognized your voice. Will left some time ago. It won't do me any good to take a message. You aren't calling tonight off, are you?"

"I'm not that kind of person. I'd never do that to Will. You do know that, don't you?"

"I was certain you wouldn't do that. Will's never had bad luck with girls, unlike Mike, who has already met two bad seeds. However, times like these change people. Likewise, decades change people. The girls in Mike's generation aren't as nice as the ones Will knows."

Celeste felt the first twinge of a headache. She didn't care to discuss anthropology. "Bev, is Ginny there? I can't be on the phone much longer."

"You must be doing a lot of cooking if a few minutes are an issue," Bev chuckled. "Will's a simple meat and potatoes man. You may know this, but, while, it's the face powder that catches a man, it's the baking powder that keeps him at home."

"Good, we are having meat and potatoes."

"No dessert?" Bev smiled. She enjoyed teasing a bit. "You know he's got a young man's appetite."

"I've got dessert and plenty of other things with which to stuff him." The idle banter was beginning to irritate Celeste. "Ah, is Ginny there?"

"Is it something I can help with?"

"Not really. I just wanted to say hello to Ginny."

"That's awfully nice of you. People always want something from people. It seems they never just call to say hello. I remember the first time Ginny brought you over here. I knew you two would be friends, but I never predicted you'd have Will buzzing up and down the highway every weekend to see you."

Oh, please, just let me hang up, Celeste wished.

"You wanted Ginny. I almost forgot. One second while I yell…Ginny! For you, long distance; it's Celeste."

Celeste could hear Ginny's voice in the background. "Tell her I'm busy in the bathroom. Have her call back! I'll be done in five. I've waited two days for this."

Celeste cringed. Didn't Ginny shut the door? She must be using that small bathroom by the kitchen.

"Ginny, your stuff isn't going anywhere. Finish up later. You have the rest of the afternoon to do that job." Celeste's cheeks were burning. She wanted earplugs. Poor Ginny would die if she knew that Celeste could hear her.

"Celeste!" Ginny squealed. "I was sorting Christmas paper and ribbons, but since it was you, I'll finish later."

"You store your paper and wrapping in the bathroom?"

"You'd be surprised how handy that room can be. It's just a speck, but it has loads of storage."

"Maybe I'll try that. It would be easier than under the kitchen sink. Say, I just want to know if Will eats sauerkraut."

Ginny excused herself to ask her mother. "Hey" she said, having returned. "Mom said he loves it. He orders Reuben sandwiches. She and Will are the only two takers in the Temple house."

"Thanks, love you, Ginny. I've got to go now." Celeste stood and shook the nerves out of her hands. "Jingle Bells" was playing was on the kitchen radio. The cheerful song brought out her energy. She made up her chef salad dressing from her 1941 *Better Homes and Garden Cookbook*, something she'd badly wanted and finally decided to splurge on.

Now for the relish, dressing, beans, and pie. Her reward would be a nice, hot bath before she dressed.

*　*　*

As much as he liked driving, seeing the same scenery week after week was boring, so Will considered a couple of different routes that passed through farm country and its communities, like Sutton, Grafton, Exeter, Fairmont, and Friend. Highway 6 took him into Lincoln. The clouds were dark with colder air, unlike summer state fair weather with sunshine until eight thirty or nine o'clock in the evening. December was a month that danced to a different beat, an icy one in this instance. He was entering Emerald, a small town just west of Lincoln when he spotted a Conoco filling station

Stepping out of the car, Will was blasted by freezing winds. The station man's pants were waving about like an angry kite. It took both hands to hold his hat on. A cheerful fellow, the attendant stuck out his hand. No one shook hands over gas, not on a night like this. What the heck? Taking the man's hand, Will returned the grin. "I'm Will. Fill her up."

"Name's Phil. Nice firm grip there. Be surprised what I get. Some of ums' like a limp dishrag. Them's the ones make me want ta say somethin'."

Will fished around in his pocket and found a dime for a bottle of orange pop. He was twenty-five minutes away from Celeste just as planned. Spotting a pay phone right outside, Will grabbed a handful of change. Needing to leave a reminder to put medicine on Wind's hoof, he called home. Ginny, the gabber, took the message. "Celeste called," she said, teasing him about tonight.

Phil checked the oil and slammed the hood shut before coming back inside the station.

"That'll be $5.75."

Will gave him the exact amount, preparing to leave. "Thanks."

"Bettcha. Say I noticed yur from Lincoln County. Where 'bouts ya from and what ya doin' way down this way?"

"I'm a rancher. Our place is south of Brady. A girl I date is fixing me dinner in Lincoln."

"You're goanna marry this one by damn!" he roared.

Momentarily jarred by such a blatant message, Will had a few moments of panic but not for long. Imagining, he pictured Celeste, her auburn hair, her blush, the red-brown eyes looking down, one long leg in front of the other, her arms folded under her breasts. His mind wandered away to their wedding night. Just thinking about her caused his pulse to speed up. He liked the idea of being the only man she trusted. He wanted her right now. He liked teasing her and watching her reaction. This very moment, he loved her more than he'd ever loved her. He shouldn't tease her. It was just her naivety. They fit together, making them a compatible puzzle.

A rough outline of Lincoln lay just ahead. Will thought about how Celeste and he would soon be locked in an embrace. Feeling a little too warm with these thoughts, he began sweating. Needing to cool off, Will smiled, remembering her on the phone a couple of nights ago. She'd spoken about a surprise for him.

"I want to make amends for what I said during the blizzard," she'd begun. "I have a surprise for you after we eat. It's hard to keep it to myself. I promised me I'd stay mum."

"Come on, Celeste," he'd goaded. "You're not being fair. Tell me. I can't stand the excitement of a mystery surprise."

"No. I can't," she squeaked. "You'll find out soon enough."

"Wait a minute. I know what your surprise is."

"You can't possibly know. You'd better not know. I won't give it to you if you guess it."

"Sure you will," he teased.

"You'll ruin that part of the evening, but go ahead and guess if you must."

"Here's my guess. You're going to have me stay overnight wrapped in your arms."

"Will, you have a corrupt mind."

"Darn. I was sure I was right. One of these times, you'll succumb to my advances. What if I said I'd leave our relationship if you didn't give in a little?"

"I'd say, take a walk. Don't bother with asking. If the time comes, have your hiking clothes handy."

Will smiled. He wouldn't need hiking clothes if things went according to his plans. They could marry in a year or so.

He'd tried but couldn't say why he found Celeste intoxicating. The girls he dated were the ones everyone wanted to date. Their pasts had been storybook tales. The dad made a decent living, and there were no cobwebs, or it seemed that way. As of now, Celeste reminded him of *Cinderella* partway there. He was the prince, the man who would bring her home to the place she loved. They so enjoyed one another's company—taking rides, going to movies, exploring the ranch, the pigs… The list was endless. He wondered if she questioned his past. Anything beyond necking had been animal attraction—lacking in substance and character. Celeste had both. She reminded him of Ginny with her standards and loyalty.

The main thing he still didn't understand was why she got scared. What had happened to cause her to kick him? Sometimes she would be fine. Other times, when he scooted close, she grew tense. He wanted to give her his strength and assure her he'd always be there for her. Whatever the fears were, she also had morals that were irretrievably unbreakable. He just hoped those fears didn't follow along on the honeymoon. As for him, he hoped his testosterone urges held out until they got married? With a girl like Celeste, they had no choice but to wait.

Will couldn't help but smile whenever thoughts of the honeymoon came to him. He had Denver in mind. The moment they left the church, she'd get all fidgety, unsure of how it would work once they got to the hotel. He'd let her fidget; he'd need to tease her as a means of caring for his own case of nerves.

Everyone, except for his mother and possibly Celeste, had removed him from the virgin category. His reputation was that of a cool Don Juan, the man who got the trophy at the rodeo. Later that night, he had his pick of the trophy women. It was how he presented himself—dancing with gorgeous ladies, giving a gal a ride home, letting this one or that one sit on his lap. It was fun but mostly for show. There was no other Celeste. Now and then, a lady would get mad, accusing him of leading her on for nothing. He didn't plan to tell Celeste anything about his status—not unless she asked, and she wouldn't ask. He was going to initiate the process, and she needed to believe in him.

His expertise would begin once they shut the door to their hotel room. This planning made him want her is his arms. He'd start things by winking and saying she could have the bathroom for changing. He smiled. Maybe he should suggest a ten-minute limit; otherwise, she'd never come out of there. Meanwhile, he'd loosen his shirt and tie, tune the radio to "Blue Moon," and pour a bit of wine—for relaxing her. He was determined that the honeymoon suite would have a radio for romance. As soon as she came out, in her black negligee, he'd be waiting with a lover's gaze—say maybe a minute or so of looking deep inside her eyes and telling her everything he felt …how he thought her too beautiful … how he would always be gentle …how he couldn't resist her…Then he'd pull her in for that first dramatic kiss. He'd lead her to the bed, and the world would stop, except for just the two of them. Much later, they'd dance.

He'd never met a woman that excited him like her; the two of them, a perfect blend. He thought about the intimacy of whispering and watching the traffic below while the snow fell softly down to the streets.

*　　*　　*

Will was ascending the West O viaduct that went over the railroad in the industrial section of Lincoln. There were plenty of food producers. Trains were a necessity; they brought goods in and sent products on their way. Will imagined sitting beside Celeste on a train, the two of them trapped side by side, sailing down the snowy tracks, while traveling over high mountains, once he and Celeste were married. For now, owning a plane and flying to faraway places sounded good. Denver would be a starter.

Reaching the top of the viaduct, he looked out over downtown Lincoln, awestruck. The scene before him could have been a painted Christmas card. Brady seemed small in comparison. Instead of a few lights, he saw hundreds of Christmas lights, a city bus with strangers sitting inside, a pool hall, its neon lights blinking, and a woman working late in a lighted upstairs office building. Cars were everywhere as people strolled along the sidewalks.

Cracking his window open, he heard "Joy to the World" playing. The corner bar had a Christmas tree in the window with the pawnshop just to the south of it. Santa, who was walking down the sidewalk, had kids chasing after him, and a dog chased them. The last thing he saw was a lady who'd dropped an armload of packages. He'd wanted to help but couldn't.

Will was glad for the opportunity to enjoy the holiday sights. However, Christmas in the country, would remain his favorite. He liked farmsteads with house lights on at night, a Christmas tree looking out the front window. During daylight, proud snowmen stood in the front yards with real pine or cedar wreaths on the front doors. Heck, several of the farm folks cut down their trees, including his family, who'd strung popcorn and cranberries around the boughs. Usually one good storm, during the holidays, would render the scenery an artist's painting.

*　　*　　*

It was now 6:15 p.m. Celeste was planning for Will to arrive at 6:30. Her beautician had styled her hair just that morning, suggesting she try a chignon. Having her hair completely pulled back, off her face, made her eyes look bigger and emphasized her high cheekbones. She really loved her new look. She was wearing a long-sleeved, brown tweed dress that hugged her in all the right places. Wearing her pearl jewelry, she imagined herself stepping out of the cover of a *Vogue* or *Bazaar* magazine.

Ten more minutes, and Will would run in the side door by where he parked. Neither Sandra nor Celeste used the long driveway. Sandra had tried backing out right after they'd moved in. Turning the steering wheel the wrong way, her car hit the side of the house. Celeste remembered sitting in the living room when a crash caused a picture grouping to tumble to the floor. Wow! Sandra had been livid over the damage to the car and even madder because of Celeste's giggles.

Examining herself in the mirror for the umpteenth time, she saw a character out of <u>Little Women,</u> but which sister was she? She wouldn't be Jo, the tomboy, or Meg, the oldest and most motherly of the sisters? Amy, the artist, was nothing like Celeste. Most likely, she was Beth, musical and shy.

She wasn't one iota musical, but it didn't matter. She'd wanted to be Beth since first reading the book in high school. In her mind, Ginny was Jo, Bonnie was Meg, and an artistic girl she'd known at Union School, was Amy. Hattie England would be the mother? Losing herself in her game of pretend, Celeste whirled about the mirror. Circling toward the door, she found herself in the kitchen with her hand holding the grease spotted, cherry dotted, flour clotted, stained, to do list.

The magical scene was set. A garland hung over the archway with a sparkling bow attached to the top. A small tree, with multi-colored lights and twenty glittering balls, sat on a stool. The table boasted a green cloth that matched the candleholders; Santa was riding in an ornate tin sleigh, draped with ruby roses and fuzzy white reindeer that were in the lead. The Christmas dishes were from–and she felt victorious— Woolworths, with green and crimson rims and a country church in the center. The church, intricately crafted in white, had miniature stained glass windows. Celeste believed the dishes looked like Lenox. Red placemats set off the table for a striking appearance. She would wait, until Will arrived, to light the candles

Stepping back for a final look at her Christmas eatery, something was missing? The wreath! She'd left it in the trunk. Fiddlesticks, she needed to rush, in order, to hang it up in time. It was loaded with sugared gumdrops, petite pinecones, mini balls and a red ribbon bow to match. Racing outside to the car and back, "There!" she said. Taking the picture of Thomas and Sandra down, she hung the wreath in its place. Almost done, she brushed her hands together, ridding them of dust. Graceful and gracious; her fingers, long and slender, like Beth's, began dancing through the air, pretending to play love songs.

Suddenly, she realized that she didn't know where Sandra kept the matches. Had Sandra said they were somewhere on her dresser?

* * *

The flame caught hold just as Will's car lights lit up the curtains. Now she had to light the other one. An unlit candle was unthinkable. Her hands fluttered about. Everything was happening at once. She dropped the candle on the plate just as Will bounded through the door. He, wrapped her in his arms, pressed her close, as he bent to kiss her. Their tongues played hide and seek, breaking apart, going close together, while tucking him against her.

When they took a breath, Celeste stepped back. Will had never looked so handsome, in his corduroy pants, navy and gray sweater, and a white collar about the neck. These last two weeks had been interminable. Both seemed on the verge of bubbling over and crying at the same time.

"Let me look at you. I like your hair. It's beautiful."

"It's a chignon. My hairdresser thought I should try it."

"I can read your beautician's thoughts. Celeste Dusty is just the girl for this quaint style, and since she's having a special guy, we'll do her up right. That's what she thought."

"Will," Celeste, laughed. "My hairdresser is a man. He doesn't know about you or tonight."

"Serves me right. I'm the one who should do the blushing."

"So, do you like my dress?"

"If I tell you how beautiful you are, you have to do the same."

"Will, what's that spicy aroma? It's masculine."

"It's some of Dad's Old Spice. Glad you like it. Tell me, did you make that dress?"

Celeste twirled around two times, offering Will a seductive stare.

"Hey, that sort of gets to me. We'd better change the subject, or you'll find yourself on the couch with me on top."

"Will, let's not go in that direction." Celeste playfully hit Will on the arm, delighted to see him.

"What's the sour smell?" Will's wrinkled nose reminded Celeste of a bloodhound. What was he sniffing? Ginny had said how much he liked sauerkraut, so she relaxed. She'd had such fun cooking the dinner and decorating, enjoying the freedom she'd longed for at Sylvie's. She'd hoped that Will would appreciate her efforts, especially the sauerkraut, saying hers was better than his mother's. But that wasn't happening. His nose continued to twitch and sniff. Had Sandra been right? Panicking, she wondered what she'd fix. She had nothing extra to cook, and her humiliation had her in frenzy.

"Are you there, Celeste?" Will asked, realizing he shouldn't have joked with her. She looked frantic. This was her first dinner. Why did he tease the way he did? he asked himself.

"I'm here," she said, wearily. "Pretend I'm not."

"Celeste, hey, I'm sorry. It smells wonderful. I love sauerkraut. It's something I don't get to eat very often. Mom and I order it when we go out. I had to call home about Wind's medicine, and Ginny told me about your call. She said you were concerned about my liking it but said not to tell you that she told me. It smells fantastic and goes with this festive atmosphere. You're an amazing hostess," he said, watching the relief on her face. "I feel like I'm in an exquisite restaurant."

"You do?" she asked, her face becoming a lily's radiance. "Oh, Will. I'm so glad. I was frightened. I almost want to dance with relief."

"I assure you that, if I didn't like it, I'd cover and pretend I did, at least I would for your first Christmas dinner. Why were you so panicked?" Again he wondered about her sensitive reactions.

Sylvie's eyes came at her, but collecting herself with a huge grin, she said, "I wasn't scared. I just wanted it to be nice. It's how I like things, and I want to please you."

"Instead of pleasing me, you should chew me out for teasing you. I thought I'd lost you," he said, lightly touching her head. "Me and my tendency to josh."

Celeste gave him a sympathetic nod, touching his cheek. "I know, Will. We can practice on it together. Sit down," she ordered; pulling out the chair for him, as though nothing had happened. "Let's talk while I set the food on the table. How was the drive?"

"It was all right. I took a new route. I enjoyed looking at the farms along the way. We need to get this Depression over with. Surely it can't go on much longer."

"I feel fortunate to have my job. We're both lucky."

"Did Tom Thumb go to the funeral with Sandra?"

"Will, please don't call him that. He and Sandra are my friends, and I don't like nick-names that might cause hurt." Celeste thought of Sylvie and all the cruel things she'd said. Sylvie's presence seemed looming which usually didn't happen.

"Mom taught Dad how to tolerate gossip. It's doable," Will smiled.

"Your poor Dad," Celeste teased. "Now, tell me what's happening back home."

"Ginny is going to do <u>A Christmas Carol</u> with her students at Union School."

"That's wonderful. Back when we did that play, I got to be the woman who was stocking the window of the grocery store when you played Scrooge. Ginny was the Ghost of Christmas Past. She scolded you; she accused you of being a tightwad—"

"You can skip this story. Ginny was talking to Scrooge, not me."

"Ginny always said there wasn't much difference in the two of you, except that you were a bit meaner and born with champagne taste."

"Celeste Dusty, it is that candor of yours that makes me crazy for you," he said, giving her a hug.

"Do you remember that harsh winter when Miss England read us <u>Old Yeller</u> and *Lassie?* We got our lunch pails and washed our hands in the pump. And while she read, we sat eating the morsels in our lunch pails."

"I remember. Which story was your favorite?"

"That's a hard question. I think my choice would be *Lassie*. You would have favored <u>Old Yeller.</u> I bet I'm right?"

"You are right. Come here, girl. Let me hold you."

She went to his open arms, and he pulled her onto his lap, kissing her, following that kiss by another, more lingering. He smelled like a combination of Juicy Fruit and Old Spice.

"I've always been curious. You'll think I'm silly, but what is it like being a guy? You're the ones who have to initiate the kissing and holding hands." Celeste was sitting on his lap, carefree and happy.

"If I wasn't a guy, I couldn't go around looking at you pretty girls."

At that, Celeste, stiffened, scooting off Will's lap.

"What did I say wrong?" Usually, Celeste wasn't as touchy as this. "Celeste, I'm sorry. I need to stop and think before I speak. I didn't mean for it to sound the way it did. I don't look at anyone but you. I can't quite imagine another someone following me around the barnyard for the rest of my life. One is enough."

Did he mean her? Her heart pounded so that she could barely breathe. She had to tell him about the past, who she was. She needed to open the closet and let out the skeletons. But how could she? Celeste was deathly worried. Once she told him, he'd leave, and there would be no stopping Will. Just like that, the love of her life would head out the door. And even if she didn't tell him, Sylvie would find a way. "What's wrong? Celeste. Something's bothering you. Is it something I said?" Pausing, he repeated himself. "I said that I could see you following me around for the rest of my life."

It was her he was talking about. She wanted to burst out crying, thinking; *I want to be there with you so much that, at this very moment, I am breathing my wish into my heart.* She never would have guessed she'd be going home with him Thanksgiving or entertaining him here tonight. So how could she know what tomorrow would bring? Who knew? Or was deception a way of wishing for the life she wanted. And his money? How much had he spent driving down here and taking her places like restaurants and movies?

Finally, she blurted her words out, rushing, not stopping for fear she would lose her courage, fleeting as it was. "I'm afraid to tell you about me and my life. I won't be elaborating on every detail. Ask if there's some specific thing you want to know, but please don't interrupt me. Call this the scariest story I've ever told."

Will reached for her hand, but she pulled hers away.

"Not this time. I need my hands to speak for me when I get to things I can't say."

"All right," Will said, confusion written on his face.

"I lied about Sylvie. Things weren't good. It began right away, even, before we got to Lincoln that first night. I couldn't say anything without Sylvie correcting me or taking whatever I said the wrong way. She would scold me, saying it was for my own good. I had to go to school that first day with a map, skip snacks, wear other's girl's clothes, stuff like that.

Sylvie thought I had problems. She hated me. I reminded her, too much, of Mom. I had no idea that she thought Mom had been the cause of her boyfriend, my dad, to leave.

"Sylvie wanted Howie and Bonnie. Since I was the wrong one, she thought she could make me become like Bonnie. So, I tried to be anyone but me. Will, I was twelve years old and doing my best."

Feeling at a loss for words, Will said, "I don't know what to say. I'm listening."

"You'll be on Highway 30 headed home in fifteen minutes. You have no idea who I really am. Who am I?"

"You are Celeste Dusty—pretty and sexy."

"This isn't funny. You think I sew and design. Instead, there are more secrets. I'm trying to tell you about me. I'm a girl who seduced a minister and enjoyed the seduction. I liked having him mentor me. He held my hands and winked at me. At home, I was thoughtless. I had no friends. And here's the shocker. Sylvie sent me to live in the attic after accusing me of seducing the pastor. She said that I caused him to hurt me. I had to take my things up two flights of stairs first thing the next morning despite the agonizing pain and hideous injuries. Before moving to the attic, I was sent to live with Elvira in the guesthouse. I was a bad influence on Howie. I can never go home; she threw me out for good."

"No one would throw you out Celeste. You're the girl who fixed this amazing dinner and the best friend of my sister. You're the girl who couldn't stand up against her shadow at Union and who cried when you found a dead mouse under that lid? You said you felt as though you'd killed Mickey Mouse. You're tender and loving."

Terrified, Celeste left. When she returned, she had her make shift diary, the one she'd made at school when she was twelve. His eyes were two ovals of fear. Studying her closely, Will took the aging pages. Not understanding Celeste, he sat down. Looking from her to the pages, he began reading. "Pastor is my stand-in father. I play paper doll family. My paper doll is the pastor's wife."

Will continued to read. Shocked by various entries, he began talking under his breath, rage emerging. "That can't be … He didn't. How could she …No, please tell me, this isn't true."

Celeste misunderstood, believing he was talking about her. He was making fun of her. He didn't even bother to look up, hold her tenderly, or to say that they would celebrate her birthday to make up for her having no birthday celebrations. Unable to bear this, she fled the room.

Will kept reading. "Pastor's touch repulses and frightens me. I don't like it." He read her full account of a child's terror and the resulting pain. "He scares me, but I don't dare say so. He's my only friend, and everyone loves him. Tonight, I asked if I could stay home." Here she wrote a full account of going for her mentoring at his pool, ending with leaving Sylvie's kitchen.

"No. Please no." Will's tears were making it hard to read what the pastor had done to her. He'd molested her in the pool.

Will read to the end. He read about her finding his valentine and about the candles and his being there. He sat and burned with shame. The final part was the most tender thing he'd ever read, complete with her naming their children. "Will and I, and the six kids, Frankie and Francie, the twins, Bobbie, Lilly, Zackery, and Betsy, went for a ride this evening. We stopped at the drugstore to get extra hankies for me and penny candy for the kids. Will bought a root beer float to share with all of us. Later we bathed them while telling stories."

He'd been so deeply absorbed in his reading that he had failed to look up, and when he did, Celeste was nowhere in sight. He found her coat and purse but not Celeste. After scouring the house in search of her, he grabbed his coat and ran to find the girl he loved.

*   *   *

He'd driven everywhere, terrified of finding a woman in the snow, frozen and dead. When Ginny's old boyfriend had refused to leave the yard, the entire family had jumped in to support her, while in truth, she'd brought on that problem by getting bored and calling him up to talk, probably enticing him into arguing, drinking, and coming out to the farm. Parked in front of the house and unwilling to leave, he'd sat there until Will brought his rifle out and shot it straight up in the air. The whole thing had put Will in a bad mood. By comparison, Celeste's entire life, since age twelve, had been a nightmare, and no one had been there for her to turn to. A filthy man had molested her.

Will had to show Celeste that there were many good kinds of love, how they blended and swirled together if decent and right. He had to help her see that love wasn't perfect, but if genuine, it was like two candles glowing side by side in rhythm. She couldn't leave him. She had to be alive. There was so much he wanted to share, things that would warm her.

She would giggle the way she did when she was thrilled at the sights and smells. He'd take her to Banner on Christmas Eve with a soup supper and dessert afterward. His mind racing with thoughts, he wanted to punish those who had treated her as though she was nothing more than a useless rag, a piece of evil, rather than a young girl being scarred forever. Yelling out to the night, he said, "Celeste, you might as well quit hiding. I will keep looking until I find you."

⋆   ⋆   ⋆

Celeste remained hidden under a blanket in the basement, pretending to be asleep. She was not about to stay and watch her life crumble into bits the way it had happened so many times. What made her feel as if her heart was bleeding was the look of disgust and disdain on Will's face. It was how he'd grunted his disapproval. Her heart was shattered.

She thought of the night he'd carried her to bed, telling her to sit and wait for him. And yet, somehow she knew it had never really happened. The whole time, he'd been over two hundred miles away, caring for cattle and other girls. Her humiliation poured over her like water galloping down the cliffs of a waterfall. She didn't want to feel. The last thing she heard was the door slamming as Will left the house. At that moment, a knife sliced her heart and hopes. She realized how she'd been hoping that he would see the truth and would know that she hadn't really done those horrible things. She had expected him to convince her of her goodness, to plug the hole that allowed doubt to enter.

Her past told her that life would continue; she would sit on a beach somewhere, maybe as a nurse overseas. Morning would come, the sun would shine, the snow would fall come winter, the world would continue to rotate, *and* she would smile again, sometime, somewhere. It just wasn't fair. He'd brought her to life these past months. Now she was losing him. She wanted him—wanted the life that awaited them.

They'd had wonderful times. However, she'd deluded herself by believing in magic. Will wasn't magic. He was real— a person, not a spirit. Will had never been there during those horrible times when she lit the candles. She had chosen to believe in that special night when he put her to bed tenderly, just as she chose to believe in the wonder of tonight. That was the real Will Temple, the man she loved. She'd used believing as a way to survive. She could still feel Will tucking her in and telling her to wait. Funny, how it all came true, but now it was over. The circus was leaving town—the head clown driving down Highway 30 homeward. Killing herself wasn't an option. Every time she had it in mind, Will showed up to spoil things. Maybe he would stay away for good now.

* * *

Will was getting more frantic. Driving every street, he looked everywhere for a frozen woman lying in the snow. It was too late now, unless by some miracle she'd gone back to the house. He had no idea her life was like that—not even a birthday party and the nightmare of a pastor going after her.

* * *

Celeste's mind was changing directions, going through all the stages of grief in one night. For now, she was entering anger. Considering the ludicrous blame she'd taken as a twelve-year-old, she'd shown very little anger. How dare he? *I was twelve*, she told herself. But, did age matter? The pain would have been there even if I was older. She'd been a lonely girl matched up with a man who preyed on her vulnerabilities.

He took that child and her future right to choose her only lover.

* * *

Will stopped at the diner to use the pay phone. Walking inside he dialed 0 for assistance. "I need a number for Sam Star," he told the operator, dreading what Sandra might say. She'd either make fun because he needed her advice or chew him out for "mistreating Celeste." The diner was empty save one old couple. The heavy smell of pancake syrup and bacon grease, accompanied by coffee fumes, clouded the place.

"Sandra! Will here. I am sorry to bother you but …"

"Will, what is it?"

"Sandra." He began to cry as he told her what happened. "I'm the only one who's read her diary."

"No! There are two of us. Don't ask me when or how I read the journal. I shouldn't have done that. It's just that when I first met her, she was severely injured. I had to understand her in order to help her. I know her; she's all right. She's the most incredible woman I know. Her brilliant mind has taken care of her. She won't harm herself. Besides, she stood up to me this morning. Let me tell you about the Christmas list the next time I … Will, she's all right."

"Sure." Deathly worried, Will halfway smiled.

"Listen, go home and wait. Maybe she's there. Check the basement. That's her spot when she feels defeated. We all have a place. I come to my parents' and go out back to my tree house; in the winter, I drive around in the country or go to the down town lunch counter. Don't tell her!

"She's the best friend I've ever had. It hurts me to say this, but you're the best thing she has, but then again, you're the only one she's had."

Will laughed. He couldn't help it. Sandra was "actually" funny and not such a bad egg.

"I need to warn you about something. If you don't take good care of her, I promise you'll wake up with a shorter leg. Don't ever hurt her. Treat her like a wild poppy."

"What? Why a wild poppy?"

"A wild poppy is a beautiful survivor. It outlasts the best of them. Celeste is a wild poppy. Her father likened her to that flower when she was a child."

*   *   *

The house was dark with one exception. Someone must have found her and come to handle the lights and oven. He felt sick. He almost didn't go inside. That's when he saw her. There she was sitting in the dining ell with two plates and one lit candle.

He'd never been so glad to see anyone. Taking a breath, he saw Celeste more closely. Everything about her looked different. She'd never looked more beautiful. She'd undone the chignon, letting her hair fall in loose, silky stands, but there was more. What was that she was wearing? Her gown took his breath away. Done in rich purples and reds, greens and turquoises, she'd embroidered dainty yellow flowers, blue butterflies, and rich orange poppies, scattering them about the gown. She reminded him of an exquisite fairy lost in the forest. He wanted to hand her a magic wand that would offer her everything she needed. He was entrenched in her sad loveliness.

"Celeste," he said in hushed tones. "You're lovely. You make me want to cry when I look at you. What happened?"

Pausing, certain he would wonder if she was sane, she whispered, "I'm the Rag Princess. Don't you remember?"

Looking at her, his blue eyes revealed a quick twinkle, just enough that she knew he hadn't forgotten. Then, as they turned a darker blue, he asked, "Why did you leave? I would never hurt you. I looked and you were gone. I wanted to tell you how deeply sorry I was for what happened to you. I was so angry at what Sylvie and the pastor did to you," he said, choking back tears.

"Will, you said things that humiliated me," she sobbed in little breaths.

"I wasn't referring to you! I'm sorry you thought that. It was that man and Sylvie. I never knew. I want to kill those two. Who in damnation was that man, the pastor?"

"He was a friend of Sylvie's. He was a pastor, but over the years, I've concluded he was bogus," she said still afraid of her secrets. Daring to look at him, Celeste saw the agony in his eyes; the boy who'd come to her in her fantasies was now a grown man who loved her. This was no dream. He was standing before her, there to touch. Reaching out, she put her hand on his lips. This was the real Will Temple.

"Can I join you?" he asked hoarsely, his eyes swollen.

Wiping at the tears that were soaking her face, she said, "I'd like that. I didn't light the other candle. It's because a candle never brought you to me. My mind did."

"I know. It's the wild poppy in you. Strong and beautiful," he said, kneeling down on one knee, his voice barely above a whisper. "It's how you survived. You were only twelve when your aunt took you there."

"There's so much more, including Howie."

"What about him?"

"He's all right. I have an old teacher friend. We discuss him on a regular basis. She keeps her eye on him. I'll tell you the whole story in the morning. Bonnie and I are unsure of what we need to do."

"Are you sure?"

"Sylvie adores him. She's not going to hurt him, not physically. The emotional damage is the part that worries me. I'd like for it to be just us tonight; tomorrow I want to discuss Howie at length."

Reaching for Celeste as though she might disappear Will swallowed. "Can I hold "Breaking into sobs, he put his hands over his face, dropping his head.

Seeing him like that, Celeste reached out, drawing Will gently to her lap.

Her skirt grew wet, with his tears, as she gazed outside where it was snowing. The lights in the window were blinking softly, lighting the night just enough to see. While he cried, she traveled back to Mother's box of long ago. As Celeste sat lightly massaging Will's hair, layers of ancient lies lifted. At last, she was able to see clearly, realizing that she wasn't evil. There was no way that a twelve year old instigated or asked to be raped. Pastor had instigated the entire thing. No one brought on a rape except the rapist. As for that day when her parent's left to see Bonnie, she'd done what any loving daughter would do. She had asked them to stay home. For a girl who got insights from her dreams and memories, she'd been doing her best. The accident happened because they chose to go and drive in a dangerous storm.

The final issue was the secrets her parent's had kept regarding Sylvie. About her mother— Celeste had already concluded that fear and rejection had motivated Mom's decision not to reveal the truth about Sylvie. Neither Bonnie nor Celeste fully understood the role Mother's letter to Sylvie, in which, she'd offered the children, had played. Bonnie, who'd been shown the letter by Sylvie, knew that the offer was made, but only if something happened to Mom. Both sisters agreed that Dad would have appeased her, wanting to ease any discomfort she felt, despite his dislike of Sylvie.

But what about Sylvie, whose aim had been revenge at all costs, a cost that included lying and other means of manipulation including brainwashing? If there was proof that Sylvie was evil, that proof could be found in her eyes, where she carried hatred strong enough to reach someone as sensitive as Celeste, someone who had extra perception. In the final analysis, Celeste saw a woman who was the personification of greed, self- centeredness, and rage. She lacked both the ability to give or forgive. Celeste wondered who Sylvie's victim was now that she and Mother were unavailable. At long last, Celeste was able to see herself as benevolent and Sylvie as the malevolent one, a woman who had left Celeste and her mother with scars.

Wiping away her tears, Celeste told herself that it was time now to drop the past and merge with the girl she'd been long ago. Life was ahead, not behind.

Knowing what she needed to do right now and not later, she reached to embrace the one for whom she'd come full circle, the child she'd been before her parents' accident.

Looking out at the flakes of snow decorating the dark, Celeste watched the scene before her unfold. She was standing in the snow beside another girl. That girl was her, at age twelve, shortly before the accident. She was in school, during recess, her cheeks red from the cold—she was laughing with Ginny and the other girls. They were building Mrs. Frosty and had added snow to her… Ginny had just put a scarf from home about Mrs. Snowman's neck.

The skies were clear and cold, and from the playground, they could see four different farms facing them. A few cattle were out eating in the distance, and vehicles passed by out on the road. The boys, loud as usual, were playing King of the Mountain. Ginny had gone over to tell them to be quiet. Celeste's world was ahead of her and felt good.

As though reading the adult Celeste's thoughts, the younger Celeste was reaching out to embrace her. "I've been waiting for you," she said, pulling Celeste in and hugging her. "You're home again. Welcome. I've missed you. Let's go inside and get warm." Hand in hand, the two climbed the schoolhouse steps and went inside, closing the door behind them. The past was gone; the future lay ahead.

Celeste realized she'd come full circle.

* * *

In the silence, Will's sobbing subsided. Momentarily, he rose, pulling a chair in close beside Celeste. Lighting the other candle, he said, "Watch the flame. It starts out small and then grows, bursting into full size just like its partner. We're those flames. We began to burn some time ago. It worked pretty well, so we burned a little further and then a little longer. Miraculously, there we were—you and me—burning in harmony. Celeste Ann Dusty, I love you."

Blushing in the dimly lit room, she whispered, "And I love you, Will Temple."

* * *

From the street, one would have seen the candle glow, softly silhouetting the outline of a man and woman, one on either side of the table. The lady, the one with the long rose-colored hair and a slender body, in the gorgeous rag gown, didn't seem to be eating. Instead, she was either leaning in toward the man or running back and forth from the kitchen, at least for a time or two, until he caught her and sat her down in her chair where she sat watching him scoop forkfuls from plate to mouth.

Finished eating, the scene changed rather drastically. The man was shaking his finger at the woman, who was giggling and pulling on him. Breaking free, he grabbed his coat and stepped onto the porch with her following behind him. "Celeste Dusty, you're trying to get me onto those cranberry sheets. You should be ashamed of yourself. What would your parents think?"

"Will," she yelled, giggling. "I was teasing. You just got scared."

"Are you kidding? I'm not afraid, but you couldn't live with yourself. I have to hand it to you; you're a good actress after all, Celeste Dusty. Tomorrow it is then—breakfast and then church," Will chuckled, heading to the car.

Stepping back inside, she bent over the candles and blew. The house went dark while a flame of light glowed within the woman named Celeste Dusty.

*   *   *

Will smiled as he drove on to his friend's place. He'd bet anything that after tonight, Celeste was going to change. He'd miss that crazy, naive girl, but a new one would emerge with confidence and poise. It wasn't going to happen overnight, but it would happen. And when it did, he hoped to be there to see every minute of it.